ENRIQUE VILA-MATAS

Enrique Vila-Matas is widely considered to be one of Spain's most important contemporary novelists. His work has been translated into thirty languages and has won numerous international literary prizes, including the Herralde Prize, the Prix Médicis étranger and the Rómulo Gallegos Prize. Vila-Matas's books have been longlisted (*Montano*) and shortlisted (*Dublinesque*) for the Independent Foreign Fiction Prize, and *Never Any End to Paris* was a finalist for the US Best Translated Book Award.

ENRIQUE VILA-MATAS

The Illogic of Kassel

TRANSLATED FROM THE SPANISH BY
Anne McLean and Anna Milsom

VINTAGE

1 3 5 7 9 10 8 6 4 2

Vintage
20 Vauxhall Bridge Road,
London SW1V 2SA

Vintage is part of the Penguin Random House group of companies
whose addresses can be found at global.penguinrandomhouse.com.

Penguin
Random House
UK

First published in Vintage in 2017
First published in trade paperback by Harvill Secker in 2015

First published with the title *Kassel no invita a la lógica*
in Spain by Seix Barral in 2014

penguin.co.uk/vintage

A CIP catalogue record for this book is
available from the British Library

ISBN 9780099597841

Printed and bound by Clays Ltd, St Ives plc

Penguin Random House is committed to a sustainable future
for our business, our readers and our planet. This book is made
from Forest Stewardship Council® certified paper.

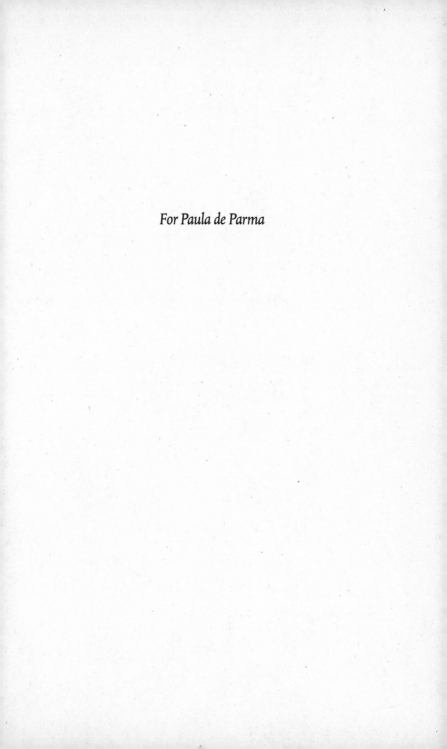

For Paula de Parma

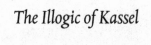

The Illogic of Kassel

The more avant-garde an author is, the less he can allow himself to be labeled as such. But who cares about that? In fact, my opening sentence is just a McGuffin having little to do with what I intend to relate, though it could be that in the long run all I can tell about my invitation to Kassel and my later trip to that city will eventually have everything to do with that sentence.

As some people know, the best way to explain what a McGuffin is has to do with a train scene: "Could you tell me what's in that package on the luggage rack above your head?" asks one passenger. And the other responds: "Oh, that's a McGuffin." The former wants to know what a McGuffin is, and the other explains: "A McGuffin is an apparatus for trapping lions in Germany." "But there are no lions in Germany," says the first. "Well, then, that's no McGuffin," replies the other.

The most perfect McGuffin is in *The Maltese Falcon*, the most misleading film in the history of cinema. John Huston's movie tells of the search for a small statue, which was the tribute the Knights of Malta paid to a Spanish king for an island. Much is said about it—they never stop talking in the film—but in the end the coveted falcon, for which some have even been murdered, turns out to be merely the element of suspense that has allowed the story to advance.

As you'll already have guessed, there are many McGuffins. The most famous one can be found in the opening scenes of Alfred Hitchcock's *Psycho*. Who can forget the robbery Janet Leigh's character commits in the first minutes? It seems so important and turns out to be irrelevant to the plot. However, it fulfills the function of keeping us riveted to the screen for the rest of the movie.

And there are McGuffins, for example, in every single episode of *The Simpsons*, where the prelude that opens any one of them has very little or nothing at all to do with the plot of the rest of the episode.

I found my first McGuffin in *The Facts of Murder*, Pietro Germi's cinematic adaptation of Carlo Emilio Gadda's novel, *That Awful Mess on Via Merulana*. In this film, Inspector Ingravallo, hyped up on coffee and lost in the labyrinth of his intricate investigation, speaks on the telephone every once in a while with his sainted wife, who we never see. Is Ingravallo married to a McGuffin?

There are so many McGuffins around that just a year ago, one infiltrated my life when I got a phone call one morning from a young woman claiming to be María Boston. She said she was the secretary of Mr. and Mrs. McGuffin, an Irish couple, who would like to invite me to dinner. She had no doubt that I would also be delighted to see them and give them my regards, since they were planning to make me an irresistible proposal.

Were the McGuffins multimillionaires? Did they want, for some obscure reason, to buy me? That's what I asked as a humorous reaction to her strange, provocative call, surely a joke someone was playing on me.

Normally I would immediately hang up on a call like that, but María Boston's voice was warm and beautiful, and I was in a good mood that morning, so I played along a little before hanging up and that was my undoing, for I gave young Boston time to drop the names of a few friends we had in common, actually the names of my best friends.

"What the McGuffins want to propose," she said suddenly, "is to reveal to you once and for all the resolution of the mystery of the universe. They know it and want to pass it on to you."

I decided to humor her. "And are the McGuffins aware that I never go out to dinner?" I responded. "Do they know that, for the last seven years, I've tended to feel happy in the mornings and in the evenings I'm hit hard by an anguish that has me imagining dark, horrible scenarios, making it absolutely inadvisable for me to go out at night?"

"The McGuffins know everything," said Boston. "They're aware you're very reluctant to go out at night." Even so, they wouldn't consider that I might want to stay home instead of finding out the solution to the mystery of the universe. It would be a very cowardly choice to make.

I've received strange phone calls in my life, but this one took the cake. And as if that weren't enough, Boston's voice grew increasingly pleasant; it really had a very special timbre that reminded me of something, though I didn't quite know what, but which made me feel even more energetic, optimistic, and content than I usually did in the mornings. I asked if she would be going to the dinner where they'd reveal that secret to me. Yes, she said, I'm planning to go; after all, I'm the couple's secretary and I have certain obligations.

Minutes later, having taken full advantage of my optimistic state of mind, she had managed to completely convince me. I wouldn't regret it, she said; the mystery of the universe is well worth the effort. My birthday was last month, I said, I'm just mentioning it in case someone is planning a surprise party and got the date wrong. No, said Boston, the surprise is in what the McGuffins are going to reveal, and it's not what you're expecting.

2

And so, three nights later, I showed up punctually for the meeting, which the Irish couple did not attend, but Boston did. She was a tall, luminous young woman with very black hair, a red dress, and marvelous golden sandals; she was intelligent and smart at the same time. As I looked at her, I couldn't hide an inner lament, which intuitively, young as she was, she caught; she seemed to know that something related to age was happening to me, a deep dejection and sorrow.

Without a doubt I had never seen her before in my life. She was at least thirty years younger than I was. Sorry for the snag, the snare, the windup, she said as soon as we met. I asked what snag, what windup she was talking about. Don't you see? I've ensnared you, the McGuffins don't exist, she said. And she explained that this had seemed the best way to get me to pay attention, for she guessed that, considering my eccentric literary fame, an extravagant call might be more likely to stir my curiosity and achieve the difficult objective of getting me to go out at night. She had to see me in person to make a proposal, since she feared she wouldn't get the response she wanted if she asked me over the telephone. And what is this proposal you want to tell me about? Is it the same thing the McGuffins would propose? Above all, she said, she felt happy knowing she had the time ahead of her to be able to set out the proposal her employers, Carolyn Christov-Bakargiev and Chus Martínez (the curators of Documenta 13) had assigned her to convey.

So then, I said, Carolyn and Chus Martínez are the McGuffins. She smiled. Exactly, she said, but now I'd like to know if you've heard of Documenta in Kassel. I've heard a lot about it, I said. What's more, some of my friends in the 1970s came back from there transformed by having seen prodigious avant-garde artworks. In fact, Kassel was—for this and other reasons—legendary and has been since the days of my youth; it is an intact legend, my generation's legend, and also, if I'm not mistaken, that of the generations that followed mine. For every five years, groundbreaking works concentrate there. Behind the legend of Kassel, I ended up telling her, is the legend of the avant-garde.

Well, María Boston said, she had the job of inviting me to participate in Documenta 13. As I could see, she added, she hadn't exactly lied when she spoke of an irresistible proposal.

That proposal did make me happy, but I contained my enthusiasm. I waited a few seconds before asking what they expected of a writer like me at an art exhibition like that. As far as I knew, writers didn't go to Kassel. And birds don't go to Peru to die, said Boston, demonstrating her conversational agility. A good McGuffin phrase, I thought.... A brief, intense silence followed, which she broke. They had assigned her to ask me to reserve three weeks at the end of the

4

summer of 2012, to spend each morning in the Chinese restaurant Dschingis Khan on the outskirts of Kassel.

"Chingis what?"

"Dschingis Khan."

"In a Chinese restaurant?"

"Yes. Writing there in front of the public."

Given my inveterate habit of writing a chronicle every time I get invited to a strange place to do something weird (over time I've realized that all places actually seem strange to me), I had the impression I was once again living through the beginning of a journey that could end up turning into a written tale, in which, as was customary, I would combine perplexity and my suspended life to describe the world as an absurd place arrived at by way of a very extravagant invitation.

I looked María Boston in the eye for a few moments. It seemed she'd done this on purpose so I would end up writing a long article about a strange invitation to Kassel to work in public in a Chinese restaurant. I looked away. And that's all, she said. Carolyn and Chus and their whole curatorial team were simply asking me to sit on a chair in a Chinese restaurant every day and carry out my normal daily activity as if I were in Barcelona. That is, they were just asking me to write and, of course, try to connect with anyone who came into the restaurant and wanted to talk to me. I mustn't forget that "interconnection" was going to be a very common concept and recommendation within Documenta 13.

And I wasn't to think, she said, that I was the only writer who was going to do that number, for they planned to invite four or five others from Europe and the Americas, perhaps one or two from Asia as well.

I was pleased to be invited to Kassel, but not at the idea of having to sit in a Chinese restaurant for three weeks. I was sure of that from the start. Fearing they'd eventually rescind my invitation, I felt obliged to tell María Boston that the offer struck me as too squalid, that she should therefore tell Carolyn Christov-Bakargiev and Chus Martínez that the very idea that hundreds of German grandparents on senior-citizen outings climbing out of their buses to see what I was writing and interconnect with me in a restaurant threw me mentally, even literally, out of joint.

Nobody said anything about German grandparents, Boston corrected me, rather severe all of a sudden. It was true, nobody had said anything about grandparents or senior-citizen outings, but in any case, I told her I would be grateful for another type of invitation to Kassel: to give a lecture there, for example, even if I had to deliver it in the Chinese dive. A talk on chaos in contemporary art, I said in a conciliatory way. Nobody said anything about chaos, interrupted Boston. It was true, no one had said anything about that. Most likely, I was one of those people who had a long-standing, unsophisticated prejudice against contemporary art and believed it was currently a real disaster or a swindle or any of the above.

Okay, I suddenly agreed, there's no chaos in current art, no crisis of ideas, no obstruction of any kind. I said that, and then I agreed to go to Kassel. I immediately felt a deep satisfaction; I couldn't forget that more than once I'd dreamed that the avant-garde considered me one of their own and would one day invite me to Kassel.

Oh, and by the way, who were the avant-garde?

3

María Boston's face gradually lit up, and for a moment she looked absolutely radiant. Perhaps she was satisfied at having achieved her mission of getting me to accept the proposal.

I knew why I'd accepted, but it would not do to be too sincere. Apart from the originality and literary nature of the invitation, I'd accepted because I had never imagined that this would one day be within my reach. It was as if they'd asked me to play soccer for my favorite professional team: something that, even if only because I'd just turned sixty-three, nobody was ever going to propose now. Also, in recent years, since overcoming a collapse brought on by the excesses of my old lifestyle, I had been recovering on all levels, and part of that process included opening my writing to arts other than literature. In other words, I was no longer obsessed with just literary material and had opened up the game to other disciplines.

For a man growing old and doing nothing to hide it, going to Kassel meant finding doors opening to a new world. Perhaps there I'd come across ideas other than my habitual ones. Maybe I'd manage to reach—with the patience of a prowler—an approximate vision of contemporary art's situation at the beginning of the twenty-first century. I was curious, besides, to see if there were many differences between the literary avant-garde—if it existed—and the artistic avant-garde that gathered every five years at Documenta. In the literary sphere, the avant-garde had lost ground, if not become almost entirely extinct, though there might still be the odd poetic project of interest. But had the same thing happened in the art world? Every five years, the great anticommercial fair of innovative art was held in Kassel. Documenta was famous for not being overly contaminated by the laws of the market.

I wanted to go to Documenta, I told her, but without having to go to the Dschingis Khan, for there I'd undoubtedly feel mislaid, completely displaced. Boston looked at me, smiled indulgently, and said I had just uttered the key word, for Carolyn Christov-Bakargiev and Chus Martínez planned to make their Documenta all about displacement, to put their heavy artillery behind this idea; they wanted to place artists outside their habitual mental comfort zones.

I didn't want to hazard a guess what "mental comfort zones" were for her, but I did want to know if there was still the slightest chance they might offer me something other than spending absurd mornings in the Chinese restaurant. It would be best if I didn't refuse to set foot in Dschingis Khan, she told me. It was to be the center of operations for successive invited writers and I couldn't be different from the others. She could reveal in advance that it would all be quite informal. I'd be left with more than enough time to devote to doing what I did best: observing, glancing, walking around like a profound idler; the organizers knew—having read my work, the entire curatorial team had interpreted it this way—that I saw myself as a sort of erratic stroller in continuous perplexed wandering.

I smiled without really knowing why. We're going to reduce your Chinese sentence, she suddenly said. I don't understand, I answered. Well, you see, she said, using the authority Carolyn Christov-Bakargiev and Chus Martínez have invested in me, I'm reducing the time you have to spend in the Chinese restaurant from three weeks to one.

From what she was telling me, I figured out that the Dschingis Khan wasn't located in a very central part of Kassel, but just the opposite. It was on the southern edge of Karlsaue Park, which in turn bordered a wooded area. In other words, the restaurant was on the outskirts of Kassel. I could take it or leave it. There were worse things than agreeing to it, because, after spending time in the restaurant, I could go for great walks through the park, through the forest. It would be a unique experience, she said, I could see unusual things, even discover (she smiled) the resolution to the mystery of the universe ...

That proposal contained very little logic, actually none. This invitation to a Chinese restaurant on the outskirts of Kassel had a slightly preposterous air about it, but the trip was a year away. I thought, or wanted to believe, that perhaps in that space of time other things for me to do there would occur to the organizers. (Or should I call them agents or curators? I wasn't experienced in these matters.)

"Will someone eventually reveal the mystery of the universe?" I asked.

She answered astutely in a voice that hadn't lost its charm all evening, and so I asked her permission to write her answer down on a napkin. I told her I'd devote myself to admiring it for the rest of my life.

"Without the McGuffins," she said, "there's not much we can do, perhaps sing hey, ho, the wind and the rain. But dinner's over."

It seemed as if she'd controlled the exact length of time for our dinner. In any case, it was much better that it should all end there because, at home before going out, I'd taken a happy pill that my old school friend Dr. Collado was trying to patent at the time. (I've changed the name of this dear and somewhat frustrated inventor of somewhat medicinal drugs.)

I'd taken that pill thinking it would help me minimize my nocturnal anguish. And although the pill did work initially, for a while now its effects had been wearing off and my situation was getting dangerous. I was starting to notice my usual bleak nighttime mood beginning to emerge, my deeply melancholic side. It seemed that at any moment Boston was going to ask me where I had left that supposed severe anguish I'd told her arrived so punctually every evening, which meant it was inadvisable for me to go out at night ... I dreaded that question and all the more so as I observed my melancholy advancing moment by moment. I even began to fear my face would turn into that of Mr. Hyde, so it seemed a very good idea that things here should end as soon as possible.

4

One evening, several weeks later, Chus Martínez and I arranged to meet. But when I arrived at the appointed place, there was María Boston, even more amusing and luminous than on the previous occasion, as if she wanted to show me she was capable of getting into the skin of a better character than the one she'd played for me the first night. I asked about Chus and there was a strange exchange of glances that struck me as incomprehensibly arduous.

"Don't you understand that I am Chus?" she said.

For a moment, she managed to make me feel like a complete idiot. I had to understand, she said, that the first time she phoned me, she thought it best to pass herself off as María Boston, a more energetic name so much more attractive than Chus Martínez, which was so Spanish and traditional. Afterward, she hadn't known how to unravel the snag, the windup that she was now trying to undo.

"I'm Chus. I've always been Chus. Got it?"

She seemed to be saying: Look, you really are stupid.

I smiled. What did one do in a case like this? Once again I had taken another euphoria-producing pill from Dr. Collado. What choice did I have? I couldn't sit there looking anguished all evening. I hoped I was taking it for the last time in my life. It had made me smile in a very natural way, although I was actually smiling, it seemed to me, like a perfect fool. The truth is I was in a fine mess. From the start, I'd noticed the mood produced by Collado's experimental pharmaceutical—what he called "the aspirin of charm"—wasn't entirely bad, but still left quite a bit to be desired.

I smiled like a poor fool.

"You're Chus, of course," I said. "You've always been Chus. Now I understand."

Over the course of this second encounter, she confirmed everything that had been said: she and Carolyn Christov-Bakargiev had agreed I could spend fewer days in Kassel, that one week would be enough, she only asked that I spend a while in the Chinese restaurant each morning. Indeed, they'd be grateful if I'd communicate as much as possible with the people I met there, with those interested in what I was writing, or rather those interested in my being a writer, and also with those simply wondering what on earth I was doing lost in that Chinese restaurant on the outskirts of Kassel.

Lost! Why did they want to see me adrift? Did they want to laugh at me? I decided to ask her why two women I barely knew—she and Carolyn—had devoted themselves to planning my loss in some faraway corner in the summer of 2012. What interest could they have in seeing me lost beside a forest? Luckily, my question coincided with an explosion of joy produced directly by the tablet, enabling me to show a more than ample smile on my face and scarcely any anxiety. I think, she said, that you're blowing things way out of proportion. There was a brief silence. I was trying to surmise, in any case, that there was something good about my being lost and also I tried to believe that deep down she, as curator of Documenta 13, was very deliberately challenging me: I had to accept her squalid proposal and not be offended, seeing the bright side of her paltry offer by virtue of my imagination.

I got up the nerve to ask her if she and Carolyn believed that, once I was at Documenta, my powers of observation would help me to probe more deeply into the amazing splendor of contemporary art. (I was being as ironic as I could.)

She stared at me. I could tell she was not going to affirm or deny anything. She simply recommended that I not lose sight of the fact that near the Chinese restaurant there was a forest, and forests were always where real stories took place. I didn't know what to say to that. I didn't know what she meant by real stories.

I told her that for years, I thought in order to write well one had to lead a bad life, and she immediately asked: What's that got to do with any of this? Nothing, Chus, it's just a McGuffin, as I suspect your phrase about real stories was. For a moment, everything got tangled up; the rhythm of our conversation was broken. We fell silent. I tried to remedy the situation, and the only thing that occurred to me was to tell her that I had a weakness for McGuffins, but that produced nothing but stupor on her part and more silence. Until she decided to diminish the tension and told me that the following day she was going to Afghanistan. The Documenta she and Carolyn were preparing with their curatorial team was taking place not only in the German city of Kassel, but also in Kabul, Alexandria, Cairo, and Banff. With the exception of the small team of organizers and a few invited guests, Documenta 13 would be too vast for any single visitor. She was sorry she had to be away for a while because she was really enjoying our conversation and she was grateful for how well I'd taken her passing herself off as María Boston one day and revealing her true identity the next.

Well, anyway, I said, it's a relief to know you're not going to change your name again. No, don't worry, she said, smiling enigmatically as she began to tell me about Documenta's road map, insisting on the spatial expansion from Kassel to Kabul, Alexandria, Cairo, and Banff. She advised me—in case it had occurred to me to think so—that I shouldn't believe she and Carolyn had a postcolonial attitude, rather that it was pure *polylogical* will.

I made a mental note of that adjective, which I'd never heard before. A short time later, I believed I saw a certain hope for my apparent dark future as a man confined to a polylogical Chinese restaurant. Among other things, she told me that a group called Critical Art Ensemble had found a recondite space far beyond the Kassel forest and was planning a series of lectures during the hundred days Documenta lasted. Talks, she told me, which probably no one will attend and no one will hear, given the remoteness of the place. I immediately realized that this space could be an ideal spot—obviously better than the blasted Chinese restaurant—to give a talk on any subject related to the avant-garde and the art of the new century. I asked her to try to get me invited as one of Critical Art Ensemble's hundred speakers, for suddenly nothing fascinated me as much as planning a talk that would be delivered beyond a forest, entitled "Lecture to Nobody."

I got very excited about this title, and here the pill, which was meant to liven me up, seemed to function perfectly. Perhaps the enthusiasm I displayed was excessive. We'll look into it, she said coldly, as if it bothered her to see me excited by the possibility of having some truly interesting activity in Kassel. But not much later she changed her tune and said she loved the title of my lecture. I could start preparing it because from that very moment it was in the program; but that wouldn't relieve me—she lowered her marvelous voice—from my daily sessions at the Chinese restaurant.

The cheerful expression on my face twisted slightly. What a huge obsession with that restaurant, I thought. *Nobody, nobody, lecture to nobody*, I heard her repeating to herself, as if suddenly the idea of a total absence of audience beyond the forest excited her as well.

We ended up finding ideal dates for my trip to Kassel: the last six days of the hundred that Documenta lasted; six days of September when the summer heat let up and the city would certainly be filled with visitors (as was the case on previous occasions) before the imminent closure of the exhibition.

As we said goodbye, she did not have the courtesy to tell me that she'd deceived me and was not Chus Martínez (as she had tricked me into believing). I did not discover that she'd been an imposter until a year later, when I arrived in Kassel and discovered the truth. I had said goodnight to her, convinced that she was Chus, and began to walk through the solitary streets on my satisfied and unhurried return home.

5

During my slow walk home, in the grip of an unstable state of mind, some words Kafka once wrote in a letter to Felice Bauer kept appearing and disappearing in my head: "Marienbad is unbelievably beautiful. I imagine if I were Chinese and were about to go home (indeed I am Chinese and I am going home), I would make sure of returning soon, and at any price."

This is the only passage in all of Kafka's writing where he says that deep down he is Chinese, which seems to indicate to us that Borges—recognizing Kafka's voice and habits in texts from diverse literatures and eras—was probably right to see Kafka's affinity with Han Yu, a ninth-century prose writer whom Borges discovered in the admirable *Anthologie raisonnée de la littérature chinoise* published in France in 1948.

According to what Kafka wrote to Felice Bauer, it's obvious that the Prague writer sensed his enigmatic relationship with China, who knows whether perhaps even including his precursor Han Yu.

That night, during my slow return home, I walked along imagining—for whatever reason, obviously I had my motives—that I was enacting Kafka's phrase; in other words, that I was Chinese and was going home. I eventually started enjoying playing that role, until there was a shift in everything and the pill's occasional positive effects stopped. Suddenly everything darkened for me, and I fell into the state of anguish and melancholy I'd wanted to avoid; I couldn't do anything to escape that slump in my mood and I muttered a thousand curses for having put myself in the hands of Dr. Collado. I remembered some old nocturnal strolls dominated by the same anguished perception that the world was full of messages in some secret code. In the middle of these negative perceptions, while I struggled in vain to recover my mood, I told myself it was very curious that a Chinese fellow like me had been invited to an Asiatic enclave in faraway Germany. While I thought all this (in a somewhat confused way of course), I remembered an absolutely intense and pivotal dream I'd had three years earlier in the town of Sarzana, in northern Italy, when I went to an international writers' event there and they put me up in an inn called Locanda dell'Angelo, way out in the countryside, eight kilometers from the town's center. Upon entering my room in this remote hotel, I immediately discovered that I'd forgotten my sleeping pills in Barcelona as well as the book I'd planned to read in bed. Even so, in spite of not having my usual sedatives, I managed to fall asleep, falling literally into a dead sleep, by remembering a Walter Benjamin essay in which he suggested that a word is not a sign, nor is it a substitute for something else, but the embodiment of an Idea. In Proust, in Kafka, in the surrealists, said Benjamin, the word parts company from meaning in the "bourgeois" sense and takes back its elemental and gestural power. Word and the gesture of naming were the same thing back in the time of Adam. Since then, language must have experienced a great fall, of which Babel, according to Benjamin, would only be a stage. The task of theology would consist of the recovery of the word, in all its mimetic originating power from the sacred texts in which it has been conserved.

I wondered there in Sarzana if fallen languages might still, all of them together, bring us closer to certain truths, truths related to the unknown origin of language. Suddenly realizing that, deep down, my whole life, without being entirely conscious of it, I had been trying to reconstruct a disarticulated discourse (the original discourse, shrouded in the mists of time), I fell asleep and into a very intense dream through which passed, with very quick steps, two of my friends, Sergio Pitol and Raúl Escari. The two of them marched electrically down the alleys of some old, possibly European, city center. The rain, however, seemed to be falling with strange sluggishness and with the same toxic appearance it has in Mexico City. The two of them went into a classroom and Sergio began to write signs I'd never seen, he wrote them with great speed on an extraordinarily vivid green chalkboard. The chalkboard transformed into a door in a pointed Arabic arch, which was an even more vivid green and on which Pitol was inscribing, slowing down the rhythm of his hand, the poetry of an unknown algebra, containing formulas and mysterious messages in cabalistic, Jewish style, although perhaps it was Islamic, Chinese Muslim, or simply Italian, from Petrarch's time; this poetic, strange, stateless algebra sent me to the center of the mystery of the universe, of a universe that seemed full of messages in some secret code.

When I woke up the next morning, I had a sensation of having been very close to an essential message, which I suspected only Pitol knew to its most profound extent. Sometimes, like today, when I return to that dream, I realize that when María Boston called to say the McGuffins wanted to reveal the mystery of the universe to me, I agreed to go to the meeting in part because my unconscious was still under the influence of the Sarzana dream. It's not out of the question that when I agreed to go to Kassel, I did so deep down (actually, very, very deep down) expecting to find there the secret of contemporary art, or maybe be initiated into the poetry of this unknown algebra, or perhaps to find what lay behind the door in a pointed Arabic arch, a door leading to a distant Chinese past, where pure language would be leading a hidden life.

6

A year after that encounter with the fake Chus, at the beginning of September 2012, and a week before I was to fly to Frankfurt to catch the train to Kassel, things had changed, and I was even doubting whether to go on this trip. After a long year in which I'd hardly had any contact with Documenta's curatorial team, there was almost nothing encouraging me to leave in a week for Germany. In that whole long year I'd received one single succinct email, from someone named Pim Durán, with my Lufthansa tickets attached and instructions for catching the train from Frankfurt to Kassel.

I had no further news from Chus Martínez (or, rather, from the person I believed to be Chus Martínez), and all my attempts to communicate with her had failed. Even so, I was completely sure I'd be seeing Chus as soon as I arrived at Documenta; a friend of hers had told me that most likely she'd been very busy co-curating the huge exhibition and hadn't had time to get back in touch with me, but in Kassel things would probably be easier.

From what I'd been able to read about Documenta 13, one thing was very clear: that is, it had far surpassed the previous occasion, the twelfth, which, among many other mistakes, had given in to the temptation of pandering to the media by inviting the Catalan chef Ferran Adrià. Its far-reaching television coverage undermined one of the unwritten laws of the twice-a-decade exhibition: to maintain a weak connection with the art market.

As if that weren't enough, I remembered that the unfortunate twelfth edition had been a venue for Ai Weiwei's media initiative that surprised everyone by bringing 1,001 Chinese citizens to Documenta. This event cast a shadow over my invitation. When I was seized by gloominess—this inevitably happened every evening and sometimes lasted way into the night—I feared, sometimes very dramatically (as comical as that might seem), that 1,001 Chinese writers were going to show up at the Dschingis Khan to see what I was writing, all standing behind me, at my back, gossiping about my handwriting and my writing behavior ...

In any case, given the lack of attention I'd received over the past year, nothing obliged me to go to Kassel, and even less thinking that the trip was only to hole up in a corner of a Chinese restaurant to show impertinent and curious people what I was writing.

With very little time left before my departure—I see myself on that day I've not forgotten, September 4, to be precise, just one week before having to leave for Germany—I remember walking in circles around my desk in Barcelona. Perhaps because of the late evening hour, feeling anxious and tormented, actually completely anguished, I'd been bothering everyone with my huge doubts about whether or not to leave for Frankfurt.

In spite of being invited to travel there, I knew absolutely nothing about Kassel, except that downtown there was a cinema called Gloria, a fascinating photograph of which I'd come across on the Internet one day. I'd saved a copy of it on my computer because there were no longer any screens like that in Barcelona, and because the Gloria seemed so very much like the neighborhood cinemas of my childhood, with continuous showings of classics on the big screens. As a boy, I'd hung around them looking at stills from the next week's films and also those announced with the ambiguous sign saying "Coming Soon."

For months, the Gloria Cinema was all of Kassel for me, since at no point did I see any other image of the city. On one occasion I even came to suppose that it was named in homage to the Van Morrison song "Gloria," that track whose beauty comes in part from the singer only speak-singing, or sing-speaking, imitating a growl like Howlin' Wolf's, that son of cotton farmers, whose voice was compared to "the sound of heavy machinery operating on a gravel road."

In fact, for a whole year, whenever I remembered that I'd soon have to travel to Kassel, all I could think of was going to the Gloria Cinema and the sound of heavy machinery.

Complicating everything on the evening of September 4, when anguish arrived punctually for its appointment with me as it did every evening, I received, through an editor of a newspaper that I habitually contribute to, a message from the Mexican writer Mario Bellatin, one of those authors I knew had preceded me in the Chinese chair at the Dschingis Khan. Bellatin had asked the editor to alert me to certain dangers that awaited me in Kassel: "If you see our mutual friend, tell him to tread carefully at Documenta, because they're quite irresponsible. The artists get accident insurance, but the writers don't. I had my computer stolen in broad daylight while I was working, and they couldn't have cared less."

When I read this, my fears got much worse and I considered not participating. So this famous Dschingis Khan, I thought, wasn't just a boring place at the far end of a park; it was also a dive where delinquents came straight in—with machine guns, one could only imagine—and took the tools of trade away from poor prose writers.

I decided I would not go to Kassel, but it didn't take me long to change my mind again when I remembered how eager I was to know what the state of the avant-garde of contemporary art was. I also thought that if I didn't go, I'd be left wondering forever what possible hidden charm there might be at the very heart of the Dschingis Khan and Carolyn Christov-Bakargiev and Chus Martínez's proposal.

Curiosity turned out to be stronger than fear, and I decided I'd go, though there was no way I was going to show up at the Chinese restaurant with my laptop. After all, nobody likes to get their gear stolen. But about three days before embarking on the journey, I sent an email to Bellatin to find out just how dangerous it was to set up in the Dschingis Khan. "Hi, Mario," I wrote, "I'd like it if you could give me more details about the circumstances surrounding the theft of your computer so I can get a better idea of the situation in which I'll find myself in a few days in that Chinese restaurant."

He answered almost instantly: "Don't worry. You just sit at a table in the back of the restaurant to write for a while. Go with a pencil and eraser and don't take your laptop, though that's not where mine got stolen ... I had another activity at the Documenta bookstore. I was working there trying to sell a hybrid book, and that's where the theft happened, someone in the middle of the throng took my briefcase with all my stuff in it."

Having learned that the danger wasn't at the restaurant, I calmed down a little and decided to write Pim Durán to inquire about certain aspects of my upcoming visit. In the email she'd sent me in April, under the letters of her name was written "Personal Assistant to the Head of Documenta and Museum Fridericianum, Veranstaltungs-GmbH, Friedrichsplatz 18." Such a long description of her position made me remember a Blaise Pascal phrase, a McGuffin about brevity, or its opposite: "The only reason this letter is so long is because I didn't have time to make it shorter."

I wrote to Pim Durán: "Dear Pim: The day on which I am theoretically to fly to Frankfurt is approaching, but the lack of news from your end makes me uneasy. All I have is a piece of paper with a round-trip ticket, and nothing else. I don't know what to expect."

As soon as I sent that email, I realized that perhaps I'd gone on too long with the text because I hadn't had time to make it shorter. I was about to send another to apologize when I received this succinct, efficient, very speedy reply from Pim Durán: "I'll get in touch with Alka, who is the person in charge of your visit to Kassel. Don't worry, you'll be well taken care of and we'll keep you apprised of everything. Alka will be waiting for you at the Frankfurt airport."

The message calmed me for a few moments, although it worried me to have to depend on Alka, which was an indecipherable name for me. I didn't know if it was a masculine or feminine name, or that of a fourth-generation German robot. On the other hand, what did this mean, a "person in charge of my visit to Kassel"? Would they not let me take a step on my own?

I did a Google search and found an Alka Kinali, a Croatian belly dancer born in 1986 and known simply as Alka; she'd been dancing since childhood and had won international recognition thanks to a variety program called *Zagreb Show*. It could be her, why not? I didn't look any further. When I met Alka, I wouldn't tell her, but I'd always associate her with the Croatian dancer. My grandmother's sister had been the lover of a Croatian dancer, but that was another story; it's probably not at all relevant, although it confirms that, as a dear second cousin, the grandson of my grandmother's sister, used to say, every story leads to another story, which in turn leads to another story, and so on into infinity.

7

Over the following hours I searched for information on the thirteenth edition, which only had a week left to run. I was interested to find out that Documenta 13 had brought together two hundred artists, philosophers, scientists, critics, and writers, who had presented an enormous number of works and been involved in all kinds of events, many of them simultaneous. Some had lasted for weeks.

They were held or conducted not only in Kassel but as far afield as Canada and Afghanistan. Nobody could even dream of seeing it all. In Kassel alone the exhibition had spread over the entire urban area, throughout Karlsaue Park, and even into the forest beyond the huge park—that is, it had spread over all the usual spaces, and was also in others never utilized before at Documenta.

Karlsaue Park was an immense space, with gardens, paths, and canals located symmetrically in front of the summer palace, the Orangerie. Evidently, I read in an online newspaper, Kassel 2012 reproduced "that sublime postmodern condition: the sense of one's own infinitude that comes from experiencing the disproportionate, pointing toward what we'll never apprehend or comprehend." I read this, and for a few moments my occasionally postmodern mind concentrated on certain "experiences of the disproportionate" I had seen up close and on the impossibility of taking in, of hanging on to, of partially or totally comprehending the world. I ended up wondering whether traveling to Kassel might not be the greatest opportunity I'd ever had to approach—almost to caress—a certain total reality: at least that of contemporary art, which was no small thing. But a little while later, I wondered why I wanted to take in so much.

Then, perhaps so I wouldn't be so scared about those six days ahead, with their more than possible promise of a radical solitude, I told myself that as soon as I arrived in Kassel, it would be advisable to find what one might call a "thinking cabin" for the evenings. It might suffice to remember the words of an enamored Czech to his fiancée: "I have often thought that the best mode of life for me would be to sit in the innermost room of a spacious, locked cellar with my writing things and a lamp." I thought I should know how to convert my hotel room at dusk into a sober isolation chamber, suitable as a place for reflection.

Please understand me. The world was in very bad shape in September 2012, in terrible shape when I traveled to Kassel. The economic and moral crises, especially in Europe, had deteriorated utterly. One had the feeling—as I write this, one still does—that the world had perished and was irremediably in bad shape, or at least would be for a long time to come. This inevitably contaminated everything and created an atmosphere of fatality, leading me to see the world as something now tragically lost. At my age, it was easier to look at things like that, because everything seemed hopeless; any idea of changing things seemed to lead one to unending, fruitless efforts.

By way of simple self-defense, I'd decided to turn my back on the lost and irreparable world, which is why the idea of trying to set up a place of meditation in the evenings in Kassel seemed sensible to me, certainly much more so than the world; in my "thinking cabin" I could devote myself to pondering joy, for example, to try to see it as something close to the nucleus of all creation. The cabin would help me to concentrate on art. Here, after all, was an opportunity to try to modestly emulate persons I'd admired for certain gestures: persons who had known in their time how to submerge themselves in those tiny spaces so suitable for solitary reflection. Wittgenstein, for example, retired to Skjolden, Norway, to a cabin he built himself in a completely isolated place. He retired there to delve into his despair: to intensify his mental and moral distress, but also to stimulate his intellect and reflect on the necessity of art and love and also on the hostility of the world toward those necessities.

The book I had first thought to take with me to my German cabin concerned precisely the joy of art when it revealed its essential seriousness (not about the world, but entirely about art). In the end, I left this book in Barcelona and brought Camilo José Cela's *Journey to the Alcarria* instead. It was an outlandish choice, because of the contrast I'd found between the modernity and sophistication of Kassel and the belfries and terrible cripples of the world of my compatriot Cela. But I wanted to take a book that told of a journey so different from my own, and that one met my criteria.

At the last moment, I also stuck a copy of Rüdiger Safranski's *Romanticism: An Odyssey of the German Spirit* into my luggage. Ever since I read it for the first time, I've always enjoyed going back to read fragments in which the author explained Nietzsche's world, how Nietzsche thought it necessary to live without illusions, and at the same time, in spite of having discovered life's great futility, to be passionately fond of it. *Romanticism* always allowed me to return to a phrase of Nietzsche's that over time had become one of my convictions: "Only as aesthetic phenomena are existence and the world eternally justified."

8

"Make sure you see the works of Tino Sehgal, Pierre Huyghe, and Janet Cardiff. I'm told they've outdone themselves." Alicia Framis, an artist friend drawn to avant-garde ideas, wrote this to me three days before I'd be leaving for Kassel. I'd never heard the names she mentioned, but understood they must be artists that might be of interest to me, and would provide me with something of which I really was entirely ignorant. (This made me enthusiastic about traveling to Germany to enter that universe.)

"William Kentridge's project *The Refusal of Time* in a warehouse at the old station is worth seeing," another friend wrote just a couple of hours after Alicia Framis's email. And a good friend from Getafe sent me, at the end of the day, a message commenting on how interesting she'd found "Mark Dion's stunning library, and, most of all, an oblique clock by an Albanian sculptor."

To convince myself that it was going to be a really great trip, I began to think that there was common ground between the great expeditions of yesteryear and the solitary one I was embarking on with my sights set on Kassel. There lay the danger, an indispensable element of any worthwhile journey. Because danger, I told myself, always brings the pleasure of feeling fear. And fear is fantastic, especially fear at the prospect of finding oneself faced with strange, unfamiliar things, maybe even new ones.

All good journeys incorporate the infinite pleasure and great excitement that moments of great fear also produce. I began to think about this and felt excited from the moment I sensed that I was traveling to Kassel with a unique sensation: an intense and maybe terrifying pleasure similar to what I felt one night casually heading down a dark alley completely unknown to me. There, I suddenly noticed a breath on the back of my neck, dry but phantasmagoric, because I spun around and there was no one there. Knowing I was actually alone in that alley, I kept walking, but found it impossible to act like I hadn't noticed; it was impossible to overlook the fact that the ghostly breathing was still there: cold, icy, rasping, discreet. How to describe it better? There was nobody there, but it felt like someone, with noticeable regularity, was huffing, and his glacial breath, in a very odd way, God knows, was landing directly on the back of my neck.

9

Two days before leaving for Documenta, I went, as I did every Sunday morning, to meet some people on the terrace of the Bar Diagonal, and there, John William Wilkinson (Wilki to his friends), mishearing and thinking that I was staying in an apartment in Kassel directly above a Chinese restaurant (from where I could look out over a forest), said to me—he said to all of us there—that what I was about to live through reminded him of the Irish poet John Millington Synge.

"Explain yourself!" we all said immediately.

This demanding repartee was characteristic of our *tertulia*. We endeavored with admirable tenacity on these Sunday mornings—naturally we knew it was in vain, but we made the effort anyway—to leave nothing unexplained.

The great Synge, Wilki told us more or less—but I'm sure he made it up, and, on top of that, now I'm twisting his words—was a guy, or, to phrase it better, a poet of notable talent, who traveled at the end of the nineteenth century to the Aran Isles, located at the mouth of Galway Bay on the west coast of Ireland. On one of these islands, Inishmaan, he stayed in a rough cottage with a beautiful view that can still be visited today. He also spent time on the second floor of a big house on Inishmaan that no longer exists. There, a discreet hole in the bedroom floor allowed him to listen to conversations and arguments, all of which were in Gaelic. For five summers, he spied on these neighbors' chats without understanding anything because he didn't know a word of that language, but he was convinced he understood everything perfectly. He was so sure that he understood anything spoken in Gaelic that he ended up producing (out of everything he heard and compiled over the summers) his famous anthropology book *The Aran Islands.* This book, which Synge finished in 1901 and published in 1907, describes the thought and customs of that remote Irish island lost in the middle of the Atlantic (that strange paradise, until then barely desecrated by any outsider). The text reflected, among other things, the belief that beneath the surface of the islanders' Catholicism it was possible to detect a "substratum" of the ancient pagan beliefs of their ancestors.

More intrigued than usual, I listened to the wonderful Wilki, for I still hadn't figured out what link he could be making between an Irish poet on an Atlantic island and me, who was only going to a sort of Chinese cubicle in Germany (though in any case I fully trusted that he might have found one).

Synge's experiences over five summers on Inishmaan, Wilki went on telling us, formed the basis of many of the plays he wrote about rural farming and fishing communities in Ireland. In fact, his works helped create the unmistakable rural style of Dublin's famous Abbey Theater for the following four decades. And everything indicated (Wilki concluded) many parallels between Synge's vagabonds and Samuel Beckett's tramps. In fact, part of Beckett's inspiration—although maybe the author of *Molloy* never came to know it—proceeded from the imagination that overpowered Synge when he "listened" to the conversations of his downstairs neighbors on Inishmaan in such a singular and inventive way.

I don't understand, I said. But a very short while later, helped by Wilki himself, I began to see more clearly when he said that he knew what I had to do in case I found myself staying by chance above the Chinese restaurant and there was a discreet hole in the floor of my room.

Very simply, Wilki answered his own question, you must never lose sight of what you hear in German or Chinese down below in the Dschingis Khan, for it could come in very handy in creating an anthropological theory on the ideas and customs of that place.

"Explain yourself! Explain yourself more!"

The other *tertulianos*, animated now by the whisky, repeated the initial demand, as if wanting to help me. And they asked him not to overburden me with so many responsibilities as well. That encouraged me to intervene, telling Wilki I did not believe it was even minimally probable that in my room I would find a hole in the floor. You'll be able to find it, he responded unflustered, you'll see with time how you manage to find that hole.

I admired his quick answers, as well as the ease with which he could introduce new concepts into the *tertulia*, as on that almost historic day when he explained—particularly to me who'd never heard of such a thing—what a McGuffin was. Maybe for this reason, I decided to reply with a McGuffin when he dropped his imperturbable sentence, predicting that I would know how to find the hole in the floor.

"Careful, Wilki," I said, "because the commander didn't marry her in the springtime."

From student to maestro. A McGuffin through and through. Nevertheless, Wilki again found a quick reply and began to tell us, just like that, the advantages of spring weddings. We were flabbergasted. What was he talking about? As incredible as it seemed, Wilki had begun to calmly list, as if knowing them by heart, the various advantages of getting married in the springtime. He made the conversation compelling, as if the Sunday morning *tertulia* actually had a much greater energy than it displayed, and moreover, a perfect internal coherence.

10

That night at home I watched a television documentary about the growing power of modern China until my wife went to bed, when I started investigating Kassel. I learned that all the telescopes in the French-sounding Orangerie Palace were pointing toward *Clocked*

Perspective, a piece by the Albanian artist Anri Sala, located in Karl-saue, two kilometers away. Beside the telescopes, an 1825 G. Ulbricht painting of a castle hung amid several clocks; the painting featured a real clock, and though the castle was seen at an angle, the clock surprisingly met the viewer face-on. Anri Sala—undoubtedly the Albanian my Getafe friend had referred to in her recent email—had corrected this error in his sculpture, and his clock told the correct time on its slanted dial, matching the angle of Ulbricht's painted castle.

Two hours later, I fell asleep thinking I was going to Kassel to look for the mystery of the lost and irreparable universe, to be initiated into an unknown algebra and to search for an oblique clock. I dreamed that someone asked me insistently if I didn't believe that the modern taste for images was nourished by an obscure opposition to knowledge. The question could be formulated more simply, I kept thinking. But in that dream, it grew increasingly twisted and bothered me infinitely, the intellectual side of it seeming so unnecessarily complex. In the end, everything was bothering me. I was returning very tired from my journey to the center of the labyrinth of contemporary art's avant-garde, where I'd found myself in a pure nightmare, within a sort of quagmire, in which the same movement was repeated over and over again: in an intensely red Chinese room, I was implacably submitting the concepts *home* and *feeling at home* to an endless, skeptical scrutiny.

The intellectual plot of the nightmare had been so intricate that I was delighted to wake up and discover the real world was much simpler, I'd even go so far as to say much more idiotic.

It was five in the morning, and, since I was suddenly wide awake, I went to my study and began to reread the copy of Kafka's *The Great Wall of China and Other Short Works* that I had in my library and hadn't opened for years. I found there, among those other short works, one I didn't remember called "Homecoming," written in Berlin in 1923. I remember the emotion I felt as soon as I started to read it, because I realized that in some way the piece contained an explanation of why, in a letter to his fiancée, Kafka had written that somewhat mysterious phrase that he was Chinese and was going home. In fact, I had the impression—strengthened by the time of day—that this story, written in 1923, had been written for me so I would read it one day, when the hour came for me to travel to a Chinese enclave in the middle of Germany:

> I have returned. I have passed under the arch and am looking around. It's my father's old yard....I have arrived. Who is going to receive me? Who is waiting behind the kitchen door? Smoke is rising from the chimney, coffee is being made for supper. Do you feel you belong, do you feel at home? I don't know. I feel most uncertain.... The longer one hesitates before the door, the more estranged one becomes. What would happen if someone were to open the door now and ask me a question? Would I not myself then behave like one who wants to keep his secret?

Did Kafka write this for me? Well, why not? I remembered that simple and guileless question he had pondered on a certain occasion: *Could it be that one can take a girl captive by writing?* Seldom has anyone formulated with such ingenuousness, such precision, and such depth the very essence of literature. It was the very task that Kafka was going to affix to writing in general, and to his own writing in particular. Because contrary to what so many believe, no one writes to entertain, although literature might be one of the most entertaining things around; no one writes to "tell stories," although literature is full of brilliant tales. No, one writes to *take the reader captive*, to possess, seduce, subjugate, to enter into the spirit of another and stay there, to touch, to win the reader's heart ...

Franz Kafka, son of the businessman Hermann Kafka, seemed there in front of his father's house to perceive that, in spite of appearances, the home did not belong to him. One can easily imagine him hesitating for hours before the big old house and finally not entering, but devoting himself to pursuing his tenacious search for a place, for a home that perhaps he'd never find by actually going home, but that he might find one day along the way.

On the morning of Tuesday, September 11, the national day of Catalonia, I left home so early, it was still nighttime, a completely dark night. A police car drove past, and I imagined that, seeing me getting furtively into a taxi with my suitcase, it would be hard for the policemen not to suspect me of some strange undertaking.They might be thinking: What reason could that guy who looks Catalan have for abandoning the city so surreptitiously on a day like today? There was to be a big patriotic demonstration in Barcelona that day and expectations were high, as was the tension, which was why police cars were circulating in the predawn hours.

Climbing into my taxi with my suitcase as quickly as possible, I looked like I was skipping town. Maybe I was the only citizen who was leaving. I was sure there was more to life than the nation; after all, I was traveling to the very center of the contemporary avant-garde, I was going to Kassel, via Frankfurt, probably to look for the mystery of the universe and be initiated into the poetry of an unknown algebra, and also to try to find an oblique clock and a Chinese restaurant and, of course, to try to find a home along the way.

When I arrived at the Frankfurt airport, contrary to what I'd been told, no one was waiting for me. At first, I was incredulous. One always fears these kinds of things are going to happen, and they often do. When they do, one even feels slightly upset: it's the same sensation as feeling lost in a strange place without knowing where to spend the night or who might shelter you in a distant city.

I tried to remember the name of the young lady who was supposed to meet me to help me get the train to Kassel. Finally I remembered: she was called Alka and was Croatian. That's what I remembered hearing from Pim Durán, whose telephone number I'd had the good idea to save in my cell phone. I called her to say I was in Frankfurt and nobody had come to meet me. How odd, said Pim Durán. Hang up, and I'll call you right back. I hung up, beginning to plan my return to Barcelona. After all, now I had a justification for leaving. Actually, I had two. The other would be that at the last moment, on arriving in

Frankfurt, I'd realized that the labyrinth of the avant-garde of contemporary art just made me laugh and I was backing out, returning that same day to Barcelona and to Catalonia's National Day celebrations. But I couldn't use that miserable excuse because I'd systematically forbidden myself to laugh, as so many do, at certain types of avant-garde art aspiring to originality. I'd forbidden myself because I knew that it was always quite easy for idiots to insult that sort of art, and I didn't want to be one of those kinds of people. I detested all those ominous voices very common in my country that displayed their supposed lucidity and frequently proclaimed fatalistically that we were living in a dead time for art. I guessed that, behind this easy tittering, there was always a hidden resentment deep down, a murky hatred toward those who occasionally try to gamble, to do something new or at least different; this tittering hides a morbid grudge against those who are aware that, as artists, they're in a privileged position to fail where the rest of the world wouldn't dare, and that's why they try to create risky works of art that would lack meaning if they didn't contain the possibility of failure at their core.

I had systematically forbidden myself to laugh at avant-garde art, though without losing sight of the possibility that today's artists were a pack of ingenues, a bunch of Candides who didn't notice anything, collaborators unaware that they were collaborating with the powers that be. Of course, so I wouldn't get entirely discouraged, I kept in mind a novel by Ignacio Vidal-Folch, *The Plastic Head*, in which he laid out a funny sketch of the business of visual arts, with its museum directors, critics, gallery owners, professors of aesthetics, and (as a dispensable element given the abundance on offer) its artists. It was a tale that intelligently and energetically set out the paradox of the most furious and radical visual arts having turned into an ornament of the nation. Vidal-Folch—who is essentially a man of letters—showed some sympathy for the poor artists, who, though they were the final and weakest links in the chain, seeming to him still in some way dangerous and powerful.

Maybe because I'm a man of letters and still believe that one can be somewhat optimistic in this world—to tell the truth, I only believe

29

that in the mornings when I enjoy an enviable mood—I was on the side of some of the artists. This was a choice I'd made at a certain point in my life and I'd promised myself that, even if I found some reason to, I'd never change. One sometimes needs to think that not all the strangers surrounding us are horrible beings. I think I was telling myself this, or something similar, when my cell phone rang.

"Alka speaking. I am here in the airport. And you?"

"Alka!"

I wanted to love her, you'll have to understand. When one spends a long time alone in the Frankfurt airport, one goes crazy at receiving even the tiniest crumbs of affection.

The strange thing is that, after I exclaimed her name, from then on, over the course of six exhausting telephone calls before she finally figured out my exact position in the airport, she never again spoke to me in my own language. She spoke in English, German, and even Croatian, languages I neither speak nor understand. Maybe that's why we took over an hour to find each other. There was no way to clarify anything. Alka had clearly memorized those first three sentences she'd said when I'd answered my phone, but she didn't know how to say anything else in Spanish.

After almost an hour of countless telephonic vicissitudes, we finally saw each other face-to-face. By then I was on the very verge of insanity. Suddenly, Alka appeared with an enormously wide smile and she was so beautiful and exotic, so irremediably sexy, that I lost all capacity for rage. I didn't complain at all about the wait, turning into a silly fool and probably moving and acting as if I'd been stupidly seduced. I followed her obediently to the train. Halfway to Kassel—perhaps because in spite of many attempts, we could only manage to understand each other through physical and sometimes quite confusing signals—I started imagining that she, in our unspoken language, was telling me it was very hot and she kept repeating this until finally showing me that she wasn't wearing anything under her skirt. I took a good look. It was true, and then I threw myself on Alka, and she encouraged me to continue and said to me: Yes, yes, destroy me, *destrózame!*

Setting aside that torrid scene, I returned to the real world, where I confirmed once again that everything was monotonous, and poor Alka, as far as I could tell from her ridiculous gestures, was describing something she'd eaten the previous night in Kassel, which was quite possibly a hamburger, although it might also have been, according to the drawing her fingers sketched out several times, an ant.

I told myself the latter was true, that her story wasn't as humdrum as I believed, but I had no way of knowing. I decided to turn my gaze toward the landscape framed by the train window: monotonous villages without church steeples to break the flat perspectives, all the houses the same height, a pure apotheosis of tedium. I remembered something Roland Barthes had written about his admired and later so reviled China, what he'd commented about the Chinese villages seen from afar: all so insipid, he said, because of their lack of steeples, all absolutely insipid, like Chinese tea.

"So, you've been eating ants," I said. I knew that luckily she wouldn't understand me.

Soon afterward, after arriving at the more modern of the two stations in Kassel, we took a taxi to the Hotel Hessenland, located at the top of Königsstrasse, an important thoroughfare in the city. I still find it difficult to forget the trip between the station and the hotel, because all along the way, it seemed like people in the street were stopping all of a sudden when they saw me go by, standing and following me with their gazes, as if saying: It's about time you got here.

Were they expecting someone and confusing me with him? That was really weird. How could I think that passersby were staring at me when in reality the opposite was happening and nobody—I well knew—was expecting me in Kassel?

Now I know what was happening to me was that I felt so alone, I had to imagine people were waiting for me to arrive like a breath of fresh air. Still unhinged from thinking everybody might be waiting for me there, I crossed the threshold of the Hessenland. I thought the receptionist, who was brokenly speaking my language, received me as if she thought it was about time I got there. Answering one of my questions, she told me that Karlsaue Park, the forest, and the Dschingis Khan restaurant were more or less on the opposite side of the city.

"*Muy lejos*," I heard her say. Very far away.

Then, she told me about the forest and explained that there was a great variety of birds and, for her taste, very few squirrels. That was what she said, and it struck me as so exaggeratedly trivial, I even suspected she'd received orders to be that way, that is, to be so banal. I decided to surprise her and ask if what she really meant to tell me was that in Kassel there were very few squirrels with a truly avant-garde soul. Alka laughed, as if she'd perfectly understood my question. But she hadn't understood, that's for sure. So it became clear that Alka was laughing because her job obliged her to laugh at everything I said. There is nothing more irritating.

"Desiring stupid women requires one to be understanding," I said.

It was just a McGuffin, but Alka laughed and laughed and her whole belly trembled.

"Alka speaking," I said to her in Spanish. "I am in the *aeropuerto*. And you?"

It was horrible because she went into such convulsions that she fell on the floor laughing. When she stood up with my help, I almost said "Alka speaking" again to see if she'd test out the cold floor of the spotless Hessenland reception area once more. But I resisted this malicious temptation.

13

When María Boston arrived at the Hessenland to relieve Alka of her mission and incidentally, I suppose, rescue me from her laughing assistance, I, logically, thought it was Chus Martínez who had arrived at the hotel. What else was I going to think? For that reason, when she warned me that she wanted to resolve an important misunderstanding, I was a little lost. It might strike me as odd, she said, but a year ago in Barcelona she had found herself forced to pass herself off as her boss, as Chus. Chus had begged her to usurp her personality, for she feared I would get angry if she didn't show up at our meeting that evening. Did I forgive them for the deceit?

First I was astonished. Then I reacted. Sure, I forgave them, I said, but had they imagined I was so sensitive, so irascible? Perhaps someone had told them that since turning sixty I'd become somewhat intransigent? Who'd told them?

I pretended that it didn't much matter, but in reality I couldn't really understand it very well. That identity exchange was surely odd, almost as odd as people, seeing my taxi go past, stopping in the streets of Kassel to approve my arrival with their gazes. No, there was nothing that could justify María Boston pretending to be Chus that evening in Barcelona. Even so, I decided not to make too much of a fuss about it. Besides, I thought, if I admitted my skepticism, I might be seen as a neurotic or not very flexible guy, maybe not very understanding of human weakness, and, most of all, as not much of a lover of what I most defended in my literature: playing games, transferring identities, the joy of being someone else …

I tried to act as naturally as possible and asked Boston about Pim Durán. What I really wanted to know was whether Pim Durán was also her, because now anything was possible.

"She's my assistant," Boston said, "and I'm Chus's assistant."

I asked her if she knew where her boss was and if her boss wasn't afraid—now that she had more reason to be than she did a year ago—that I'd get angry that I still hadn't met her.

What happened, María Boston hurried to explain, was that the incredibly busy Chus had to go to Berlin that very morning, but I mustn't worry, since she was coming back just to have dinner with me on Thursday evening, at eight on the dot. She urged me to write it down: at the Osteria restaurant on Jordanstrasse; everything was foreseen, planned, organized with true Germanic order.

I wanted to know where the works of Tino Sehgal, Pierre Huyghe, and Janet Cardiff could be found. I pronounced those names as if I'd known them all my life when actually I had no idea who they were.

Tino Sehgal's contribution to Documenta, said Boston, was taking place in the building right next door to the hotel, and, if I wanted, she'd go there with me. It was called *This Variation*. It was, in fact, of all the works presented in Kassel, the only one that was very close; it was just there, in an old annex of the hotel, now unused and currently one of Documenta's venues. Was I a Sehgal fan? I preferred to tell her the humble truth, that I knew nothing of that artist's activity, actually I knew nothing of any of the participants in Documenta 13.

"This is so contemporary!" she exclaimed.

She meant that in the world it was more and more normal not to know about what was truly contemporary. Her phrase was also a sort of a wink, she said later, to a recent Tino Sehgal performance in Madrid, where a group of museum guards—to the visitors' surprise—suddenly came to life, began to dance, and then softly sang the phrase *This is so contemporary* while pointing toward the Sehgal piece.

What people appreciated so much about this trendy artist, Boston said, was that the museum workers seemed to be part of the work of art, maybe they were even the work itself.

I didn't yet know the greatness and genius of Sehgal. I just thought that placing museum workers as artworks was not the least bit original. After all, who hasn't at some point thought that museum guards were the real works of art? As for putting life before art, that was something I had the impression it was all well and good and even healthy to do but had very much been seen before.

Later, I began to take more interest in Sehgal, especially when I saw that his principal motto could be: "When art goes by like life." Sehgal proposed that only by participating in his performance could a person say he or she had seen his work. If you think about it, that's really good. When art goes by like life. It sounded perfect.

Boston and I went outside and into the old tumbledown annex next door to the Hessenland. After walking down a short corridor, we arrived at a small garden, where on the left-hand side was the room in which nothing could be seen and where you could, if you wanted, venture into the darkness itself to see what happened, what kind of experience awaited you. It was a dark room, Boston warned me, a room you entered thinking no one was there, perhaps just another visitor who had preceded you, but after being inside for a while, we started to perceive, without being able to see anybody, the presence of some young people, like otherworldly spirits, singing and dancing and seeming to live among the shadows. They were performers of sometimes enigmatic, sometimes fluid movements, occasionally stealthy and then frenetic, in any case invisible.

Although many other things could be said about that dark room, in principle I could summarize: Tino Sehgal was presenting *This Variation*, a space in darkness, a hidden place in which a series of people awaited visitors and, when the moment was right, sang songs and offered the experience of living a piece of art as something fully sensory.

Sehgal, Boston reminded me, rejected the idea that art had to have a physical expression, that is, it had to be a painting, a sculpture, an artifact or installation; he treated the idea of a written explanation of his work with equal disdain. Therefore, as she'd told me before, the only way to be able to say that you'd seen a Sehgal work was to see it live. For example, there wasn't even a record of that piece in the thick Documenta 13 catalogue, as Sehgal had asked Carolyn Christov-Bakargiev and Chus Martínez to respect his desire to be invisible.

Pure Duchamp, I thought. And I remembered that sunshade Duchamp was working on one summer in Cadaqués, which, in the end, turned out to be to shelter him from the sun or, to put it a better way, so he could settle into the shadows, his favorite territory. Where was that sun shelter now? Only in the minds of those who saw it or enjoyed the shade beneath it. Since they'd all been dying off, there were very few left—if any—before that "canvas" (once a silent work of art) would disappear from living memory.

Yes, it was clear: art goes by like life. And Sehgal was an illustrious heir to Duchamp. But was he innovating? Could it be said that he belonged to some avant-garde?

No, I decided, he wasn't really innovating. But since when was it necessary for art to be dedicated to innovation? This is exactly what I was wondering when I walked into *This Variation*, Sehgal's dark room.

(That night, I coincidentally stumbled upon a long interview with Chus Martínez on my computer—finally I saw her face—and her declarations helped me gauge whether today's artists were innovators or not. In the interview Chus explained that Documenta 13 wasn't like other exhibitions; it wasn't just for looking at, but could also be *lived*. And when she was asked if art was still being innovative or if it was more schematic, she answered: "In art we don't innovate, that happens in an industry. Art is neither creative nor innovative. That we leave to the world of shoes, cars, aeronautics. It's an industrial vocabulary. Art is art, and what you make of it is up to you. Art, of course, neither innovates nor creates.")

Not yet knowing that Documenta 13 was for *living* and, especially, not knowing "art is art, and what you make of it is up to you," I walked into *This Variation* and advanced through the dark room without seeing anything or sensing anyone's presence. I even forgot that there might be more than one person or ghost in there.

Soon I found out I was not alone. Suddenly, someone, who seemed more accustomed to the semidarkness of the place, went past me and intentionally brushed against my shoulder. I reacted, prepared to put up some resistance if anyone tried to touch me again. But it didn't happen. For the rest of the day, I wouldn't be able to get the feel of that touch out of my head.

Soon afterward, I thought I noticed—it was impossible to see anything but darkness—that the person who'd brushed up against me was dancing away toward the back of the room, gathering there with other souls, who, when they distinguished my presence in that impenetrable obscurity, abandoned their silence and also began to dance, humming strange, slight songs or chants, almost like Hare Krishna.

I walked out of there thinking it had all been more than odd and that, depending on how you looked at it, it was terrible to discover the significance of a stranger brushing against one's shoulder.

"Well?" was all Boston asked when she saw me.

I understood that she wanted to know how my experience inside the gloomy room had been, but I found it difficult to communicate what had happened to me there. I had the impression I'd just seen something that wasn't art *about* some matter, that wasn't discursive or about anything weighty that I'd spent a lifetime fleeing and not managing to get away from; it seemed to me that I'd just seen *art itself*. But I didn't know exactly how to explain that to Boston; I had to think more about it; so I opted to answer evasively, telling her I'd just been reminded of the canon of Poitiers.

The word *canon* sounded strange in that context. Of what? she asked. Someone Montaigne wrote about, I said, a preacher who didn't leave his room for thirty years and gave some extraordinary excuses for not leaving. Sounds like Ratzinger, remarked Boston; they say he never moves from his office in the Vatican.

14

Leaving Sehgal's room behind, we crossed the garden of the old annex, walking along the corridor that led to the street.

Boston said she was a fan of strolling, of journeying on foot. It seemed so odd to her that the most natural and basic way of getting around could become the most luminous of activities; perhaps it was such a creative thing to do because it took place at human speed. Going for a walk, she told me, seemed to produce a clear mental syntax, a narrative of its own.

After this brief reflection, she went back to worrying about the impression Sehgal's room might have made on me, she wanted to know how I'd felt.

"Well, look," I said point-blank, "I have to tell you that without England's resistance to Hitler, I wouldn't be here today."

That sentence was clearly a McGuffin, perhaps arising directly from the very art of walking. It came out as the first thing that entered my head. I realized that this art of *journeying on foot* facilitated, among other things, the ability to say things without thinking about them first; you said things, letting them literally fly out of your mouth.

Unlike what we say after we've carefully formulated an idea, polishing it until we feel ready to let it go, the sentence that is unconsidered and born directly from a walk may be daring, strange, and seem at times as though it is not ours. On other occasions, it may even have an unexpected syntax that sometimes surprises us, because we discover it was overwhelmingly ours without our knowing it.

"Without England's resistance?" Boston queried.

I kept quiet, I didn't know what to say; in truth that McGuffin hadn't felt like mine at any point. I kept quiet, but it was not an embarrassing silence. When two people walk along conversing, the silences are never tense, violent, or serious. It doesn't matter, for example, if you don't respond to something, because in fact everything follows its course without any excessive dramatization.

On our left-hand side, on an avenue that crossed Königsstrasse, Boston pointed out the stop for the Documenta bus. In the mornings, it could drop me for free at the door of the Dschingis Khan in fifteen minutes.

These were the words I most feared: Dschingis Khan.

Going to that Chinese restaurant felt like a schoolroom chore, and, on top of that, I had no desire to show anybody at all what I was writing. Perhaps that's why I pretended I hadn't heard, staying very focused on my walk.

A few seconds followed, during which I looked solemnly at the ground. We were heading down Königsstrasse toward the Fridericianum, the central museum, or temple of Documenta. I felt I was walking along resisting everything and particularly going into the Dschingis Khan.

"Sehgal's dark room is the closest room you have to your hotel bedroom," Boston said, accompanying her convoluted sentence with beguiling diction and an attractive slight smile.

I didn't understand why she said that, but for precisely that reason the sentence stayed more firmly engraved on my memory; I think I retained it in the hope of understanding it later on, as in fact did happen. When I returned to the hotel two hours later and went to my room with the idea of starting to turn it into a "thinking cabin,"

I remembered her phrase straightaway. I remembered it as soon as I saw that, in effect, you really could lean into the street from the balcony and see the entrance to the building where the dark room was to be found.

"And are you going to write about this?" she asked, as we slowly continued making our way down Königsstrasse toward the Fridericianum, about a twelve-minute walk. Write about what? Oh, she said, I'm asking whether you're thinking of writing about your direct connection with Sehgal's dark room. Well, possibly, was all I said in reply, perhaps a little thrown because the question seemed related to the idea of showing my texts to visitors at the Dschingis Khan. But later I realized that perhaps what she was really asking me was to write for her. Why not? Was it then true that one could take a girl captive by writing? Luckily, thinking things through more carefully, I very soon saw I'd get nowhere if I considered wanting to take Boston captive. So, making the most of my common sense, I calmed down, telling myself that by no means had she asked me to subjugate her. I then chose to explain to her that I planned to shut myself up in my hotel room in the evenings and turn it into a place of isolation, a space well-suited to reflection: a place similar in the imagination to a cabin where it would be easy to devote myself to thinking, to meditating on joy, for example, and seeing it as something possibly within the nucleus of all creation; the location was as similar as possible to a space where I could think of my relationship with the lost and irreparable world. Perhaps I would write something there but I didn't think so; my objective in that room-turned-cabin was not to write, but to think.

On hearing this, Boston couldn't refrain from a kind, beautiful laugh, really very friendly. She shot me a friendly glance. (I'd started to uncomplainingly put up with that type of fond glance "toward the old man," which some women had thrown my way with sad affection lately.) And I realized that sometimes her natural happiness surpassed the charm of her marvelous voice, which was really saying something. It seemed to her, she said without letting slip her expression of strange satisfaction, that there was nothing less conducive to meditation than staying sitting in a closed room or a "thinking cabin," or a fretting cabin, or whatever I wanted to call it.

She said it in such a captivating way, it might even be the case, I thought, that she was absolutely right. But I did not want her to notice I'd admired the wisdom of her words, so I acted as if I'd heard nothing. I pretended not to have taken in what she'd said. And while I was pretending, I started to turn over in my mind the fact that somebody had brushed up against me in Sehgal's dark room and that I had thought at the time about resisting a second touch. It was not something to pass over with indifference. Maybe this was a touch, I said to myself, I would find hard to forget.

Today, I think things would have gone better for me if at that juncture I'd already read—I did not read Chus's piece until that evening—that "art is art, and what you make of it is up to you," that peculiar McGuffin from Chus Martínez that could also be interpreted in this way: "The touch has already happened, and now it all depends on you, let's see what you can make of it."

But at that point I still hadn't come across Chus's sentence. Happening on it that night, I associated it with something Boston had said to me during the afternoon about Carolyn Christov-Bakargiev's desire that participants in Documenta 13 *be left to make something*, and that there should be no artistic brief to mold their intervention. Through that association, everything caused me to wonder if perhaps Carolyn and Chus, with their strange invitation to the Dschingis Khan (an invitation without sense or instructions) had deliberately *brushed up against me*, to see if I were capable of turning their Chinese proposal into something creative, or what amounted to the same thing: a fertile and properly productive way of *making something of it*.

15

I did not have *Locus Solus* by Raymond Roussel in my luggage, a novel I adore but didn't bring with me. It was as though I had, because I knew it almost all by heart. I'd read it an infinite number of times and always had the feeling that memorizing it instead of taking it with me constituted a sort of strange, and no doubt singular, good luck charm. For me, Roussel's whole book has always been, above all, a summary of walks. Over the course of an afternoon—which takes on the character of an itinerant initiation rite—the learned Martial Canterel goes along expounding each one of the rarities dotted around his property, the lovely villa at Montmorency.

Sometimes, I find it amusing to feel as though I'm in other people's novels. Perhaps because of this, when María Boston and I finally arrived, after a brief walk, at the great esplanade of the Friedrichsplatz, I remembered the beginning of the second chapter of *Locus Solus* when they "came in sight of a broad promenade which was completely bare and very smooth."

In fact, that route traveled with Boston was the prologue to other walks that would come later and would in part turn my trip to Kassel into the story of a journey punctuated by strolls, during which I saw, in the style of *Locus Solus*, a good number of rarities, many marvels.

On arriving at the grand esplanade, we arrived at a point on Friedrichsplatz where we could literally go no farther due to the huge crowd waiting to enter the Fridericianum, the oldest public museum in Europe and the heart of Documenta since its beginning in 1955. It was unthinkable to visit the whole exhibition and not enter the impressive neoclassical building (one of the few to survive the brutal devastation of the war), since that would have been like traveling to Germany and not even hearing about a city called Berlin.

In short, I had never seen such a gigantic line in my life. The pleasant temperatures for August, along with the fact that Documenta was only on for another four days, had filled Kassel with a host of last-minute visitors. In the line I seemed to once more see, with astonishment, that there were people looking at me with a strange fixation. They were all but saying: It's about time you deigned to get here. Once again I felt I could be someone they were expecting: an impression entirely lacking any sense, but from which I could not escape, which allowed me to suspect that everything I thought I was observing had some hidden basis in truth, a truth I would not necessarily one day know.

Of course, they might simply be mistaking me for somebody else.

We've got these brilliant passes, Boston said, and we can skip all the lines. When I heard her say this, I could have jumped for joy. The thing is, this type of maneuvering, in which you get ahead of the crowd, has always seemed to me very good therapeutically, perhaps because we drag too many frustrations around with us. From time to time, it's good to skip the humiliation of standing in a monotonous line, which evokes for us the single file we all stand in sooner or later to enter Death's domain.

This sort of ploy was always well received by me, and so I welcomed the news with satisfaction, while remembering that the only useful bit of advice my paternal grandfather ever gave me was that if I wanted to be someone in life, I should always jump right over people standing in bothersome lines.

While the security guards were looking at our passes with more than rigorous attention and simultaneously containing the fury of those who complained we were jumping the queue, Boston told me of Carolyn Christov-Bakargiev's conviction that one could change reality with art, although one could not force that change: Carolyn had been in favor of change from the outset, but without putting pressure on the participating artists, not exerting excessive control over their work, letting them be the ones who, if they so desired, revealed new paths.

We passed through security and headed into the mythical Fridericianum. Once inside, we started to cross vast exhibition rooms on the ground floor, rooms that had been left empty and seemed to be, Boston said, a reflection on saturation and emptying out; in this main exhibition space of a big international show, the emptiness was far more noticeable than in any other setting.

Faced with such emptying out I couldn't help but remember the Sunday morning a few years back now when they opened the newly built museum of contemporary art in Barcelona (the MACBA) to the public with evident haste; they threw it open to the citizens, but without pictures, not a single painting or sculpture, nothing inside it. The people of Barcelona wandered through the museum admiring the white walls, the solidity of the construction, and other architectural details, proud of having paid for it with their taxes and telling themselves that the works of art could wait.

I was thinking of all this in the Fridericianum, thinking of that happy period for Barcelona, when Boston, noticing I was being bothered by the current of wind circulating around those vacant rooms, which had obliged me to turn up my collar, led me over to a small, inconspicuous plaque set in the corner between two bleak white walls.

There on the plaque I saw, with surprise, that the current was artificial and signed by Ryan Gander. Brilliant, I thought. Somebody was putting their signature to a draft! Fantastic. Although, naturally, I couldn't avoid thinking of the detractors of contemporary art: no doubt they would find inspiration for all-out mockery in that plaque.

Boston confirmed that Gander had titled that ethereal breeze—which seemed to lightly push visitors along, giving them a gentle unexpected strength—an extra impetus: *The Invisible Pull*. I found that current of air very interesting and at first connected it to Duchamp, with his perfume *Air de Paris*, then to the geometry textbook he gave his sister when she got married, that she had to hang outside the kitchen window, letting the wind flick through to choose the geometry problems to solve: that volume Duchamp titled *Unhappy Readymade*, guessing its fate, as in the end the wind left not a single trace of the gift.

However Duchampian *The Invisible Pull* might be, that did not stop them from placing that breeze at the heart of Documenta 13, placing it at its spiritual center. It was a brilliant notion on its own account and even generated a certain happiness. Actually, it also allowed me to experience at moments a hint of an "aesthetic instant," something I recalled was one of the things I'd come to Kassel to find: a sort of instant of harmony. I didn't quite know what that might consist of, but I was keen to sample it. Still, what the hell, I thought: that invisible breeze filled me with a strange but interesting sense of well-being. It seemed to me that this on its own already justified my whole journey to Kassel. I was fascinated by it. I didn't need to know why it exercised such a hold over me, it was enough to know that it put me in a good mood, which was the same thing that happened with the intrinsic pleasure of mornings—I compared this to the art of forgetting, that art of forgetfulness as light as the first morning air and always liberating—while the evenings and above all the nights only drove me into a malaise inasmuch as they turned out grim and bitter, like the very art of remembering. That art of remembering brought only the tenacious memory of the past and, in tandem with resentment and melancholy, was terrible.

The bad thing about this divide between mornings and evenings—between these states of mind that in themselves signaled whether it was daytime or night—was that it was so systematic in nature: in over five years, there had not been a single day during which I managed to escape from this monotonous rule of well-being in the mornings and anguish as night fell.

I turned and went back to where the plaque was, reread it, smiled happily, and then returned to my previous position beside Boston, standing looking at her golden sandals, the same ones I'd found so charming in Barcelona. Now they seduced me less and her voice, too, seemed to have lost something of its devastating force on the day of our first meeting; but all this was to be expected and, in any case, she still seemed to me an extremely agreeable presence (though I never lost sight of our age difference and, above all, the "fond glance toward the old man," which, as if it were a question of target practice, seemed to be her favorite pastime).

For this and other reasons, I decided to concentrate on the invisible breeze. And then, aware of what it meant to go down a certain path, I wondered about that sentence by some author about the space a work of genius leaves behind, when it burns this space away, which is always a good place to light one's own small flame. I didn't remember who the author was, nor do I recall it now. The fact is, for that current of air, there was a before and an after, and that current seemed to me, over and above everything else, to be the creator of its own light.

Perhaps it wasn't the best work of art in that Documenta—how could I tell, after all, when I'd only seen two pieces up to that point and one of them was a darkened room?—but a light issued from there, settling firmly within me, and it did not leave me again for the duration of my stay in Kassel.

From the work of genius, I thought, something always springs that inspires us, pushes us forward, leading us not only to imitate what has dazzled us, but to go much further, to discover our own world....
There was nothing that could be done now to change my opinion about the genius of that breeze. Boston at no point tried to quell an enthusiasm she perhaps secretly shared with me. Although she did, it's true, see fit to warn me that "genius" was an overly used term, as it had ended up meaning too many things. Nevertheless, she said, the word "genius" was indeed useful for understanding people.

Still, with Boston at my side, I weighed up the possibility that I'd maybe made a mistake, acted rashly, perhaps I'd been wrong to lay on my enthusiasm for the breeze so thick; but none of that mattered now. If my attraction to the invisible push was somewhat unfounded, all that was happening to me was what happens to us so often in love, the great realm of the unfounded and the uncalled-for.
Did I no longer remember, for instance, the enamoring of Stendhal, who traveled around Italy and fell for that country with such force, such gratuitousness that his love at first sight took the face of an actress who sang Cimarosa's *Secret Marriage* in Ivrea? That actress had a broken front tooth, but the truth was that this hardly mattered, with that invisible push contained in every *amour fou*. Or did I no longer remember that Werther, when he fell in love with Carlota, only glimpsed her through a doorway while she was cutting slices of bread for her siblings, and that first sight, although trivial, drove him a very long way, carrying him off to the greatest of passions and to suicide?

That extra, invisible impetus might already be an object of mockery for thousands of idiots all over the world, but that didn't matter in the slightest now, what difference did it make? I had fallen in love with that breeze, that pull, and, what's more, I suspected that in its force, its pull, was hidden something that escaped me, perhaps a coded message.

"Where did you buy those sandals?" I asked Boston.

"Why? Do you like them?"

"They go well with the breeze. Yes, I like them. But"—I put on an affected voice, making out I was joking—"there are moments when I think they might drive me to the greatest of passions."

"To love?" she asked, conspicuously wary.

"Or to suicide. Can you imagine? Killing yourself over a pair of golden sandals?"

16

Feeling helped along by the invisible pull, I arrived at the rotunda of the Fridericianum, where I saw a work that was christened *The Brain* by Carolyn Christov-Bakargiev. Installed by Carolyn herself, what was exhibited there—separated from the rest of the museum behind glass—attempted in some way to summarize the lines of thought developed in Documenta 13. It was a microcosm representing the puzzle posed by the whole huge exhibition. It seemed to me perhaps an excessively arbitrary *brain*, given that it brought together Giorgio Morandi's bottles painted in Fascist Bologna with sculptures by Giuseppe Penone, linking them with objects damaged during the Lebanese civil war, or books carved out of stone from the Afghan valley (where the Taliban wrought destruction on age-old Buddhas), and the last bottle of perfume that had belonged to Eva Braun.

That *brain*, I felt, lacked a certain internal coherence. It gave the impression that other, very different artistic elements could have been brought together and the result would have been similar. Everything exhibited in *The Brain* seemed more piled up than selected. I remarked on this to Boston, and she said I could be wrong, above all if I wasn't considering the fact that Carolyn Christov-Bakargiev believed that confusion in art was a truly marvelous thing.

Confusion? I remembered having read that many visitors to Documenta 13 took a firm stand on the confusion they felt viewing the eclecticism of the large display, although many mentioned it not as a criticism, but to emphasize the brilliant plurality of its focal points, the sweeping scope that the assemblage managed to achieve, and the fact that it was an interesting metaphor for our historical moment.

I remembered this, but I continued to be among those who found *The Brain* baffling. Perhaps because of that, I sought further information. With the intention of discovering more about that rotunda, I asked additional questions. I soon found out, for example, that Braun's perfume bottle—undoubtedly the object that most caught my attention—had made it to our day in one piece because it had been found in April 1945 by the American war correspondent and artist Lee Miller in the dictator's bathroom, in the apartment Hitler and Braun occupied on Prinzregentenplatz in Munich.

In a vitrine in the Fridericianum there was also a bath towel monogrammed with Adolf Hitler's initials. Towel and perfume had been carried off by Lee Miller to her Munich hotel, and one could never know whether she ended up using those peculiar, possibly fetishistic, trophies of war in her daily life. Did it matter? Not much, in fact not at all. In any case, I thought if I'd found the towel, I wouldn't have even touched it, it would have utterly repelled me. But that was me. In the same display case as the perfume and the towel with the initials A. H. were four photos of Lee Miller cheerfully immersed in Hitler's bathtub. Apparently, the images had been judged frivolous and created a certain amount of polemic when they were published in the *New York Times* at the end of the war. I'd never seen those pictures before or even heard about them. They might be frivolous, I thought, but that wasn't something that was overly obvious. What *was* very clear was that the bathtub was far more modern than any I'd ever had in all the different houses in my life. That is what I thought. It seemed a trifling detail, but maybe not. That bathtub was more modern than any bathtub of mine.

Soon afterward—as if I were ashamed of having thought that—I rubbed my face like I was trying to forget what had gone before. After that rubbing, I looked behind me toward the invisible breeze, as if it might be seen, and little by little a sinking feeling came over me. My sense of loss was the same as a person feels when, along the way, he turns back and sees the stretch he's covered: the indifferent path is visible, its unbending trajectory expressing the irreversibility of time.

In the end that's all that's left, I thought, the backward glance perceiving nothingness. Perhaps that's why I suddenly wanted, desperately, to look forward. But what I encountered was what I was running away from: the bad vibe Braun's perfume bottle gave me and, of course, the same irreversible past that I had thought I left behind, including my steps around the *brain* that was preserved in that rotunda in the Fridericianum.

I was in Germany; it was the first time during the whole trip that I started to feel somewhat conscious of being there. We recognize that in journeys to countries by plane, we take time to truly land where we've set ourselves down. In my case, it wasn't until I came upon A.H.'s towel and Braun's perfume that I had the feeling for the first time that perhaps I had now landed on German soil. The Nazi artifacts and the presence of the irreversible past succeeded in making me come down to earth all at once, with a bump. There was the old horror, the giant stigma of interminable Nazi guilt. But did that constitute a landing? Perhaps I hadn't completely set down and I should keep asking myself whether I was in Germany.

Shortly before leaving the Fridericianum, María Boston insisted on taking me to a separate room to see *Sleeping Sickness*, the strange work of a Thai artist, Pratchaya Phinthong. At first, what I thought I saw was a black smudge caught at the center of a large sheet of glass on top of a large table. But when I got closer I saw it wasn't a little smudge. According to what was written on a small plaque, it was two tsetse flies, a fertile female and her sterile consort. In that instant— later on I would see more oddities—the work seemed extremely weird to me, very far from my idealized concept of avant-garde art.

Pratchaya Phinthong, Boston told me, was researching the ecological control of the tsetse fly, which spread sleeping sickness in humans. I was left confused, not knowing what to say, thinking of people I'd known who behaved just as though they had been bitten by that deadly fly.

Afterward, leaving the vicinity of the Fridericianum, I thought again of Eva Braun's perfume bottle and ended up going off on the subject of guilt. That question came back to me like flies returning to an infected person in order to infect them twice as much. In my home country—a nation especially famous for its macabre civil war—guilt barely existed; that vulgarity was left to the ingenuous Germans. Nobody in Spain wasted time regretting having been a Nazi, or pro-Franco, or even a Catalan collaborator with the dictator in Madrid, an accomplice himself to the assassins of the Third Reich. In my country, we have always lived with our backs to the drama of Europe's demise, possibly because—as we didn't directly take part in either of the two world wars—all that was seen as other people's business. Perhaps also it is because at bottom we've almost always lived in our own decline; we are so sunk in it, we don't even recognize it.

You are in Germany, an inner voice seemed to want to repeat to me, reminding me somehow of the voice running through *Europa*, that Lars von Trier film that speaks to us, powerfully and obsessively, of the brutal ruination of the old continent.

"You are in Europa" was heard insistently in that film, and what the cameras showed us was a continent turned into a vast, infinite hospital.

As I came out of the Fridericianum, the voice telling me I was in Germany became unrelenting, and I felt it was likely that I had now finally, really landed. If that were so, I was in a country famous for combining intelligence and barbarism, one deeply familiar with remorse, which had spent years hesitating between feeling great pain for its sins and trying to feel a lesser regret; in short, a country whose citizens tried to find a reasonable balance between going overboard and placing too little emphasis on it, perhaps aware, on the one hand, that without memory they ran the risk of turning monstrous again, but also with too much memory, the risk was that they'd remain firmly stuck in the horror of the past.

17

I was in Germany wondering all the while whether I was really in Germany. When María Boston and I left the Fridericianum and headed straight down Königsstrasse in a southerly direction toward the Hotel Hessenland, I began to ask myself what sort of relationship there could be between avant-garde art and the bottle of perfume that had belonged to Eva Braun.

To put it succinctly, it pained me to see that war criminals and contemporary art could be related, even if it was only through art. I was turning this question over in my mind. Almost without realizing it, I drifted off not just mentally, but physically, and was on the verge of losing my balance and crashing—fortunately María Boston didn't notice—into the window of a large department store.

A minute later—in the instant when, not without understandable concern over what had happened, I managed to peel myself away from the wretched window—I was dazzled to see in the store's plate glass the false glitter of an utterly improbable summer light, and I realized that, contrary to what I'd thought, I still couldn't say with complete certainty that I'd landed in Kassel or anywhere else.

That was when, to feel more as though I was in Germany, I started to pretend—just to myself, of course—that I felt a certain nostalgia for the starry nights of this country: for the deep blues of the wide German sky, the gently curved sickle of the Aryan moon, and the somber whisper of the pine trees in all the forests of that mighty land.

The moon isn't Aryan, I corrected myself at once. And then I told myself that too many things had got muddled up in my head, and all the tiredness from the day was making them pop up in the most alarming way.

I was starting to feel really worn out, and at that stage even greater muddles can end up materializing in my mind. I'd gotten up terribly early in Barcelona to catch the plane to Frankfurt, and over the course of the day the fatigue of the flight, the lengthy Croatian incident and other tribulations had been piling up. On top of that, I didn't want to bother Boston any longer, whom they seemed to have obliged to carry out these welcoming acts of courtesy toward me; as she herself had been half-hinting, she was expected as soon as possible in the central office, where she'd left a host of work matters pending.

It was time to start saying goodbye to her and devote myself to setting up the "thinking cabin" in my room in the Hessenland. Soon it would be getting dark, and, what's more, I believed I could feel tiredness stealing over my body. It followed that the glitter of summer light in the store window could only be false (that sparkle I'd glimpsed a moment ago). Already in the grip of the imminent appearance of anguish, I was reminded of the philosophers of the Tlön school, who declared that, if we mortals didn't already know it, it was as well for us to understand that all the time in the world had already transpired, and our life was only the crepuscular and no doubt falsified and mutilated memory or reflection of an irrecoverable process.

In a chain of events that took place out of my control, I saw myself as a worthless twilight reflection and fell into a state of unease that I guessed would not now be assuaged for the rest of the day, not even by the genuine glitter of the truest summer sun. And all this, naturally, was putting off the moment when I could at last feel I was fully in Germany. Depending on how I chose mentally to tackle the problem of my definitive landing, Germany might even come to seem like the other side of the moon to me, with its craters and its great seas.

18

On the terrace of a bar on Theaterstrasse, we stopped to eat some frankfurters, and I recovered more than I expected to, although it so happened that, once again, I couldn't avoid a silly memory coming back to me. Since boyhood, it has been hard for me to eat a frankfurter without thinking of the two pounds of mud my grandfather claimed to have accumulated on the soles of his shoes near Frankfurt during World War I.

If the anecdote was ridiculous, its absurd tendency to come back every time I was about to swallow that sort of snack was even more so. Trying to escape the muddy memory by fleeing it mentally, I said the first thing to Boston that popped into my head. This was as spontaneous as it was outlandish and, seen from my present perspective, perhaps somewhat suicidal (although, not wishing to punish myself too much, I prefer to see the question as utter whimsy, like a McGuffin):

"Do you think there can be any point of connection between the avant-garde and Aryan perfume?"

Nobody has ever looked at me with such rage as Boston did hearing this question.

"What concept do you have of the avant-garde?" she asked.

At that moment it was hard to imagine what consequences this question would have for me.

19

I didn't know what crime I had committed. I was almost scared. I took the opportunity to remind Boston that since my physical collapse some years back, I had taken exceptionally good care of my health, and, because of this, in spite of having just recovered my strength, even though I knew it was still early, I was going to retire to my hotel to rest until the following day. Surely, I thought, my question had originated in my accumulated tiredness of that day.

Boston objected, asking me at the same time if I was really so sure I had to go. I told her that I was, indeed, very tired. And then, in a very friendly tone, I reminded her that in Barcelona I'd made exceptions going out for dinner with her twice, and I could make another one or two, but not that evening because I felt worn out and needed to recover.

She laughed. I wanted to know what about. "Because," she said, "you spoke in terms of 'physical collapse' and 'recovering your strength' and your language coincided with the motif of Documenta 13, which is precisely *Collapse and Recovery*."

I reacted with what must have been a dense-looking expression.

"Collapse and Recovery," she reiterated, still smiling.

Then she paused, as if she might need to take a deep breath. "That theme seems almost custom-made for you," she insisted, not hiding a touch of sarcasm. We were at this juncture when a tall guy with dark hair and a beard passed by. He greeted Boston in German, discussing something with her that I thought, from his exaggerated gestures, could only be a weighty matter, something beyond measure. I understood nothing of what they said, but I imagined they were talking in tragic tones about the powerful force of the storms around the Irish Aran Isles. I imagined the entire conversation she had with that man whose eyes—to tell the truth—were unusually deep-set and gloomy, enjoying myself during that imaginative exercise. After they spoke for a few minutes, the man went on his way as if returning to his distant homeland. "He's a sad one," was all Boston said after he had moved off. This gentleman seems very worried about the storms in his country, I was about to say, although in the end, I contained myself; it was not the moment to make things worse.

Not long afterward, the greatest possible contrast to the sad man passed by that corner of Theaterstrasse: along came joy personified, Pim Durán, a very attractive brunette, from Seville, Boston's assistant in the office and the same person who had sent me the Lufthansa tickets in Barcelona. She was the person I'd spoken to at the Frankfurt airport when Alka didn't show up. I'm the one who sent you emails and talked to you on the phone, she said with a lovely smile. She spoke into María Boston's ear about what was surely a work-related matter, then continued on her way. She was off to a post office, if I wasn't mistaken. She seemed a fundamentally happy woman and would have made me envious if it weren't for the fact that I wasn't exactly seeking happiness.

When we were alone once more, I asked Boston where the name Pim came from. She thought about it for a moment, and it turned out she didn't know. I would have to ask Pim myself. Then she deftly reintroduced the theme of collapse and recovery, which, according to her, ran through Documenta 13 the same way that it ran through Kassel's tragic wartime past and its regeneration since then. It would not do, she added, to lose sight of the fact that these concepts—

collapse, recovery—didn't necessarily have to proceed consecutively, but could also take place simultaneously.

The two processes, she told me, could *occur at once*, in the same way that existential insecurity lately had become the norm for everyone and so we were living in a permanent state of crisis punctuated by situations of emergency and exception; we recovered, but violent collapse returned at the very same moment, and then it could be the other way around, and so on, without end, all the time. Nobody seemed immune from the general upheaval of the world, which was precisely what—unofficially, but ultimately significantly—that edition of Kassel was most concerned with.

More than just talking about Documenta, Boston instructed me about what was happening there. It seemed they had charged her with doing so. I decided to cooperate and make her undertaking easier, asking her for more details about the city's past. Straightaway, I saw I'd made it plain with my request that I was entirely ignorant about the place, which shocked her in a way, almost as much as my question minutes earlier about Aryan perfume and the avant-garde.

The Nazis, she ended up explaining to me somewhat tersely, produced a great deal of military hardware in Kassel, especially tanks, so the city and its environs were a priority target for allied bombing raids in 1943. In fact, the bombs wiped out ninety percent of the city's thousand-year history.

The fateful evening hour was now very close at hand, and I noticed that, perhaps even a little earlier than usual, anguish and melancholy were beginning to take hold of me. I would have to wait until the following morning to recover a decent state of mind. I was thinking about the tragedy of this split life, the life of morning joy and nocturnal collapse I seemed destined to live out for the rest of my days, when I saw that the man with the unusually deep-set and gloomy eyes was circling around us (although on this occasion he had not even bothered to greet us). He looked different to me now, seeming suddenly exhausted, as if he were already overcome by the worry he'd probably been dragging around with him since the day he left the Aran Isles. But I preferred not to say anything. All at once, I started to feel unsure whether it was the same German I'd seen before.

Minutes later, looking more closely at this man with the unusually deep-set eyes, I saw that I couldn't have been more mistaken, as it wasn't the same guy who'd spoken to María Boston earlier; I'd simply been speculating about a complete stranger. We were getting ready to leave the terrace on Theaterstrasse, and María Boston asked me if I'd ever reflected on the fact that walking was almost the only activity not appropriated by people who devoted themselves to the world of business, that is, capitalists. I paused to think. It had been ages since I'd heard that word, so clear-cut and so unambiguous: capitalists. Look, she said, there's nothing special that's sold for walking, and yet there's a whole market around eating, running, sleeping, having sex, reading, even drinking water.... Well, I said, I liked walking very much, I loved the idea of going for a stroll. That's all I said. Just that. I remember it perfectly, because it was from that moment on that things started to go downhill, as if following the same rhythm of decline that daylight does when dusk overtakes it.

Strangely, the more María Boston said there was lots of work waiting for her in the curatorial team office (seeming to indicate to me that she had to leave without further delay), the more she insisted on setting off with me on a new walk. It was as if leaving me or not leaving me, staying or abandoning me, amounted to the same thing; and there was something in that contradiction that reminded me of the idea that I could very well experience collapse and recovery simultaneously.

That was an interesting idea, no doubt, but one which anyone could see didn't really work when applied to normal life, because it made no sense at all. For example, she must clearly perceive I was tired but still suggested we go on walking; who knew if she meant to the end of the world? I found out later she meant only to the end of a train platform, although it wasn't one that was exactly around the corner.

I looked at Boston, and she did everything in her power not to return my gaze. "I thought the sad man came from the Aran Isles," I said, just to try out a bit of mischief. This was a somewhat desperate McGuffin, only to make her feel sorry about how tired and irrational I was and to get her to let me withdraw to the hotel and set up my "thinking cabin."

As might be expected, Boston said she didn't know what islands I was talking about, and so it fell to me to explain that they were found on the west coast of Ireland, washed by the Atlantic, in Galway Bay. "I thought that you and he were discussing what was happening on those remote islands," I said. "Who was I talking to?" she asked. "To that sad man earlier," I said. In the end, it became clear I was referring to that sorrowful German who'd stopped to speak to her. "But poor Hans and I only philosophized a bit; he explained to me that the idea of 'trying to survive' was just for megalomaniacs, and I didn't know what to say to him. What would you have said?" "That I didn't understand him," I replied, "but not to worry because, when all is said and done, life is governed by all sorts of misunderstandings, and the natives of Galway Bay know everything, absolutely everything, there is to know about that."

If it had been Alka, she would definitely have split her sides laughing at what I'd said, not understanding a thing. But in that whole trip, I never again saw Boston as serious as she was at that moment. To tell the truth, it was an almost terrifying moment. And that was despite the fact that I still couldn't even imagine the sort of heavy pressure Boston was going to put on me in the ensuing minutes to go to that train platform she considered vital for me to see that very evening.

20

It seemed to me a more than demonstrable fact that every time communication problems arose between the two of us and our relationship collapsed, it recovered immediately. It was as if the acts of ruin and recuperation really could make up a single entity and share the instant perfectly well.

And so, talking of this and that, in reality philosophizing or aspiring to philosophize—possibly the most pivotal activity in contemporary art—darkness was falling over Kassel and extinguishing
everything sluggishly, like any old Tuesday on Earth.

Suddenly, Boston showed signs of taking a leap forward, embarking on a surprising new ode to walking, at the same time proposing
we go and see a *sound installation*, which, according to her, was not
far, but actually required another long stroll. We had to get to the
old central station, the end of platform 10.

During the war, she said, that platform had been the main setting for
the deportation of Jews; now it was the setting for the resonant sound
installation *Study for Strings*, by the Scottish artist Susan Philipsz.

I balked gently at this new initiative, telling her that, as she had
work to do, I didn't want to bother her any longer and, moreover, I
had to get to the hotel, because I was beginning to feel my energy
running out. She seemed not to have heard me, so I stressed my
need to go to my room in the Hessenland and immediately set up a
cabin, insulating myself at that early evening hour from any sign of
the continuity of life outside.

I didn't tell her, but among other things I had a terrible fear of her
seeing the unpleasant expression I habitually started to have at that
hour; I knew if I let a few more minutes go by, my face was going to
get gloomy, my personality turn bitter, everything was going to get
extremely complicated, and this time I couldn't rely on the help of
Dr. Collado's tablets.

And while I was insisting, I remembered *The Walk*, by Robert
Walser, where, after the more than lengthy description of a happy
day's wandering by the rambler who walks his way through the
book, we arrive at a final page as perfect as it is gloomy, with some
last words containing a revealing change of mood on the part of the
walker: "I had risen up, to go home, for it was late now and everything was dark."

Walser's tiny dodge reverses the rules of the game for the book,
and the happy wandering comes to a sudden end. The streets go
completely dark. If up to that point the walker had always professed

to feeling good (tremendously good), to being constantly delighted by everything, all of a sudden he tells us it has grown dark and things have changed, to the extent that the book has reached its end and the rambler wishes to take refuge in his den.

Soon after this, I was going on about my health to María Boston when abruptly—as if night were falling on my words—she interrupted me to say that *Study for Strings* was a better place than anywhere else to meditate on the great Collapse. Her delivery was so forceful, I was left rather mired in the boggy state brought on by my fragility, as if carrying my grandfather's two pounds of mud on the soles of my shoes. And this caused me to wonder whether Boston was attempting to keep hold of me, or if she only insisted on the walk so I'd say no and that way couldn't subsequently claim she'd had no intention of spending further time with me.

I soon saw that things were heading in a different direction, perhaps still a touch darker than I had imagined, and perhaps even more complicated. It was necessary, vital, that I go to that platform, Boston said, looking at me with the same rage she had on that previous, horrible occasion. Never before in my life had anyone pressed me in such a manner to go to a train station. I asked, timidly, why this displacement was so essential. The sun was setting almost completely and the clouds over Kassel had been turning an intense scarlet. Because, Boston said, almost chewing her words, I want to go on walking awhile, I like walking, and also it's about time you finally understand you're not in a Mediterranean country, but a profoundly tragic one. It's unbelievable you don't know the relationship between a bottle of Aryan perfume and avant-garde art, she said, revealing at last why she was so angry with me.

That had surely been my big mistake of the day: not being convinced that Braun's perfume could be related to avant-garde art. Although a new question arose: did avant-garde art really exist? Much was said about an art that was ahead of its time, but for me it was far from clear it existed. The very expression *avant-garde* seemed to have a different meaning now from what it had meant at the beginning of the last century ... but this wasn't the right time to talk about that.

During the arduous walk that followed, I was able to discover, among other things, that Kassel's great postwar reconstruction didn't come about until 1955, when its citizens bravely opted to take a much more insecure path than the one other compatriots had chosen; instead of industrial development, they decided on rebirth of a cultural nature, putting Arnold Bode—an architect and lecturer—in charge of the first Documenta, which had a clearly restorative character. Germany under Hitler had classified contemporary art as degenerate, expelling and murdering its artists, but now it paid tribute to the art of the twenties and thirties, with an exhibition that, according to Bode, "finally brought art to the workers."

When at last we arrived at the city's old central station, we headed with slow steps to the far end of platform 10. Once there, I was able to understand almost in an instant why that sound installation, *Study for Strings*, was a better place than any other to think about the Nazi years (what Boston called the great Collapse).

Everybody knows that most so-called avant-garde art these days requires one part that is visual and another that is discursive to back it up and try to explain what we are seeing. Curiously, nothing of the latter was in evidence in *Study for Strings*. At Susan Philipsz's installation, it was enough to simply position oneself at the end of platform 10 to understand it all at once; there was no need for a leaflet that would finish off the story being told there.

Study for Strings was a somber installation, a simple piece that went directly to the heart of the great tragedy, the end of the utopia of a humanizing world. Philipsz had situated loudspeakers in an enclosed area of Kassel's Hauptbahnhof that were audible to people walking to the end of that stretch of platform—exactly the same stretch on which a great number of Jewish families waited for the train that would transport them to concentration camps; from these loudspeakers came beautiful but devastatingly sad music: a sort of funeral march for those who died before their time called *Study for Strings*. It was a composition that in Kassel 2012 harked back to the memory of the Holocaust. Its composer, the Czech musician Pavel Haas, wrote the piece for the chamber orchestra in Theresienstadt, shortly before being transferred to Auschwitz, where he died.

We listened to the piece standing, with the same grave expressions as everyone else gathered there, watching other spectators come join that railway music performance that lasted under half an hour, one of many identical performances that were separated by short time intervals and played one after the other on the cheerless platform every day. In the end, a group of around thirty people formed, who had followed the concert of violins and cellos with emotion, remaining motionless and sunk in thought, moved, profoundly silent, as if recovering from the collapse provoked by what they had heard, and also by what they remembered, what had been evoked, almost reenacted, I'd go so far as to say experienced, because it wasn't difficult to feel vulnerable and tragic there, like a deportee.

I would have liked to confess to Boston that it seemed incredible to me I hadn't been aware from the outset that the political, or more accurately the eternal illusion of a humanized world was inseparable from artistic endeavors, from the most forward-thinking art. But I said nothing because underneath it all I felt a certain resentment toward her. At that point in the evening, I still hadn't been able to get over the fact that my question about the Nazi perfume and avant-garde art had led her to punish me, to literally punish me, and, consequently, to oblige me to take one walk too many, perhaps with the severe notion that I'd correct such thoughtlessness at the far end of this platform.

I would have liked to say to her: How could I have been so stupid? Or perhaps the opposite: to reproach her for the fact that she had wanted to scold me like that, albeit in such a subtle manner. Whatever the case, I opted to keep quiet and devote myself to carefully observing the general mental recovery of the people gathered there. I ended up identifying an intense communion between all those strangers, who, having surely come from such different places, had congregated there. It was as if they were all thinking, we were all thinking: we've been the moment, and this is the place, and now we know what our problem is. It was as if a spirit, a breeze, a current of morally bracing air, an invisible impetus, were pushing us toward the future, forging forever the union between the diverse members of that spontaneous, suddenly subversive-seeming group.

This is the kind of thing, I thought, that we can never see on television news programs. There are silent conspiracies between people who seem to understand one another without talking, quiet rebellions that take place in the world every minute without being noticed; groups form by chance, unplanned reunions in the middle of the park or on a dark corner, occasionally allowing us to be optimistic about the future of humanity. They join together for a few minutes and then go their separate ways, all enlisting in the hidden fight against moral misery. One day, they will rise up with unheard-of fury and blow everything to bits.

21

I already knew how to get back to the Hessenland unaided, I told Boston, I just had to stay on Königsstrasse. Two kisses and farewell. Boston didn't specify a time, but she said she'd come pick me up from the hotel the next morning to take me to the Chinese restaurant. Just as I'd feared, it was clear no one was going to save me from the trip to the Dschingis Khan. Over the course of the afternoon, I'd avoided asking her anything to do with what I privately called "the Chinese number." I'd done so, foolishly thinking that I'd get out of the whole nuisance that way. But the ostrich approach doesn't always turn out to be useful and, ultimately, when we were saying goodbye, I saw how "the Chinese number" ended up bobbing to the surface and, what's more, it did so at the moment that packed the most punch, just when I thought I'd outmaneuvered it completely.

It was late now, and everything was starting to get dark.

I observed that for the first time in my whole life it wasn't fun to feel as though I were inside someone else's novel, in this case, a book by Robert Walser. Although it was poetic to think that, as in *The Walk*, it was late and everything was getting dark, it nevertheless seemed more appropriate for this to be experienced by

61

whoever wrote it, in other words by Walser, and not me. And yet it was unsettling to see that what was happening to me was exactly what happened to the happy narrator in that book: it got dark, and I suddenly thought it better to stop walking. Usually I was already at home when darkness fell, so it followed that my melancholy there in Kassel was in fact similar to Walser's.

Maybe not everything is so sinister and strange, I said to myself, trying to keep from having an anxiety attack in the middle of the street. Right then, it was a question of being able to cover—relatively calmly, with all the calm in the world—the distance separating me from the Hessenland. A somewhat forced calm, perhaps, but it could be useful if I at least managed to stave off the first onslaught of melancholy. And I did, I deflected it; I observed I was still enjoying everything I saw in the street instead of being depressed by it. But very soon afterward, sensing I was all alone, I began to feel low. Underneath it all, I am Chinese and I'm going home, I thought. And those things became still further complicated for me, as I did not dare to look at the people on the street, because once more it seemed some of them were saying: it's about time you got here.

"Were you expecting me?" I wanted to shout at them.

I was sure they were looking at me strangely. Might it not be the case that some of them really were waiting for me and had made an agreement to pretend otherwise if I finally decided to inquire about it? I wanted so much to say to them: "I know you've been expecting me for days. I noticed it as soon as I got here."

Maybe the most surprising thing was noticing that out of the blue I was recovering a sort of energy I'd describe as almost like solar power. The fact is, all at once I saw myself on Königsstrasse not knowing what to do with that sudden invisible impetus, which sort of came over me and was more than I needed. I felt like my arms had become excessively long and my legs were too far away from me. I couldn't manage to locate myself, and the movements I was making contributed to that fact. Walking down the road in such a peculiar way gave the sensation of being insane as much as it did of being blown about by a breeze as invisible as it probably was invincible.

Some of the people who had seemed to be looking at me before now seemed to be saying: It's about time you got here, but you've made it in bad shape—you won't recover from this now.

Luckily, a few meters from the hotel, my energy disappeared as quickly as it had arrived, and I went back to simply being the man who collapsed in the evenings and recovered in the mornings. Sometimes returning to normality, even if it's to a pitiful former state, does us good. Who'd have thought it, but I felt calmer on seeing that the absurd, sudden energy had evaporated; I much preferred plain old anguish to having to feel my arms had grown excessively long, like the arms of a Quixotesque giant confounded by a windmill.

I entered the Hessenland and headed straight to number 27, my second-floor room; I went out on the balcony and immediately remembered what Boston had told me a few hours earlier: that from up there, I'd be able to see the entrance to the building that contained Sehgal's dark room.

So what she had predicted came to pass. In addition I had proved that solitude was impossible, because it was inhabited by ghosts. I'd said goodbye to Boston, but in a way she was still there, now in my memory. I was on the balcony just long enough to establish a mental connection with the hotel annex, with the gloomy building next door that housed Sehgal's room, a chamber I converted into a sort of lighthouse in the night, off in a direction I could look toward by going out on the balcony if I felt I was drowning in so much solitude (with ghosts) in my cabin.

It was better to have that invisible lighthouse than nothing, though, true enough, the cabin still remained to be built. Or not, since the best way to construct it was to imagine a life of thought in that hotel room. I must do this without further ado.

My model for the cabin was Skjolden, the place where Wittgenstein managed to isolate himself to hear his own voice and to prove he could think better there than from his chair in the university. Indeed, from the cabin, Wittgenstein began to address those wanting to start seeing things in a new way and not the scientific community or the general public. For him, thought could reach the level of an artistic gesture. His philosophical ideal was the pursuit of a liberating clarity, the opening up of consciousness and of the world; he did not wish to offer truth, but truthfulness; he wanted to offer examples rather than reasons, motives rather than causes, fragments rather than systems.

While I was thinking about Skjolden, I lay on the bed with my hands linked behind my head, looking at the ceiling. And then I remembered a friend who once told me that any form of exile for a spiritual man became a prompt for inner reflection. How good that phrase could have felt if I'd thought of it or remembered it in the morning, when I tended to be in a better mood. Even so, it did help keep me going. In the long run, I thought, one realizes that attending to one's personal matters in a productive way is the most important thing in the world.

I looked at the clock and saw it was a good time to call Barcelona. My elderly parents told me the nationalist demonstration in Barcelona hadn't been exactly nationalist but more pro-independence, at least that's what the local television stations repeated ad infinitum.

It suddenly occurred to me to think that you can't defend the freedom of the masses, only your own. Perhaps because I found myself on the threshold of my inner reflection, of the creation of the cabin, it was logical that talk of mass movements should startle me, just when the move I was preparing to make demanded individuality.

Then I phoned my wife and told her my day had in no way resembled an action novel, but things had constantly been happening to me. When she asked me what things, I could only say I had been joking. I didn't want to tell her, for example, that I had no sooner arrived than the people of Kassel seemed to be expecting me, and this misapprehension had made me think of the day I drove to Antwerp with my nephew Paolo and, near the pretty train station, began to feel a wave of presentiment that the city would suffer some sort of retribution. These visions seemed anchored in reality, but from what ancestor's remote past did they spring? Was it preposterous to imagine that I'd lived out previous existences in European cities and seen catastrophes coming? Was it crazy to sense I was back on streets I had traveled repeatedly in other times? Nothing could be ruled out in a place like Kassel, which, opening its doors to the ideas of the avant-garde, was implicitly rejecting any invitation to logic.

I didn't want to tell my wife any of this, perhaps because these were things you don't say over the phone. So I said goodbye and soon afterward began to notice—no doubt this was brought on by the lonely state I'd plunged into—that from outside, through curtains stirred by a gentle current of air, could be heard isolated cries, cradled on the wind. The reflections of light dancing on the ceiling seemed to forecast that a crack was about to open all the way across it at any moment. Perhaps the conversations of the guests in the room above would reach me clearly through that chink. When I was in Barcelona with John William Wilkinson, we'd thought I might set myself up on the top floor of the Chinese restaurant facing the forest, but now I could see that none of that was happening or would happen, rather the complete opposite: the place the dark forces seemed to have offered me to spy on wasn't beneath, but above; it was as if Galway Bay were out there above the ceiling of that room. And there was one more problem. Seeing it properly, it was clear no such scenario existed, that the reflections of light on the ceiling had simply created it, perhaps connected with my lighthouse in the hotel annex, my lighthouse in the night.

22

I got up from the bed in order to escape from my private Galway Bay, and I had a depraved glance at Cela's *Journey to the Alcarria*: "The peddler has perfectly naked eyelids, without a single lash, and a wooden leg crudely fixed to the stump with thongs."

Afterward, I played the game of pretending to myself that what I'd read astonished me. Peddler, naked eyelids, wooden leg. I feigned surprise when I knew perfectly well that in reading Cela I was bound to encounter the medieval: another world a thousand light-years from where I found myself.

Then I went straight to the computer and looked up information about the city I was in, and the first thing I came across was material about the Documenta of 1972. If I read that 72 backwards, I got my room number. This didn't exactly compel me to keep reading, but it did make me take more interest in what I read. An admirer of "that historic Documenta"—the one in '72—claimed to have discovered in it that the latest members of the avant-garde belonged to the purest strain of romanticism, the beatniks in particular.

Suddenly, for reasons that still escape me today, my attention focused entirely on the beatniks. What did I know about those people? For a moment, I was disorientated by my own question. I only managed to leave the muddle of the beatnik mystery behind when I remembered I had that old copy of *Romanticism*, by Rüdiger Safranski, lying in my suitcase. Once again, I hadn't made a mistake in choosing it for company. I opened it to the page where I could read that only as aesthetic phenomena are the world and existence eternally justified.

I thought: Didn't I come to Kassel precisely to seek the aesthetic instant? Yes, but not only that. Besides, I'd never found that instant in my entire life so far, and everything seemed to indicate that things would go on the same for me after passing through Kassel. In fact, I didn't even know what an aesthetic instant might really be, since up to that point I'd only managed to get glimpses of it, not much more. I paused to think. Why had I traveled to that city? I've come, I told myself, purely to think. I paused thoughtfully. I've come to mentally construct a cabin, a human refuge in which I can meditate on the lost world. I paused thoughtfully. I've come to read something about a peddler and his stump and an incurably gloomy Spain. I've come to discover the mystery of the universe, to initiate myself into the poetry of an unknown algebra, to seek an oblique clock, and to read about Romanticism. I paused thoughtfully. I've come to investigate what the essence, the pure, hard nucleus of contemporary art is. I've come to find out if there still is an avant-garde. In fact, I've come to carry out research on Kassel. I paused thoughtfully. I've come simply so that on my return home I can tell people what I've seen. I've come to find out what beatniks are. I paused thoughtfully again. I've come to get acquainted with the general condition of the arts. Again, I paused thoughtfully. I've come to recover enthusiasm. I paused a little less thoughtfully. I've come so I can narrate my journey later on, as if I'd been to the country estate in *Locus Solus*, or to the Alcarria, an Alcarria described by Roussel, for example. I've come to gain access to that instant when a man seems to take on, once and for all, who he is. I paused thoughtfully. I've come to leave my wife in peace for a few days. I paused thoughtfully again. I've come to hesitate. I paused doubtfully. I've come to find out whether there is any logic in being invited to Kassel to pull off a Chinese number. I paused thoughtfully.

I paused for even more reflection when I noticed that the pessimism that came over me so inexorably at that hour had begun to strongly take hold. I was beginning to see that the so famous aesthetic instant (I had thought that one day I would or wouldn't know what it was) would never be within my grasp. Was it normal for my pessimism to increase so much in so few minutes? Unfortunately, yes. The onset of the black hours always erupted without warning, and straightaway I got to thinking that I didn't have many years left and everything in my life had gone by very fast; why, just a few days ago, I was young and carefree, but it had all changed in a short time, this was now an incontrovertible fact, and I felt sad. When the black hours flared up almost punctually evening after evening, I could never avoid sliding relentlessly down the slippery slope of the most pessimistic and dangerous thoughts.

To top it all, I remembered something a friend told me (not such a good friend, to judge by his actions) whenever he wanted to depress me. He'd do this when he noticed I was already depressed. He said that during the night the essence of night does not let us sleep. I have never understood very well what the sentence meant, but I found it terrifying. I turned it over in my mind a few times. Preventing us from sleeping. Was that something at the very core of the night? Did the night only make sense when it managed to stop us resting?

It was early to go to bed, but I was worn out; the final punishment of the walk to platform 10 had been brutal, and the dawning of consciousness there was so intense it had left me in bits. I now thought only of sleep, though I was very afraid I wouldn't be able to attain it. In spite of the desire to lie down, I found the strength for something that turned out to be very banal compared to Pavel Haas's music on the platform.

I found the strength for a final foray into Google, where I stumbled upon a photograph of Chus Martínez, whose face seemed to me essentially lively, making me guess (I wasn't in the least bit mistaken) that this was someone who'd internalized her ability to have ideas as profoundly as someone once said that the whaler in *Moby-Dick* had internalized his harpoon.

I don't know how long I spent, half asleep, looking at the photo of Chus; she had invited me to Kassel and we still hadn't met, though there was every indication I'd have dinner with her on Thursday. The more I looked at her face, the more I saw it brimming with ideas, and ultimately that made me think about them thoroughly—about ideas, I mean, and their presence and absence in modern art. I remembered that, in the mid nineteenth century, no European artist was ignorant of the fact that, if he wanted to prosper, he had to interest the intellectuals (the new class), which turned culture into the topic most often addressed by its creators, and the sole objective of art became the suggesting and inspiring of ideas. Strolling around Kassel, one was left in no doubt that there at least, things were still under the influence of that mid-nineteenth-century transformation. Elsewhere, no. Because almost all over the rest of the world the intellectual had taken a nosedive, and culture had become extraordinarily trivialized. But in Kassel a certain romantic and Duchampian aura remained; it was a paradise for those who loved intellectual conjecture, theoretical discussions, and the elegance of certain speculations.

I've always been enormously entertained by theories, so I could feel satisfied. For a long time I didn't get contemporary art, but here in Kassel I was overloaded with stimuli to investigate the position of that art. That said, as a young man, it bored me to look at a Rembrandt. Confronted with a painting by that admirable artist, I didn't know what to say. But, if I saw a *readymade* by a humble imitator of Duchamp, all sorts of commentaries poured out of me and I started to feel, once and for all, like an artist too. The same thing, I recall, happened to me with Manet, an artist very influenced by Mallarmé and whose most significant disciple may have been—I dare say—Marcel Duchamp. Mallarmé told Manet: "Paint, not the thing, but the effect it produces." That sentence prefigured the modern abandonment of the two-dimensional plane and the ascent of the conceptual to a position of dominance.

Back in the days when Rembrandt left me mute, I already loved lofty theories (I didn't understand any of them, but that was another matter). Above all, I loved the interviews in which the main topic was Theory, in that case with a capital "T." I'd been fascinated at the beginning of the seventies by some questions that had been put to Alain Robbe-Grillet, which made him writhe against theories like an upside-down cat: "Let's say I'm old-fashioned. For me, all that counts are the works of art."

The works of art! These days such ingenuousness would trigger laughter. At Documenta 13, separating work and theory would have been seen as very old-fashioned, because there, according to all the information I had, you saw a great many works under the ambiguous umbrella of innovation presented as theory and vice versa. It was the triumphant and now almost definitive reign of the marriage between practice and theory, to such an extent that if you casually came across a rather classical-looking piece, you'd soon discover it was nothing more than theory camouflaged as a work. Or a work camouflaged as theory.

Was there any artist at Kassel with sufficient courage to just hang a painting on the wall, a straightforward painting? I imagined the great peals of laughter that would ring out if it occurred to some poor brave devil to hang a canvas on a wall in the Fridericianum. It seemed nobody there wanted to be regarded as terribly old-fashioned, so there was no way of seeing a painting anywhere.

I stopped looking sleepily at the photo of Chus Martínez and started to read her interview about whether art had to be innovative or not. My attention was caught by the final sentence—"Art is art, and what you make of it is up to you"—which was possibly just a McGuffin. Perhaps it had been said so that I should read it in my room at the Hessenland and finally understand what I'd been asked to do in Kassel. It was as if those last words ultimately meant this: "Here's an invitation to a Chinese restaurant, we're asking you for art, now let's see what you make of it."

23

I was now deep in the black hours, but I took refuge in my computer a few minutes longer. I was surfing around lost corners of the web when the memory of the music of Pavel Haas and the Holocaust came back to me. Many times on TV I'd been intrigued by some documentary footage frequently broadcast on all channels, especially Catalan ones, that showed Hitler and his staff soaking up the sun on a terrace—a sort of luxurious look-out in the Alps—in a place called Berghof. There were women in the film, women who posed and laughed, that was what had always struck me the most. Hitler, moreover, was seen taking some children by the hand and stroking some dogs. Everything was spectacularly strange and sinister up there on that terrace of the powerful. The weirdest thing, though, was that due to the elevation of the place, each scene was ringed with a light that virtually bounced off the screen, an exaggerated light, almost like that from the beyond.

The first time I'd seen those images I'd been surprised by the extreme beauty of the alpine landscape and the fact that the Nazi murderers were carrying on a peaceful and ordinary bourgeois Sunday morning at that look-out. I'd asked myself many times what had become of that fabulous terrace with its splendid, white-framed windows, behind which something distinctly dark and unhealthy could be guessed at. And I decided it was now the time to try and find out what could be seen today at that scene so fixed in my mind, in that alpine spot where a handful of criminals were one day placed in a frame.

The route Google took me showed the day in April 1945 when the house was bombed by the British Royal Air Force, and then the day at the beginning of May when some ruddy-cheeked American soldiers took photographs of themselves amid the ruins of the terrace while bragging about drinking "Hitler's wine." And finally the search engine led me to eight years later, after that Nazi cellar ran dry: more than a thousand tons of explosives left not a single clue that there had been a house there with a luminous terrace projecting menacingly out over the world.

Where the look-out had been is today an innocuous rectangle of well-cut grass. Nobody would guess there had once been a house there and a lofty terrace and some children who waved their little hands, waving their purity at you, smiling sweetly at the women who posed, also smilingly, beside their beloved murderers.

I looked carefully: the innocuous rectangle of well-cut grass might be a metaphor for this country I found myself in. But perhaps I looked at that rectangle for too long. I ended up so utterly exhausted I kept thinking that, if it were possible, I'd lie down right there on that inconsequential grass deprived of history, right on that computer screen.

Everything happened very fast. In the midst of an anguish that didn't stop growing and reminding me obsessively of my age, how my time had already been cut irretrievably short, I imagined myself lying like a pariah on the bland rectangle, and ended up falling asleep.

I dreamed of fields of grass where beatniks were grazing, fields that split into more fields and then into killing fields like a sprawling nightmare. And then I dreamed (in the part of the night closest to my waking and, therefore, to my cheerful morning mood) that somebody stole my shoes in those fields and told me that the common, revered model of the "great man" was the opposite of poetry and the irreducible individuality of being unique. This view was the opposite of the poetry of the unique existence (ephemeral, unrepeatable), which did not need to be written, but only—and above all—to be lived. This second part of the dream, with its agreeable observations

71

on the poetry of individuality, must have influenced my excellent mood the following morning, which was indeed the norm.

Collapse and recovery.

In the hotel bar, I had a triple espresso, which gave my energy and joy such a boost I was almost chuckling to myself. I decided to go outside straightaway to calm a certain tension. It was early, very early. There was hardly anyone around. In fact I saw only an old woman leaning in toward a shop window with a finger to her lips. Apart from this odd, potentially disturbing image, there was not much else to be seen on the street.

Feeling extraordinarily humorous, I said to myself: Just as well there's hardly anyone around, that way nobody will look at me and say, It's about time you got here, son—we were waiting for you to start giving contemporary art, which is half-asleep, a new direction.

Half-asleep?

I realized I still carried within me the classic fatalistic tics of the intellectuals of my country, especially those of the "lucid intellectuals." I was still influenced by those determined to find that contemporary art was half-asleep and an absolute disaster.

Wasn't it? It was not at its peak, you had to admit. But except during my black hours, I was bothered that some of my friends were so radically defeatist about contemporary art. I could see that it found itself in crisis and, in fact, I imagined Documenta 13 might perhaps illustrate this tricky state of affairs very well; even so, contact with some of the works at Kassel had been very stimulating so far. What's more, I had absorbed much of what I'd seen; it had injected me with an optimistic energy right at the height of my usual dead time.

I looked at the street, which was deserted at that early morning hour, and I told myself that the lucid voices of some of my compatriots, so self-satisfied, weren't telling the whole truth either. They were articulate and sometimes went all out to dazzle. They did so, but you couldn't ignore the fact that they reveled in fatalism, some of them simply because they themselves hadn't been given the gift of creativity, and this pitched them furiously up against other voices and, in passing, against contemporary culture as a whole. In the very end, I thought, so much lucidity leads them to cliché. Some maintain that we find ourselves at a slack moment, that there have been no new ideas since the seventies. Some claim that since the eighties, there have been no worthwhile novels or anything else. But some of these fatalists were already radical defeatists in the seventies, devoting themselves to preventing anyone with ideas from trying to do anything.

I carried on walking, at first with no particular destination in mind. It may be true, I mused, that there are few young people today who draw inspiration for their lives from what contemporary poets are saying, while in the seventies an interesting minority took poetry as the most dependable guide to life. It may also be true that at the end of the eighties something very serious happened, which resulted in the arts, especially poetry, losing its leading role. That might all be correct, but if there was something I had long detested, it was those fatalistic voices gathering to project their own personal catastrophes upon the world. I prefer to enter Tino Sehgal's dark room to see how some people are rescuing art from such a lamentably sure collapse.

Very soon afterward, I decided to head for that dark room, which was my sinister lighthouse in the night. That morning I began to see it as a place that could also be stimulating by day. And making my way toward it, I started to wonder whether our fatalists' lucid impression that we're experiencing a dead time in art meant one had to live through it alarmed, scandalized, distressed, and without humor.

I was reminded of Stanislaw Lem and of his *History of Bitic Literature*, published in Paris in five volumes. In his book about the future (in this case, now our past), Stanislaw Lem said that from the end of the 1980s, from the "fifteenth *bynasty*" of "talking computers" onward, it was shown to be a technical necessity to give the machines periods of rest during which, free from "programming instructions," they could fall to "babbling" and "random shuffling," and, thanks to this erratic activity, regenerate their capacity.

As if Lem's prediction had come true, it couldn't be clearer that in the eighties, creators of all sorts were freed from "programming instructions" and entered into paused, dead time. In fact, I'd heard it said to students of "bitic literature" that relaxation was as indispensable for talking machines as an awareness of the danger of losing the power of speech was for the literature of the future.

I was walking down the last stretch of corridor to the garden of the Hessenland annex when I asked myself if it might be the case that, in the creative field, we had found ourselves in a period of repose born out of technical necessity, a period from which—talking machines as we undeniably were—we would all emerge more than revived. So why so much ominous chatter? Was it so infuriating to live in a time of "babble"? Perhaps we were in a moment in which we were recovering speech. Was it really so painful to be "randomly shuffling"?

I seemed to see that underneath it all, this dead time was still a more than positive place, a laboratory in a state of ferment, a perfect space in which to greet the returning poets who had perhaps already started to transform our life. Didn't we sense them already among us? Hadn't I detected them on my first visit to that room of Sehgal's that I was now preparing to visit again? And if they hadn't come back, that didn't mean we had to despair. By bringing us such interesting relaxation, this period of repose that was technically necessary might even do us some good.

24

It was becoming increasingly obvious to me that walking cleared my head and allowed me to dare to speculate with an open mind. I was going along so intent on what I was thinking, I bumped into a chair in the corridor leading to Sehgal's room, and somebody looked at me as if to say: It's about time you got here, but you blunder around.

Finally, I went into *This Variation*, my second incursion into the place that generated in me so many contradictory feelings. I thought because of the early hour, there would be nobody in there, and I entered too confidently. I marched in blindly, but somehow sure. I chose to go in a straight line, moving forward about two meters and, just when I was about to turn around, I heard some singing issuing faintly from the back of the room; then it started to get a little higher pitched and began to seem like a sort of reedy Hare Krishna chant with a mellow and surprising reggae beat, which eventually transformed into what I thought sounded like a foxtrot.

It started to become clear to me that there were people, or phantoms, in the dark practicing dance steps. Suddenly, two of these people, whom I could only sense, of course, became my escorts. Taking me by both arms, they gently whisked me much farther into the room and left me at what I imagined was its far end. They achieved what usually never happened to me in the morning: my anguish resurfaced bit by bit; it didn't stay for long, but it brought with it certain consequences.

Standing probably at the far end of the room, in the most absolute darkness, I remembered a day in a village in La Mancha, close to the Ruidera Lakes, when I saw two men in black jackets with silver buttons removing a coffin from a back courtyard; inside the coffin, beneath a floral-patterned cloth, lay what looked by any reckoning to be the body of a man over seventy years of age.

In Sehgal's room, the singing suddenly stopped. Impenetrable silence. I felt nostalgia for the foxtrot. The dancers, who had been in the dark so long and could possibly see me, seemed to have paused, standing absolutely still, like ghosts. Not wanting to lose the mood, but with a certain amount of trepidation, I said out loud: "You are in Germany."

And then I tried to touch the wall that might be in front of me with both hands but I didn't find one. I swiped around, like a poor tiger in the gloom. I decided it made no sense to go any farther, and in the end I laughed in the darkness. Not long after, I felt what one perhaps feels the day it's all over: completely outside of this world, which at the same time had me thinking I had grasped the internal structure of life, as if a lightning bolt were lighting it up. Nothing more. It was brief, but extremely intense. Now I knew everything I needed to know about my death, although I quickly forgot it. Then I left the dark room and saw that the daylight was like the bolt of lightning that had momentarily illuminated me inside the room.

I took a turn around the block trying to reflect on what I'd just experienced. I felt the chill of an early September morning. Could the contemporary avant-garde frighten a person to death? I realized there was still absolutely nobody out on the street, so I returned to the Hessenland.

I had not only regained my usual morning cheer but also found myself far more euphoric than usual; I took no notice of this, not wanting to give it any importance. There, in the very doorway of the hotel, I literally bumped into Alka, who was bringing me a note telling me María Boston couldn't come to fetch me that morning (she was backed up with work at the office), and Pim Durán would come instead, arriving about eleven o'clock.

There was more than an hour until the cheerful Pim arrived. I didn't want to spend all that time with Alka in the lobby, so I decided to go ahead with what I'd planned, which was to go up to my room. I noticed that a Chinese man in reception—probably an artist or journalist—was checking in and incessantly asking questions nobody knew how to answer. I jotted that down in a small red notebook I'd called *Impressions of Kassel*. It wasn't the first time I wrote something in that book. In fact, since leaving Barcelona, I'd been sketching scenes—I don't draw well, but it doesn't matter—and noting plenty of things down, as if I guessed that maybe one day I'd decide to work up some impressions of it all.

In the elevator, two plump Chinese women, who were quite young, with no apparent link to the man of a thousand questions, got in as the metal doors were closing. They got out at the same floor as me and went into room 26. Seeing we were neighbors, they smiled broadly, which made me think there must be something ridiculous about me, or rather, that in China the fondness for laughing and smiling was prodigious, although we somewhat befuddled Westerners were still not in a position to understand what they were laughing about or what could make them so happy.

Now in my room, I went out on the balcony and established a new mental connection with Sehgal's dark room. It was my special way of letting my lighthouse in the dark know I was thinking of returning to visit it a third time, but that I wouldn't be able to bear any more frights. Then I went back into my room and, listening through the wall, devoted myself to spying on, or rather, imagining what the two Chinese girls were saying.

One of them said: "When winter came, he always assumed you'd die of cold." And the other replied: "But he was the one who died." I could not know then that the "Synge method"—my personal system for finding out what was being said by anyone it was impossible to understand—had only just fired up and in the long run would become the method—I was going to describe it as *infallible*, but it would be a mistake to classify it that way—that I would use in the Dschingis Khan to comprehend what the customers and waiters were talking about.

I stopped listening to my neighbors, who—from the solitude of my room—I imagined even bigger and rounder than they were. I returned to my computer to try to discover whether Critical Art Ensemble had announced the time and place of my "Lecture to Nobody" yet. I was unsure whether they'd included my talk in the program after all, as the previous afternoon Boston hadn't even mentioned the subject. I searched but found nothing about the talk that I'd agreed to give in a remote spot beyond the farthest forest, on the outskirts of Kassel.

I found nothing about that, but instead came across another interview with Chus Martínez. The photographs accompanying the text all had one thing in common: Chus wasn't laughing in any of them. She was asked how she thought Spain had taken the economic crisis. Dreadfully, she said. On a psychological level, she continued, it was sort of like the end of the world. The politician Durão Barroso had said the situation in Portugal couldn't be compared to Spain, because Spanish gloom and doom was ferocious. According to Chus, her compatriots did not know how to be easygoing: "We thought ourselves really crazy, but it turned out we were nothing of the sort. It's precisely madness and a sense of humor that are lacking. Humor, as a fundamental element of the modern, has been laid claim to since Cervantes. A way of life that's a bit more relaxed, open, flexible ... I wonder, was Don Quixote's humor ever Spanish?"

Next, I began to hatch a plan, so that no one in the Dschingis Khan who wanted to spy on my work would be able to get the slightest idea what I was writing. To this end, I invented a character very different from myself: a writer obsessed with two problems, with two themes that held him captive. I'd have no problem developing them in full view of the entire audience. The invented author, then, would sit in a corner of the Dschingis Khan in front of the visitors and tackle two stories that would hound him, but never me. And as that Barcelona author would be a nervous man, afraid his computer might get stolen in the Chinese restaurant, he'd just write his stories in a notebook—let's say a red one, mine, why go looking for another, I could save myself the cost, financial and mental, and use a pencil and an eraser. The author would be far from intellectual (not being an intellectual was abominable in Kassel, although in the rest of the world being illiterate, or appearing to be so, made one immensely successful); this might make communication easier with the people who came to see him writing on the spot. The author would be a man in whom ingenuousness and raw intelligence would coexist perfectly. A rather simple man, who would set his characters very simple problems, that he, with his lack of sophistication, would think tremendously complicated.

The first of the simple stories holding him captive revolved around the conundrum that we are so many million people in the world, and yet communication—real communication—is absolutely impossible between any two of us. A most tragic theme, Autre thought (Autre was the provisional surname I gave my nonintellectual author until something better came along). Anxiety about noncommunication went way back for that good man, in fact it had worried him greatly as a boy when his intense loneliness had produced in him the desire to start bellowing. Maybe because of this he had taken up this momentous question an infinite number of times.

The other theme that held Autre captive was that of fleeing. A journalist had once asked for a précis of the story that had occurred to him on this theme, and he'd said something solemn, convinced of his talent (although at night he cried when he discovered in dreams that he altogether lacked genius): "Change your life completely in two days, without caring in the slightest what has gone before, leave without further ado. Do you know what I'm referring to?"

"Starting again?" the journalist asked.

"Not even that. Going toward nothing."

I'd just finished inventing this Barcelona author who was in possession of two such serious themes (communication and flight—I laughed out loud) when they notified me from reception that Pim Durán had arrived. I quickly took the red notebook, pencil, and eraser from my bedside table, and went down to reception, already in my role as a nonintellectual author "with two problems." As I went, I felt I was being activated by an invisible breeze from the Fridericianum.

25

They say nobody sleeps on their way to the scaffold. I can only speak for myself and say that I was more than wide awake that Wednesday morning on the free Documenta bus heading toward my fast-approaching Chinese gallows. Alka and Pim kept laughing at what I was telling them with my morning good humor. I was witty, or at least I thought I was, though I didn't manage to forget I was actually a prisoner.

The bus soon left the network of the city center, which had been entirely rebuilt since the war. It took a road that I think looped around the city, an unobtrusive ring road. It also looped around the baroque-style Karlsaue Park, which was Kassel's vast and beautiful extension. Entering this open space multiplied my optimism and joy, although I didn't forget the shadow of the Chinese gallows continuing to loom over the present.

And that's how we ended up going onto the Auedamm, a lovely road running beside the Fulda River and along which walked hordes of retired Germans. Pim told me that Germany was a country for old people. The old knew how to have fun there, how to travel en masse better than anyone. It was enough to see them euphoric on the terraces beside the Fulda drinking beer, defying a world that otherwise believed only in youth.

For a while I'd been wondering what Autre had meant with that comment about "not even starting again, but going toward nothing" and I ended up asking my two jovial companions how they would interpret a man of a certain age suddenly showing a desire to go "toward nothing."

A difficult question, I thought, a question to make you laugh or cry. Alka and Pim looked at me with mistrust and then backed away from me on that half-empty bus; they stood still a second, and then, like automatons, said something into each other's ears and burst out laughing simultaneously.

The uncalled-for synchronization of their laughter and their movements made me rather uncomfortable, although a distinction had to be made between Alka—who laughed not understanding anything (once more, she was laughing only because she thought that was what her job entailed)—and Pim, who reacted that way because, it seemed to me at that moment, she was dictated to by what we might call the downside of her charm, which obliged her to show herself, without the slightest letup, always delighted by life.

Anyway, it was drizzling when we got off the bus at kilometer 19 of the Auedamm. On one side of the highway, a beer terrace with views over the river was crammed with German pensioners. On the other was the most miserable-looking Chinese restaurant I'd ever seen in my life. Karlsaue Park spread out behind it.

The Dschingis Khan, I thought, was a place for the evenings when anxiety gripped me; it had not been designed for my jubilant mornings. I was left hoping this first impression was false—I had to add, moreover, that I was convinced of finding myself confronting my own personal gallows. Perhaps it was all down to the drizzle that made the whole place look unwanted and disastrously glum.

In for a penny, in for a pound. Whatever the circumstances, I've never been one to turn and run if I didn't like something; I've always known there's only one battlefield with no way out. I say this because as soon as I went in to the Dschingis Khan, I spotted the old-fashioned round table, a sort of Spanish warming-table, and could barely believe it: pushed to the back of the dismal corner they'd assigned me, it was one of those tables with a space underneath for a heater and had a hideous vase and a worn, old yellow sign that read: "Writer in Residence." Despite all this, I did not run away.

I had been so many men (I thought, parodying Borges), and now I was just a resident writer they'd invited to come and do a Chinese number. To cap it off, you could tell the sign had been handled by a large number of writers who'd been invited in the preceding weeks, some of whose names I remembered: Adania Shibli, Mario Bellatin, Aaron Peck, Alejandro Zambra, Marie Darrieussecq, Holly Pester.

I thought I'd be able to bear it.

I would sit at my gallows with dignity.

I knew some of those writers. I had preferred not to email them to ask how they'd artistically come to terms with the obligation to sit in that disagreeable corner each day. The fact of the matter is that writers can get drunk with one another, but they can never resolve together the technical problems they have with their respective lives or novels or Chinese residencies. Watching two writers talk of these matters is as excruciating as watching two future mothers swap details of their respective pregnancies, believing they're talking about one and the same thing.

At that time of the morning, there were no customers in the dark, not terribly attractive restaurant, and there were just a few employees: some cooks and some waiters. There was also a Chinese woman at a table piled high with papers next to a large fish tank, who was devoting herself, in full view of everyone, to doing the accounts.

Not a single employee bothered to greet me; they all behaved with notable indifference, if not aversion. I understood right away that they saw me as a dangerous element: one more link in a frightening chain of scribblers, which made me surmise that the ones before me had, in general, left dreadful memories behind them. Furthermore, from certain disparaging looks I thought some of the cooks were sending in my direction, it seemed that more than a thousand different reasons to steer clear of writers had built up in their minds.

I took advantage of the unwelcoming atmosphere to ask Pim what she thought I should do with my pencil and my eraser and my red notebook in that somewhat inhospitable spot. No reader had come along at that mid-morning hour to see me, which wasn't surprising, considering the fact that my appearance at the table in the Chinese restaurant hadn't been announced anywhere in the city or on the Internet, and only one sign on the restaurant door and another on my table indicated I was there, at the mercy of any idiot with a vocation for gossip or who wanted to snoop at what I was writing.

"Who do you think is going to bother taking the Auedamm bus this miserable Wednesday to come spy on what I write here?" I asked Pim, with all the common sense in the world.

I was waiting for her answer, when a German woman weighing over 260 pounds came in and spoke briefly to Alka or, more accurately, Alka spoke to her very sharply. She must have said something to her about me, because, seconds later, the woman came resolutely forward and, in the most effusive manner, proceeded to embrace me with rare enthusiasm.

"Writer, writer, writer!" she shouted gleefully, as if she'd never seen one before in her life.

She let me go, but then embraced me again. Again she shouted, Writer, writer.

I heard Alka's needless laughter.

"Yes, I'm a writer," I said, annoyed. "What of it?"

26

When I got a grip on myself, Frau Writer-Writer was saying goodbye to Alka and Pim and leaving. Her absence was immediately noticeable, as I was stuck without potential admirers who would want to spy on what I wrote. The woman went without saying anything to me, as if she had forgotten me immediately after her second savage squeeze.

A German experience, I thought.

And I was left relying on what really interested me: whether Pim, the cheerful girl whose name reminded me of a beach in the Azores called Porto Pim, would take responsibility for the absurdity of my situation, given that there weren't any people there now to annoy me.

I was going to ask her again what she thought I should do there with my pencil and my eraser and my red notebook on the outskirts of Kassel. Up to that point I hadn't been interested, but now I wondered if she could give me any idea how those who'd preceded me in this Chinese number had worked out this peculiar situation. I was going to ask, but at the last moment, I decided to inquire about my talk with the title "Lecture to Nobody." I wanted to know if it had been scheduled for a particular time, as I was keen to give it, even if, I said to myself, it was possibly only to make up for the conspicuously shabby "Chinese number" that they'd entrusted to me. What's more, it seemed that only if I gave my "Lecture to Nobody" would I feel as though I'd really taken part in Documenta.

It took Pim a while to understand my question, but finally the penny dropped. I was to give the talk on Friday, she said, but they'd changed the venue and I would not do it out beyond a forest without an audience, but in the very center of Kassel, in the conference room of the Ständehaus.

"Then I can't call it 'Lecture to Nobody.'"

"If it'll make you happy, we'll stop the public coming in."

I laughed and asked what kind of place the Ständehaus was. It was the old Hesse parliament, she said, and one of the few buildings left more or less standing at the end of the war. She'd show me around inside whenever I wanted to get a good idea of where I'd be speaking.

I didn't want to let the opportunity pass me by and asked whether that meant we could go and see the Ständehaus right that minute.

"Don't even think about it!" Pim barked.

Bit by bit, she lost her smile, which up to that point had suited her so nicely. Seeing her like that made an impression on me. Noticing that her reaction surprised me, she took it badly, not knowing how to get back to her permanent exuberance, the *downside of her charm*. The return to that state had seemed expected.

83

"But we're not doing a thing here in this Chinese restaurant," I said.

"What do you mean we're not doing a thing?" Pim said. She seemed put out.

Far from venting my rage on her *false charm* or accusing her of taking orders from superiors about what she had to do with me, I kept quiet. Perhaps it was for the best. I smiled, took a step toward her, and positioned myself very close to her face; then I retreated, making out nothing had happened, that I hadn't noticed she wasn't always charming. But something had happened, and then some. There was something shockingly horrible about the unpredictable Pim's face. When it's artificial, I thought, joy can fall apart in an extremely alarming manner. And what's more, how frightening people are who suddenly show a side of themselves we'd never imagined (as sometimes happens to me, which is why I try not to be seen out too much at night).

27

Minutes later, I was seated behind the dog-eared "Writer in Residence" sign, like someone who is waiting for a very absentminded customer to come into his disastrous shop. Three tables away, Pim and Alka were drinking Chinese tea while talking about mysterious matters. Everything led me to suspect they had instructions to observe *what I made of it* (and from a certain distance in order to ensure the whole thing worked). The ball, they seemed to be saying to me, is in your court now, so *what you make of it is up to you.* You could see perfectly well they were thinking this or something along those lines, because occasionally their glances were somewhat sadistic, as if they were expecting a real gallows expression to take hold of me.

I wrote in the red notebook:

"Change your life completely in two days without caring in the slightest what has gone before; leave without further ado. When all's said and done, the right thing to do is take off."

I wrote this just in case. It would be a total miracle if anybody came in and was interested to know what I was working on. At least I would give that visitor the impression I was really writing there at my table in the Chinese restaurant. If anyone asked me, I would speak at length in Autre's voice about the creation of a character in a novel, who was an average man, naive and intelligent at the same time: a man who lived through a particular moment and wasn't even looking to start again, but wanted to leave without further ado and *go toward nothing*.

And what did going toward nothing mean? I didn't have the slightest idea. In my role as Autre, I would ask the first person who inquired about it. Of course, that person might never turn up. In short, in the highly unlikely event that anyone should approach my table, my idea was to act as though I were a writer seeking the collaboration of his fans. It goes without saying that having to ask readers for their help seems a pretty unattractive method to me, but I knew I could allow myself to do it if the circumstances arose. I would feel not that it was me myself who was doing it, but the guile-less Autre. Moreover, I was indifferent to a desire to change life and leave without further ado: in the end, that was somebody else's de-sire, expressed in somebody else's work, in the book being written by a man from Barcelona whose name was (provisionally) Autre.

While I was waiting for I'm not exactly sure what, I entertained myself by writing an autobiographical note for poor Autre, letting him borrow several details from my own life so he wouldn't turn out too radically different from me. I focused the text on his early relationship with art and revealed that cinema had been a big thing for him long before literature was:

> From the window of the living room in the house where I was born, you could see the Metropol. I followed the changes on the marquee from there and the pasting up of huge posters of Bogart, for example. At the age of five I saw Humphrey Bogart a hundred times a day. I was only

three when I saw my first movie one summer in Llavaneres, a village north of Barcelona, a kilometer from the
beach. My mother's family had settled in that village four
centuries ago. My first film was *Magnolia*, with Ava Gard-
ner. I remember that, on leaving the cinema, I began to
imitate William Warfield, the black singer who sang "Ol'
Man River" at the end of the film in an extremely deep
voice (which I aspired to, I suppose, the voice of a man).
The event was much celebrated in my family. More than
that, it seems they thought I wanted to be a black singer
when I grew up ...

Alka and Pim came to see me to say they were going outside to
smoke, and after their interruption I was no longer capable of carrying on with my autobiographical note. It'd be best if they went a
long way away, I thought. That's all I thought.

Then I plunged into a text in the style of Jonathan Swift's *Resolutions When I Come to Be Old*. I barely diverged from the original: "Not to
marry a young woman. Not to be peevish or morose or suspicious.
Not to be too free with advice, nor to trouble any but those who desire it. Not to be too severe with the young, but make allowances for
their youthful follies. Not to be categorical or stubborn. Not to insist
on keeping so many rules for fear you should keep none of them."

I preferred to attribute these *Resolutions* to Autre too. As well as
preparing everything so that, if any reader-spy were to appear, the
writing I showed wouldn't be mine but my double's (that is, poor
Autre's), I dumped the whole drama of the extreme proximity of
old age onto him.

Of the two women, only Pim came back, but not until almost an
hour later. I wouldn't see Alka again for the rest of that day. During
the hour spent alone, with the girls smoking outside, I had more
than enough time to lament, a thousand times over, not having
brought *Romanticism* or *Journey to the Alcarria* with me. As I had nothing to read, I devoted myself to *remembering* something I'd read: a letter from Kafka to his girlfriend Felice Bauer, in which he expressed

his fear that, when they married, she would spy on everything he wrote. (Indeed, Bauer had affectionately written to him of her desire to sit beside him in the future while he was writing.)

Perhaps my terror of being spied on in the Dschingis Khan was humbly and distantly related to Kafka's panic at the mere possibility that Felice Bauer wouldn't let him write in solitude. I had the feeling that part of my problem with the invitation to Documenta had been just that fear of mine. If I remembered correctly, Kafka's panic was mixed with some Chinese business in a January 1913 letter, in which he wrote something along these lines to Bauer: "You once said you would like to sit beside me while I write. Listen. In that case I could not write at all. One can never be alone enough when one writes, there can never be enough silence when one writes, even night is not night enough." And these words mingled with far-off China because, in the same letter, Kafka used the anecdote of a poem to mark a separation between himself and Felice, and in passing he showed her that even in that distant Oriental land, working at night was the exclusive preserve of men. The poem sketched the lovely image of the scholar bent over his book who'd completely forgotten to go to bed; the Chinese man's companion, who had made a huge effort to keep her anger under control up to that point, snatched the lamp away and asked him whether he knew what time it was. But he was absorbed, engrossed in his fascinating task.... With this in mind, I also became engrossed and missed all the things I was used to having around me. When I was able to react, I once again felt ridiculous grasping my true situation: waiting for some very absentminded customer to come into my disastrous business. Business? Yes, the business of a man of letters, seated at his own gallows.

28

As the hour approached when Germany has lunch, the Dschingis Khan started to liven up, as you might expect, and customers began coming in: people chose tables near mine. I was so alone there (in theory Alka and Pim were still smoking outside, although I'd soon discover Alka had taken the bus back). For a while, I entertained myself by pretending everyone in the place was an acquaintance or a friend, a really surprising gathering of people linked to different periods of my life.

As everyone asked for the menu, so did I, though in my case it was just to have something to read. They might be old acquaintances or friends, but none of them spoke to me, which never ceased to be a relief. I was worried they might all want to head for me at once and I'd have to choose between friends or acquaintances from one period or another; the truth is, I've always hated favoritism.

I'm not sure how it came about that I bent down and started looking for a hole under the table. Knowing that Marie Darrieussecq knew that I, too, liked those jail scenes in which prisoners leave useful messages for their successors in their cells, I was trying to find a cranny into which she might have slipped some instructions about how to survive in those tricky Chinese circumstances. As you might guess, I didn't find anything, but I did spend quite a while pleasantly entertained, mostly by imagining I did find a scrap of paper, which turned out to be a message for Holly Pester, not for me. She was another of the writers who'd passed through here. I'd been able to read some of her poetry on the Internet and enjoyed it a lot.

On deciding the fruitless search was over, and also purely to fill the time, I turned to doing something else. I devoted myself to listening to the conversations in German and Chinese that I could hear in the restaurant, as well as those between customers and waiters that mixed the two languages together. They might be acquaintances or friends, but they all spoke in German and Chinese. Supposing our paths had crossed over the years, my friends certainly seemed to have changed a good deal, at the very least to have changed languages.

I rang a friend in Barcelona to ask if he could possibly imagine the idea of a Catalan taking up the Chinese language and renouncing his own forever. Luckily for my friend, he wasn't at home. I didn't feel like calling anyone else after that.

Soon the whole restaurant had turned itself into a new Galway

Bay as I began to use my fantastical "Synge method": that special technique that allowed me to believe I understood everything everyone was saying so perfectly that I could even draw conclusions about what was going on there.

For a moment I went so far as to believe that, if the circumstances were right, I could someday work as an interpreter in meetings between Chinese and German entrepreneurs. I heard, for example, a German customer telling his wife that her face, usually washed out and tending toward a sort of eggish hue, had acquired an incandescent tone. And I heard the wife replying that he was a dead man. I heard a Chinese cook tell a waiter he wanted to get over his sexual extravaganzas and that he was fed up with his horrible girdle. What girdle was he talking about? Did I really know what a girdle was? I heard another waiter tell a customer he understood his desire to stand out when there were ladies around and I heard the customer promise him a big tip if he managed to make him stand out even more. I heard one of the Chinese cooks tell a German kitchen boy he was a greaseball and that they'd end up finding him in a sewer and have to scrape a layer of filth off in order to identify him. I heard the kitchen boy tell the cook she had a lovely big ass. He congratulated her on having such a large one but said that every day she wasted half her time stuck in the doorway, as it was so hard for her to get into the kitchen.

From everything I heard and translated using the Synge method, I came to the conclusion that there was an undercurrent of violence about the place. A tension between the German and Chinese citizens—both countries stars on their own continents—ran almost covertly in every corner. It was as if all the immense tension between the Chinese and the Germans over dividing up the world as soon as the United States lost it was concentrated there in the limited space of that establishment.

You could feel that tension, and the dialogue somehow reproduced it with a hefty emotional charge. It ended up leading to my notable physical exhaustion, and only that morning's excellent mental state saved me from a weariness and anguish premature at that time of day. It was obvious I couldn't bear being in that absurd place any longer, where perhaps the worst thing of all was that I wasn't doing anything. Nobody came to see me, despite how ghastly that would have been. Maybe because of this, when I saw Pim reappear I actually felt happy. At first, I thought Alka had got left behind. But I soon discovered that not only was Alka no longer there, but she was perhaps several miles away. It was obvious Pim had sent Alka off to laugh elsewhere; but I didn't inquire, I didn't want to know. I preferred to remain ignorant of what had become of the marvelous Croatian woman who laughed because she thought her job obliged her to. I was more concerned with things of a different order, most particularly my weird situation waiting at that table with its monstrous vase.

As if being there all by myself with the red notebook weren't enough, Pim angrily remarked that nobody was coming to see me. I've always thought it most unnecessary that she told me so. I contained myself as best I could and, letting myself be carried along by my generally good state of mind, I simply said that I found her immensely amusing and somehow was going to put her into my next novel.

I expected she would at least want to know what my next book was about and that might even cause her to lean over my table to see what I'd jotted in my notebook (that way, a feeling that people were interested in me would be created, and this might possibly help with the formation of a line; it's well known that people tend to be imitative); but not only did she not glance toward my notebook, she half turned around, and after saying she was going back outside to carry on smoking, she disappeared from sight so quickly I almost felt offended. I was so annoyed by her attitude that I couldn't bring myself to follow her. I didn't even want to get up from that absurd table and catch a breath of fresh air, or concentrate on the sprightliness of the pensioners on the terrace by the Fulda.

The minutes that followed have all vividly stayed with me, even though nothing happened. The mysterious mind sometimes seizes on moments that are simply dead or appear quite banal, but which, for reasons that escape us, stay in our memory and end up leaving us uneasy. These memories seem to be ineradicable, making us think these moments mean more than we first believed, and perhaps we just didn't succeed in seeing it all at the time. In fact, if we take stock, all the moments of our lives are like that; in other words, more happens than we think. But there are some moments that surprisingly tend to be dull and yet mysteriously lodge in the memory, perhaps so we might investigate later on what buried reality ran through it all.

I was there a long time in this second phase of strange lingering; I was basically hanging around, waiting for Pim to return from her latest cloud of smoke. And during that time nothing happened, but taking into account the fact that I remember it minute by minute, I tend to think much more took place than seems possible to get down on paper. Throughout that period of time, boring and memorable at once, I devoted myself to recalling an unexciting impasse experienced on a now dimly remembered group trip to Dublin: I was trying to buy film for my camera, but we were in the suburbs and in a hurry to get up some metal steps leading to a bridge we had to cross to reach a train station.... Well, I won't go on, because nothing happened. Or, more accurately, I didn't know how to identify what it was that really happened and left me intrigued for life.

I was just thinking of this when Pim came back in, this time to tell me she was considering seeing a hypnotist to give up smoking.

"As nobody's coming to see me, don't you think we could go now?" I said.

"It's not all about you being seen," she replied, aghast.

It was unnecessary for her to tell me this, too, but it did sound like she was reproaching me for not getting down to writing, which ultimately, she seemed to think, was what I should really be doing.

29

A few minutes later, a guy of medium height came in, overweight and sporting a mustache, around forty years of age. He was dressed in a conventional gray suit: a guy, I would soon see, who was coarse and refined at the same time. He was heavy, but also seemed light;

his personality was sporadically graced by a certain crackpot charm.

On seeing him, I went so far as to wish the whiskery fellow was not a restaurant customer, but someone coming in to pester me. That shows what a bad state I was in at that moment. I was desperately lonely. My unique existence no longer seemed poetic after all these ludicrous minutes playing writer to an empty spectators' gallery.

"I feel terrific, how are you?" said the guy with the crackpot air about him. It gave me enormous joy to find he was talking to me, and it was a nice surprise that he was speaking in my mother tongue, in Catalan. His surname was Serra, and he said he was from Igualada, near Barcelona. He had come from the sanatorium, he explained. At first, I thought he was talking about an outpatients' unit or a hospital, maybe an asylum, but no, far from it—the fat man in gray came from a Documenta installation called *Sanatorium*, a project by the Mexican artist Pedro Reyes. *Sanatorium* was a pavilion in the middle of Karlsaue Park, an improvised clinic with seven rooms for psychotherapy, with specialists attending those who needed to overcome stress, solitude, and fear. The visitors, if they so requested, were cared for as patients and could be treated with *goodoo* therapies (positive voodoo); they were encouraged to stick small objects onto cloth dolls. *Sanatorium* was right in the south of Karlsaue Park, in other words, almost adjacent to the Dschingis Khan.

The fat man with the crackpot air had just emerged completely cured (not crude) from there. At least, that's what he told us, as though trying to crack a joke. He also wanted to play with the word *goodoo*. I'll be healthy later, he said, but it's *good-oo* to be healthy now. He'd read something of mine once but didn't remember the title. I'm delighted you're in a good mood too, he said. I've been sticking super-positive things onto a rag doll. Sticking? I queried. Don't go thinking I said *slicking*, he said. No, you said *sticking*, I heard you perfectly. I've been gluing things to the doll, he said, now do you understand me?

Standing beside the table, Pim seemed interested to see what I made of things with the man who came along so *good-oo* from *Sanatorium*. And tell me, the jovial fellow said, is it true you're going to let me see what you write? Even though I knew I had set myself up for this to happen, I'd discounted the possibility, so the request took me very much by surprise, even rattling me more than usual, but I reacted in time. I'll let you read the latest thing to occur to me, I said; in fact I just wrote it down here. I passed him the red notebook, and he read aloud: "Change your life completely in two days, without caring at all about what has gone before, leave without further ado. When all's said and done, the right thing to do is take off."

He read it out and said he would have written: "Change your life completely in two hours with glue from the *Sanatorium*." Although I wasn't exactly Autre, I felt offended and leaped to the defense of the beleaguered professional I knew to be inside that long-suffering writer, humiliated at his table in the Chinese restaurant. I'm trying to write about an average man, I told him, who's going through a difficult time and doesn't even look to start again. He plans to go toward nothing. And tell me, Señor Serra, what do you imagine going toward nothing means? No idea, he answered, I live with success and every day I go further toward that.

If I had any doubt, he'd just made everything perfectly clear; once again, a strange situation had cropped up in my life with an oddball included. Nothing new there. For reasons that escape me, I've attracted crazies my whole life.

You should know that just a few months ago, he said, I was able to leave behind a perfectly uninteresting forty-year-old life and start to savor success as a writer. I began to experience it in the only place in the world I wanted to triumph, New York. Here Serra paused (I'd say perversely and with malicious intent) in order to ask if I proposed to triumph in this Chinese restaurant. He didn't give me time to reply, not even just a tenth of a second, to say that the verb *savor* didn't indicate he was such a good writer as he himself declared. Because if you do propose to triumph here, Serra went on, unperturbed, I have to advise you that New York is more suitable. You're not going to get anywhere with a Chinese ambition. I trust, I said, already rather peeved, that's not just because New York is more central than this crappy restaurant. He laughed and I was again aware of that crazy side of him. I wondered if it wouldn't be better to say suddenly that I was going to the bathroom and wouldn't be back, or suggest he order a *babao fan* at the bar, which, if I hadn't read wrong, was the dessert that nourished the first Chinese cosmonaut on his space voyage. Alternatively I could suggest he order—I'd memorized the menu—an "eight-treasures rice pudding."

I don't know if you can imagine, he said, suddenly sounding somewhat pained and serious, what it is to astound Greenwich Village with your novels and publish brilliant articles in the *New Yorker* and the *Coffin Factory* and the *Southern Review* at the same time, and for your appearance to be simultaneously slovenly and splendid and your mind to ebb and flow the whole time like water, and the blond waves of your hair to spring up rebelliously around your head, and to finish nights chatting with the editorial team of *Screen Gossip* finding out the latest rumors or arguing with Rockefeller Senior to ascertain which of you best carries the burden of success.

I didn't need to hear another word. He spoke a more than distinguished Catalan with a wide vocabulary, but how many years had it been since *Screen Gossip* was last published? Fat, gray Serra was even loonier than his overly conventional appearance suggested. This seemed to me to offer a more than good enough excuse to run away. Providentially, I saw Pim signaling to me from the doorway, as if indicating I should pop out with her to take some air, and I remember very well how it felt: as if someone had just proposed I should get out of Hell on my own two feet before it was too late.

I left.

The right thing to do was take off.

We went out to the back of the restaurant and from there started to descend a pronounced slope of green grass, heading to the southern end of Karlsaue Park. After a while, we began to follow the arrows on scrappy signs pointing toward *Sanatorium*. It wasn't drizzling anymore. The unfriendly restaurant was being left behind, and for me it was like losing sight of Sing Sing. As we went farther and farther into the park and at the same time into Documenta territory, "the Chinese number" also felt increasingly far away.

"Do you think the Chinese couldn't even see me?" I asked Pim.

She didn't answer, which didn't particularly worry me. I preferred to remember that when you're walking along with another person you don't feel obliged to respond to everything that's said to you and that's why a lot of sentences end up unanswered.

Half a minute later, Pim finally decided to speak. She did so to say that she'd talked to Boston on the phone the last time she'd gone out to smoke and they'd told her from the curatorial team office that there was really no need to overdo things, that the time spent in the restaurant was flexible, was up to the writer in residence, and the last thing that must be allowed to happen was for the invited writer to feel under pressure at any point.

You could have said that sooner, I thought. But I said nothing, I just kept walking. I would rather everything followed its course. After all, we were getting farther away from the Chinese restaurant, which was the most important thing just then. At least for that day I would not be returning to Hell. Nothing could feel better than that calm push of the invisible current.

30

We were walking along peacefully through Karlsaue Park for what must have been a tremendously long time. Suddenly, looking to the left, I thought I saw a series of tiny individuals—sometimes singly, sometimes in pairs or groups—all inside a gigantic glass of water. Like Cartesian divers, the little people rose vertically in the liquid and immediately, without having reached the surface, plunged toward the bottom, where they rested an instant before starting a new ascent.

I was very thirsty because it had already been a long walk, and I thought I might be suffering from a passing spot of sunstroke. It seemed to me that Pim had told me the glass was really an athlete holding back the flight of a great bird and contained drowned dwarves, who, trained in crime, were trying to strangle Raymond Roussel.

Okay, I said. And we carried on walking.

When I realized I was hallucinating, I put all my hopes into being able to sit and rest as soon as we got to the terrace of the café-bar at the Orangerie Palace. You could already see the terrace on the horizon casting a strange and lovely oasis-like light, in this case it wasn't hallucinatory. We were heading for that terrace, and one might assume we'd have a good rest in the bar, but in the meantime my thirst was getting worse. I longed for water more with every moment. This did not outweigh my impression that at the same time, I was increasingly firmly in the grip of a very enthusiastic mood. The sensation was unusual for me: I was extremely tired, but at the same time I kept up my almost inordinate enthusiasm with just as much vigor as I had hours before, most especially for anything to do with Documenta. I maintained a critical attitude toward certain installations and pieces but, in general, felt very interested in what I was seeing. Entirely happy, I'd say, to stroll around a city turned upside down by avant-garde art, or contemporary art, or whatever it was.

No doubt it was this same enthusiasm that led me to want to locate the work of Pierre Huyghe, one of the artists who had been recommended to me.

"Make sure you see the work of Tino Sehgal, Pierre Huyghe, and Janet Cardiff," Alicia Framis had written me.

Not even five minutes had passed, and we were already on the path through the park leading to the installation by Huyghe, a French artist who was, as Pim started to explain, hard to classify. In any case, here was a guy who had challenged the narrow, ambiguous relationship between reality and fiction and was, moreover, adored by people who loved playfulness in all manifestations of art. He was mad about Dada and Perec and Louison Bobet (the latter was the oddest, as he was a famous cyclist whom Huyghe considered a Dadaist); in fact, he was crazy about everything that struck him as displaying unfettered imagination and an unruly capacity for invention. He liked reality to turn itself into fiction and vice versa, for it to be hard to tell the difference between the two. Huyghe had been working outside the framework of the museum or gallery for over ten years, Pim went on to tell me, fleeing all that was conventional, and his work sometimes seemed related to that of the Belgian Maurice Maeterlinck.

I was surprised by that name cropping up, I hadn't heard him mentioned for decades. For a time, I'd actually studied Maeterlinck in depth. He was the author of philosophical essays about the natural world: *The Life of the Bee, The Intelligence of Flowers, The Life of the White Ant.* Under a very clear German influence, this Belgian writer was adept at creating atmospheres in his books that were thick with invisible forces and very somber. Víctor Erice, the Basque filmmaker, took the title of his much-admired movie *The Spirit of the Beehive* from the beginning of a paragraph from *The Life of the Bee.* And I myself had ended up writing a long article about the curious relationship between certain film titles and certain insects.

It was significant, Pim said, to see how Huyghe's previous installations, in spite of his efforts to emphasize sociological questions, turned out to throw much more light on those somber and invisible powers already examined by Maeterlinck in his time. There was in Huyghe a constant concern with the forces that are so often hidden in fog, smoke, and the clouds.

This last observation led me to wonder about the many times I also employed poetic images of fog or the diverse iconography of smoke in my novels. Some of my tales have been set in overcast, foggy countries. Yet, while mist and smoke attracted me most, I never wanted to analyze the causes too deeply.

Clouds appealed to me less, perhaps they seemed not to possess so much mystery, or perhaps because too much had been written about them. A friend of mine from Barcelona once exhausted the subject of clouds. Sitting beside me in the cinema one day watching little puffs of white cloud cross behind the Washington Capitol in a film by Otto Preminger, he said: "A minor detail, but not irrelevant: those clouds passed that way over thirty years ago."

I never saw anyone so focused on one of the billions of useless details from the past; never anyone so immobile in a cinema, so still, so literally *in the clouds* as my friend was that day. Since then, clouds haven't played much of a role in my books; perhaps I fear that readers will become similarly immobilized or perhaps I don't want them guessing I wish to immobilize them.

Fog, on the other hand, has always been one of the things that fascinated me most in this world. There have been times when it's seemed to me that everything was contained within it. Curiously, I never managed to see any on my first trip to London, and I still haven't gotten over that disappointment. Smoke, by contrast, isn't as beautiful or as mystical, but it also appeals to me. I don't know the reasons, much as I sometimes think I've guessed them. I remember that my father didn't envy the unbearably competitive guy next door in the least, but he was jealous of the smoke that issued from that horrible neighbor's chimney. I've always thought I could perhaps begin with that memory in order to understand why smoke interested me so much, at least as literary material.

We were descending a muddy path. Smoke was the first thing I saw as we started to get close to the corner of the park where Huyghe's incredible, unforgettable *Untilled* was located. Land to cultivate, to farm, to plough? More than anything, on my first visit to that space I found so disturbing, I was able to appreciate the consummate oddness of the place. A person couldn't remain indifferent there. One immediately realized it was one of the foremost spaces in the whole of Documenta.

Not even Raymond Roussel could have improved on that atmosphere of extreme weirdness. Indeed, Huyghe had just quoted Roussel in an interview, though saying that the phrase might possibly be apocryphal: "The best place to travel is your own room." (Apocryphal it is, though not entirely. I am a humble expert on Roussel and permit myself to clarify here that the sentence was actually much longer and expressed something slightly different: in it Roussel explained he'd gone all the way around the world twice, and even so, none of those journeys had provided any material for his books, which he thought worth pointing out, because it demonstrated in a very tangible way the importance of the creative imagination in his work.)

What Huyghe had installed within the confines of the Karlsaue was a compost pile for producing humus. I didn't find this out myself but from Pim, as I barely knew what humus might be. Later, at night in the cabin, I looked up more information about the mulch apparently being made there and about other unsettling questions related to the place. The French artist had managed to transform an area of French garden, that is, an area of well-ordered nature within the park, into a space in the process of construction/destruction, suspended in time, with both live and inanimate elements. The presence of two dogs wandering around as part of the work was conspicuous. One of them (the one with its leg painted pink) was extremely famous, the best-known dog in Europe at that time and an absolute icon for Documenta 13.

One of the odd things that occurred to me about that weird place was that it seemed to have been created especially for me, or for people very like me, in order for us to better reflect (via the all-pervading smell of the humus) on the mortal weariness of the West, the many instances of devastating fatigue that were running through the continent.

Near the compost pile was the statue of a reclining woman on a pedestal; the statue's head was full of bees—real live ones—buzzing inside a great honeycomb. The statue was part of the compost pile and vice versa. Through the humus, that is, everything obtained by the biochemical decomposition of organic waste—roved the media hound, the lithe and extremely skinny dog with one leg painted pink. That hound loved being photographed. It posed as soon as it saw a camera. It seemed, at that late stage of the summer, to be delighted by the cameras pursuing it and even more delighted by all the changes brought about by its great fame.

Pim told me they'd gone to Spain to find that dog, because the legislation governing animals there was more relaxed than in Germany, where they did not grant licenses to paint an animal's leg pink. The hound, photographers aside, moved with surprising agility all over that peculiar area, in which there were also hallucinogenic plants (which I didn't manage to see), logs piled up like mountains, slabs of cement, and even a big sink full of stagnant water. Chemical reactions, repetition, reproduction, formation, and vitality were all present in the work, but the existence of a system was quite uncertain. Nothing was allocated; there was no organization, no representation, no exhibition.

I remember that place was very different from all the rest. I've never seen more poetically expressed, with such horror and elegance, the idea of rupture with the classical beauty always so associated with art. It was astonishing how, stone by stone, even with the tire tracks of a truck in the mud, Huyghe had reconstructed everything in that strange spot that seemed abandoned; yet it was actually extremely well cared for. After being there just a short time, you could see the place demanded constant maintenance, which in the long run ultimately revealed how complex it was to maintain this preconceived chaos.

As I describe it now, thinking of the place, I realize that as time goes by, I'm getting better at understanding what I managed to see there on my first visit. I can't deny that the first time I went in person to that unexpected compost pile (which didn't hold too many spectators for long, given its smell and its disquieting disorder, the clear perception of a terrifying absence of any system whatsoever), I reacted very superficially. Not knowing what I had in front of me (or rather, what I did *not* have in front of me), I devoted myself to observing the peculiar life of that skinny Spanish hound with the pink leg amid the mulch.

Perhaps to complement the undeniable disquiet, the notable rejection generated by everything in front of us, a young blonde German woman—who seemed quite unhinged and was dressed in strict mourning—crossed impulsively before us, got up on a pile of rubble, and began to preach vehemently and at length about what we were seeing.

Pim told me the young woman was well known throughout Kassel and was just then expounding aesthetic theories on the weeds in the area, on what was natural and what was not in our rotten world. She claimed and proclaimed repeatedly that Europe had taken a wrong turn more than two centuries back with the triumph of reason and the idea of progress in the age of Enlightenment.

We looked at the statue of the woman with the large, active bee-hive for a head from a distance because, although there were some completely entranced passersby over in that direction, it didn't seem a very good idea to approach her.

I recall the instant when the young madwoman and the statue appeared to have identical mental seething going on in their respective heads. Then they went back to having nothing in common, and all I know is that, as we moved away from the installation, the tragic voice of the madwoman talking of the ruin of Europe echoed continually in my ears.

31

We strolled along, and it was becoming increasingly obvious that walking cleared the mind, or ordered it to run more freely, helping us to speak more genuine sentences, perhaps because they were less carefully crafted. But from time to time, a phrase slipped out that was spontaneous, which nonetheless sounded complex, so much so that it even seemed preplanned and dropped like lead into a pool of uranium. I remember one that I let loose when we were still two hundred meters from the beautiful, French-style Orangerie Palace. I wonder, I said, whether a compost pile can be a work of art; I'm not saying it can't be, indeed, maybe even the fact that it's so far from being able to be art is precisely what makes it so. Pim didn't answer. Her silence was interrupted by a phone call from Chus Martínez in Berlin. I realized straightaway it was the first time I was properly close to the person actually responsible for my invitation, unless Boston was toying with me again, phoning Pim and pretending to be Chus. But I soon saw it really was Chus on the other end of the line. Pim passed her over to me, and, luckily, I decided not to ask what she was expecting me to do at the antiquated table in the Dschingis Khan. That would have been a mistake. I saved myself from a scolding—from being asked, for example, how it was possible I didn't have any ideas, when she'd entrusted me with the

Chinese number so I could find out how to make good creative use of the absurdity of the commission.

I think that underneath it all, I was afraid Chus would say she had a feeling they'd tricked her when they told her I was one of the few avant-garde people around in boring old Spain. I'm glad I didn't for a moment lose sight of the far from unlikely possibility that Chus— famous for being very clever—had invited me to Documenta to put me to the test. It was better to see things that way and not make mistakes I might regret later on; better to pitch myself onto that wild path of the most positive side and believe that with her illogical invitation to the Chinese restaurant, she'd endeavored to give my creativity a push, that is, she'd endeavored to see what I made of it when confronted with this oriental commission that made no sense.

I opted to see things this way and not more bitterly. I talked to Chus about something else, about Barcelona and the pro-independence rally. Chus knew my city well because she'd lived there for many years; it was a comfortable topic for a telephone conversation. I studied at a school in La Pedrera, she said, and it was really cool. I was surprised, not that she'd said "cool," but that she'd studied in a school inside a Gaudí building. I'd never met anyone before who'd studied at such a curious school. Fortunately, at this point in the conversation I was also careful not to succumb to the temptation to make cheap psychological interpretations, saying, for example, that her vocation as curator or art agent must have been born between the four walls of her Gaudiesque school.

The problem was that, biting my tongue in order not to make any mistakes, I sank into excessive silence. She too was silent at times. And I suffered a brief moment of panic, a sort of sudden terror that must have run, trembling, all the way along the invisible wire linking our respective phones.

That silence was like a powder keg. Well, Chus said finally, we'll see each other tomorrow night for dinner. I relaxed. I was going to ask the address of the restaurant, but that would have once again shown poor reflexes and imagination, as the curatorial team office had already sent it to me various times by email. I decided to fall back on a McGuffin, though none occurred to me, and right at that moment, unable to avoid it, I sneezed deafeningly. Twice. Sorry about the smudges in the air, I said. She laughed, and I took the opportunity to somehow end it there, passing the phone back to Pim, who caught it in midair without dropping her constant false smile.

The occurrence of smudges in the air had possibly saved the day and perhaps I could feel rather smug. But my happiness didn't last long. While Pim was talking to Chus about what a lovely morning it was—yes, that's what they talked about—I began to slip dangerously toward that torment reserved for anxious minds that the French call l'esprit de l'escalier (staircase wit), which consists of thinking of the right thing to say too late: going through the moment when you find the perfect response, but it's no longer any use to you because you're already on your way down the stairs and should have given the ingenious reply sooner, when you were at the top. And so, reviewing the brief conversation with Chus, reconstructing it piece by piece, word by word, I began to see what I could have said but didn't, and ended up wondering whether, when I went back to Barcelona on Saturday and told people about my trip to Kassel, I'd realize what I should have said or done in the city but didn't.... And, well, if I wrote the story of this journey one day, I went on thinking, I'd no doubt work with that staircase wit. I should be so lucky ...

Minutes later, Pim pointed out a mound in the distance that seemed part of the park but was actually a strange garden in the shape of a hill: *Doing Nothing Garden,* the work of Song Dong, almost the only Chinese artist—apart from Yan Lei—invited to Documenta.

The most logical thing for our walk would have been to pass alongside that hill-turned-garden before we got to the Orangerie, but very soon afterward, something unexpected took us out of our way.

I am going to digress here a moment, just briefly, to skip ahead to something that happened later that night in my cabin, when I changed my name and started to call myself Piniowsky.

Yes, Piniowsky.

That happened at night, when Autre lost his provisional surname and started to call himself Piniowsky too, a minor character in a story by Joseph Roth called *The Bust of the Emperor*.

All I'm going to say in advance is that after the sudden change, I began to feel relieved, happy too, because my own name that I'd had for so many years had come to feel like a dead weight and was really nothing more than something from a youth I'd spun out too long, in my opinion. In fact, my own name, in my mouth, always gave me a funny feeling.

I will also say that during that night, now as Piniowsky, I thought deeply about Huyghe and his installation *Untilled*. It seemed obvious to me that only art at the margins, distanced from galleries and museums, could be truly innovative. Huyghe showed discreet wisdom by taking the last route that appeared open to the avant-garde, as well as foresight in seeking out a tucked-away place in the Karlsaue for his pessimistic landscape of humus and a pink-legged Spanish dog; perhaps it was a tribute to a hypothetical art of the outskirts of the outskirts.

Maybe, I thought that night in my room, *Untilled* created an idea of a return to a time before art. In an age as uncertain as the current one in which everything was changing at incredible speed, it spoke of the necessity of no longer making art as we'd understood it up to now, of the need to learn to *stand apart*, perhaps to be like Tino Sehgal (Sehgal didn't wish to be visible and seemed to propose returning to the mortal dark room that's always been there). It was as if Huyghe were telling us: when all's said and done, hasn't the avant-garde fundamentally always sprung from a need to sweep everything away, to get back to the obscurity of the beginning?

And might not that flight from a dead art be an attempt by Huyghe to go beyond simply sweeping everything aside: to head toward the outskirts of the outskirts and then on toward nothing, literally toward nothing? Was the most innovative art of my day going toward nothing? Or was it going toward something I still hadn't found and that it would perhaps do me a lot of good to discover?

But let's get back to the morning of that same day, when Autre and I were still in one piece and Piniowsky hadn't yet even raised his head. My mind hadn't become so tangled in so many questions as it had that night in the "attempted thinking cabin" of my room.

Let's get back to that fine morning when I still allowed myself to be carried along by my passion for walking around and glancing at things like a profound idler, like a passerby who might be happy. Everything was going quite well, and even though I was dying of thirst, I was catching the smile (possibly false at times) that hardly seemed to leave Pim's lips. I ended up in such a great mood, I was even able to laugh thinking of the anguish that assaulted me almost punctually in the evenings. It was easy to do that early in the day, by which I mean that the very easy, heartfelt mockery of my melancholy tribulations wasn't so commendable.

How did I get on such a high? There are always means. I made use of a McGuffin—let's call it an intimate, secret one—a McGuffin that parodied the most horrendous kitsch language and consisted—I held back a giggling fit—of telling myself that there would be no shadows if the sun were not shining. It was enough to make a person laugh his head off, shedding four pounds of solemnity all at once.

32

In *Doing Nothing Garden*, Pim said, plants had been grown on a mound of organic waste. If I understood correctly, Song Dong had found the rubbish piled up in her mother's house in northern China and had it transported to Kassel, where she planted seeds and left it so that, over time, it turned into a little landscaped hill. A not very well-informed viewer might see it from a distance as he headed for the Orangerie—someone very thirsty, like me, for example—and have no idea that in under two months, that very peculiar little hill had taken on the deceptive appearance of having been part of the park for years.

This is where we were when the distant rumble of a bombardment interrupted our walk toward the Orangerie (where, according to Pim, there was a bar and also an astronomy museum with collections of clocks and antique stargazing instruments).

I was thirsty, more thirsty than anything, and even now I distinctly remember that terrible thirst. The bombing noise, Pim said, is from Janet Cardiff and George Bures Miller's loudspeakers. And she said no more. A bit later on, she conceded the installation had the enveloping sound of the tumult of battle, mixed with a symphony orchestra and rustlings from the forest, and in some manner it re-created the bombing raids Karlsaue Park and the city of Kassel had suffered during the Second World War.

For the first time that whole morning, I saw not a trace of Pim's constant cloying smile, because what she'd just told me really didn't allow for joy, either genuine or false. Until a minute ago, she'd been the epitome of joy. And I remembered that meditating on joy in my German cabin had been, since the beginning, one of the objectives of my trip: to reflect on the possibility that in joy could be found the central nucleus of all creation.

A pity, I said to myself, that at the last minute I'd packed *Journey to the Alcarria* instead of the book on joy I was going to bring. Nevertheless, just thinking of that "book about walking and seeing," as the author himself called it, reminded me that my stay in Kassel had the structure of a stroll, during which I was contemplating the natural as well as human landscape, while not neglecting to also study the landscape's theoretical heft, something that, by the way, was conspicuously absent in Cela's book.

Art about walking and seeing, I thought, while we continued strolling toward the cheerful terrace of the Orangerie bar. We were heading that way, but hearing what was coming from Janet Cardiff and George Bures Miller's loudspeakers, we ended up acceding to their demands and taking a path that led us to an area with a large lake. (This was where the bombardment seemed to originate.) It was a beautiful place, this lake with a small romantic temple, surely the finest part of Karlsaue Park, with a vibrant nature reserve full of birds on one side. On the other, I was at last able to see what looked most like a forest, most like the leafy area that in Barcelona I had imagined I'd see all the time I was in Kassel.

For me, there's nothing as German as this forest, I said to Pim, who didn't answer, or preferred to refrain from making any reply. Even better, she pointed to a water fountain at a bend in the path. I must have had a sign on my forehead saying I was dreadfully thirsty and that was why I said crazy things, revealing what felt like a hairy bear living inside me. In any event, I drank water like never before, feeling, in addition, that the fountain was a perfect miracle on our way. I drank for a long time, like someone who has been hypnotized by water.

Then we resumed our walk somewhat uncertainly toward the clamor of war. Little by little, the sounds issuing from the loudspeakers grew louder, and you were better able to appreciate that they were re-creating the din of an immense battle: it sounded like shells were dropping all through the forest. The birds in the nature reserve were going crazy. Pim ended up explaining to me—she seemed to have been there before with other writers and it bored her to have to say it again—that we were heading toward *FOREST (for a thousand years …)*. The title, she said, referred to the thousand years that Hitler proclaimed the Third Reich would endure and perhaps also to the thousand years of age the city of Kassel had reached when it was almost entirely destroyed by British firepower.

I remembered Janet Cardiff was part of the holy trinity in Alicia Framis's email ("Make sure you see the work of …"), but I didn't expect that any installation would shake me up the way that one did. I was struck—hard to forget it—by the discovery of a group of about forty people in the middle of the forest. They were sitting on tree stumps—forty mute, emotional people—terrified but secretly conspiratorial at the same time, as if a subversive, invisible thread passed through them, an immaterial impulse, an infinite breeze reminiscent of Ryan Gander's: forty people sitting in the great shade of the trees, listening to the brutal sound of an aerial bombardment that, thanks to the speakers installed in the tops of the oaks, created the compelling sensation that it was all happening right there exactly where we stood.

That was, without doubt, the most impressive thing. You ended up believing yourself the target of the bombs because you felt them approaching by an auditory sleight of hand; you felt the very real sensation of being in the middle of a battlefield. You heard everything as if it were actually taking place beside you: the hair-raising yells of men in hand-to-hand combat, the overflying airplanes, the breathing, the shouts, the footsteps through dry leaves, the nervous laughter, the wind, petals blown on the rain and squall, the enigmatic rustling in the forest, thunderstorms moving off, the din of ancient battles, bayonets tearing through the air, shots, explosions, shrapnel...

And then, suddenly, came the heavy blow of silence, and with it the reflection on the rediscovery of music: a classical symphony issued from the loudspeakers and allowed for pondering and recuperation. After the intellectual impact of the bombardment, there followed minutes of meditation and powerful recovery after the great collapse; during these minutes I was able to think things over and put an end to any further questions I might still ask myself about the possible, or impossible, relationship between innovative art and a bottle of perfume belonging to a Nazi woman, about the possible relationship between innovative art and our historical past and present. I seemed to guess that I wouldn't revisit the matter for a long time to come. It had become clear to me that art and historical memory were inseparable.

Any activity connected to the avant-garde—assuming the avant-garde still existed (which I doubted more with each passing hour)—must never lose sight of the *political dimension*: one that required us to bear in mind that perhaps nothing would do us poor mortals more good than for the avant-garde to disappear, not because it was worn out, but because, through an invisible current, it had turned into a source of pure energy, transforming itself into our own fascinating life.

33

For a moment, I thought I saw the invisible impulse cross the area and flow through that community of strangers seated in the middle of the forest. I remember thinking of the efforts of popular revolutions trying to make a name for themselves, while secret groups like this one in the woods in Kassel, or those formed during sporadic bursts of fighting, had, by contrast, never tended to be photographed or to leave a trace. I recalled Sebastià Jovani, a writer from Barcelona, who said that revolutions spawned postcards and all sorts of souvenirs, while guerrilla warfare and spontaneous groups involved in clandestine struggles—volatile groups, *situationists* if you looked at them that way—generated emotions, common feelings that didn't require a picture framed up on the wall. Jovani also said, if I remember rightly, that it was worth asking if anyone would really want a signed urinal in their living room. Perhaps, in that question, the difference between art exhibited in museums and art without a fixed home—art that is out in the open, so visible in Kassel, in more than one installation—couldn't be better summed up. Art of the outskirts. Or of the outskirts of the outskirts. Like Huyghe's work, with his humus and pink-legged dog, with his remote quagmire, where there was no organization, no representation, no exhibition—although I suspected things were more interconnected there than they appeared to be.

And while I was thinking about all this, I realized how that silent revolt of the spirit was making a move at that precise instant and letting itself be seen, too: the almost imperceptible was making everyone suddenly *get younger on the spot*.

This reminded me of that episode in Proust's *Remembrance of Things Past* where you see members of the old aristocracy grimacing in a Paris salon, *getting older on the spot*, becoming mummies of themselves.

For a while, I didn't stop looking around me. The music's attempt to get us over the collapse seemed very fortuitous. That motif of death Schubert had placed at the center of *Winter Journey*, which we were all listening to there in shy silence, collided head-on with the idea of that voyage. Each of us allowed ourselves to be assailed by our solitude, which expanded timelessly in the evening light, the sun reflecting among the clouds, and it did so like the nightmare I most feared, the one in which I felt at constant risk of seeing everything invaded by frost and dead nature.

Death was before us like the bird singing just then, filtering through in an unequal contest with Schubert's music. Death was playing no tricks and plainly visible, but the general resistance, the effort not to succumb to its awful, murderous song, was admirable. The imperceptible breeze ran serenely throughout, getting stronger every minute, perhaps because it was a current that advocated life. Indeed, the conspirators in the forest appeared to be getting stronger and stronger in this lull. Even so, my disquiet didn't seem about to evaporate so easily. There were flashes of vitality within the forest group, but a certain inner disquiet persisted. I remember the circumstances of that moment well. The truth is, I always remember my own unforeseen anguish with mathematical precision: I was in the forest, I lost myself mentally in a tangle of undergrowth. I heard the cry of a tawny owl in the area bordering the woodland, and then nothing, absolutely nothing. I went on to the esplanade and saw that Europe was a lifeless expanse and then accepted that the dawn light of morning had turned into darkest night. I think I perceived a song far off in the distance that I learned in childhood and that comes back to me from time to time, above all now that I'm getting old. It's a song that disturbs me because it says there is no escape: to get out of the forest we have to get out of Europe, but to get out of Europe we have to get out of the forest.

34

Hours later, in the basement of the supermarket Pim recommended for buying food for my "thinking cabin," I was assailed by staircase wit.

Crafty as this staircase wit always was, it didn't let up until I remembered Pim's words as we were saying goodbye to each other at the Orangerie, when she told me that this edition of Documenta, so extravagant, ended up imposing a Shakespearean truth: this time was out of joint. I had shown myself in complete agreement with that, but down there in the basement, suddenly forced to reexamine the moment of my parting from Pim, I began to think about what I might have added or even countered had I been a little more agile in that instant.

Why hadn't I said this or that to her? Once again, I told myself that writing was born out of that staircase wit and was essentially the story of a slow-maturing revenge, the long-winded tale of putting into writing what we should have put, at the time, into life.

I could have said some of this to Pim in the Orangerie when she spoke to me of time being out of joint. She had told me they wouldn't be able to catch up with me again until three o'clock the next afternoon, that either she would call me, or maybe Boston, whoever was able to get away from the office first …

I could have said so many things at that moment, but I said nothing, maybe I was too taken aback at the news I was going to be all on my own for so many hours, which at first (without my being overly aware of it) brought on a slight desperation, which later gave rise to a need to find ways to fill the empty hours ahead and make out it didn't matter to me that, for example, I'd have to go to the Dschingis Khan the next morning alone and, once there, literally have to *make something of it*.

That need to sidestep anguish decisively marked the hours that followed, during which I went slightly crazy. Noticeably disoriented on emerging from the supermarket, I dashed out of there so fast that two minutes later, I'd already discovered in a panic I was going down the wrong street: I found myself on Goethestrasse, a Kassel thoroughfare I didn't know at all, and this despite having committed to memory, almost by fire and sword, the instructions Pim gave me in case it so happened that, on leaving the supermarket, I made a mistake and ended up getting hopelessly lost. Nobody had mentioned the name of *that* street to me. I was completely lost. Pim had foreseen various errors I might make and even drawn an improvised map, but Goethestrasse wasn't included in any of her possibilities for getting lost. This aggravated my feeling of abandonment. Then I was surprised to realize that clearly, one way or another, there in Kassel, the inhabitants of the place, instead of telling me it was about time

I'd got there, had begun to see me as just another native of the city, and because of that, it would be difficult for me to get anyone to understand, *being so obviously from there*, how I had gotten lost and might have to ask the way to the exceptionally central Hotel Hessenland.

It was curious, of course, to observe that my doubts about whether or not I was in Germany had unexpectedly developed into the clear perception that everyone there saw me as just another German.

Urgently needing to see whether I could find Königsstrasse again, I went full speed ahead past a whole host of places, including the Bellevue Palace—with a museum dedicated to the brothers Grimm (pride of the city, those two wrote their best stories in old Kassel)—and also the Bali Cinema (I didn't even look to see what was playing, though I later learned that the Catalan filmmaker Albert Serra was showing episodes of *The Three Little Pigs* there, a two-hundred-hour-long movie, the title of which alluded ironically to three moments of great significance in the creation of Europe, embodied in the figures of Johann Wolfgang Goethe, Adolf Hitler, and Rainer Werner Fassbinder). I went so fast, I passed a lot of places without being able to pay attention to anything other than the intensity of the light in the street, which was diminishing by the minute in a terrifying manner. I breathed more easily when I came upon a short alley that gave me a glimpse down a side street, at the end of which I thought I could see the longed-for Königsstrasse. The dark alley wasn't as dark as the one where I'd once discovered delight in an icy breathing, a dry, glacial blast that went straight to the back of my neck and let me know the pleasure of fear all at once, in its purest and most sublime form.

While I was heading down that murky alley, I remembered my friend who said that you never arrived at literature by chance. Never, never, he repeated, it's pure destiny, a dark destiny, a series of circumstances that make you choose, and you always knew it was the path. Nice thinking, I said to myself. It was highly likely I had arrived at literature due to that blast to the back of my neck in the dark alley; in other words, I got there because of my delight in that icy, glacial breathing, suddenly received as a dry blast, a blast from no one in that solitary place.

A while later, I entered my cabin and went right out on the balcony to greet Sehgal's work, *This Variation*. It was drizzling again, as it had been hours earlier, and I felt the presence of a current of fresh air, not at all unpleasant, but ultimately chilly, and decided to go straight back into the room. Once inside, I lay on the bed with my hands linked behind my head, and after a few moments of which I remember nothing, I went back to thinking that for the artists with the most innovative spirit, the truth was simply out there. But this time I asked myself where these outskirts lay. From inside my discreet delirium—to tell the truth, it was the result of my fear of the solitude in store for me—I struggled to recover my proper equilibrium. Anguish and melancholy, for their part, had advanced inexorably, and as the shadows loomed more profoundly over the city, my whole mind became even more confused.

Where did I think the outskirts were? I answered myself as well as I could, thinking that first one had to know how to move through unexplored territory, far from the center of culture, from the market, which was as well known as it was hackneyed, that this was something that should be asked of everybody with disruptive ideas. But I wasn't long in asking myself what exactly "unexplored territory" and "everybody with disruptive ideas" might mean.

I was not consoled by the knowledge that I had the whole cabin, the whole night, in which to find that out; perhaps I had the premonition that besides those essentially simple questions (simple questions posed only in order to avoid trickier ones), the night might be a difficult one. It was. In fact, it was very difficult, a night of complete anguish. It turned out hard and grueling, filled with insomnia, terror, an imaginary journey down a strange track with grassy dunes and great cliffs. Nothing that I saw or imagined or breathed in this environment helped to sweeten things. I soon understood it had very probably been a mistake to try to set up a cabin precisely for those hours when melancholy most controlled me.

How could I have been so stupid? For hours on end, I was tormented in that darkened room by the image of two orangutans, one fertile and the other sterile, that I believed I'd seen somewhere that morning. It was not an easy night. The melancholy of the evening wasn't content to remain until the wee hours when I normally started to feel sleepy, but extended itself practically until dawn.

Having slept for just an hour, I got up the next day and immediately discovered, unexpected as it may be, that I was once again in an excellent mood, perhaps because the very idea that a new day was beginning, that splendid Thursday, could not have been more pleasant to me.

Collapse and Recovery, I thought. I couldn't help thinking that Documenta's motto was being played out by my own body.

Later, after a lengthy breakfast, I visited Sehgal's *This Variation*. I'd proposed to myself the idea of going every morning of my stay in Kassel without fail. I entered the large building adjacent to my hotel and walked down the short corridor, now almost familiar to me, toward that neglected garden, to the left of which was the entrance to the dark room. According to the receptionist at the Hessenland, the room had been a modest dance hall in its day.

Now right inside Sehgal's dim space, I took six rapid steps toward the back of the room of spirits. Nobody brushed against me this time, and again I made the mistake of thinking there were no dancers in there. I paused in the pitch dark. As on the previous occasion, I laughed into the darkness. And suddenly, everything changed. I noticed with horror that someone at the back of the room tried to imitate a whinny and I was given or imagined a mental picture of a woman two centuries back, sitting in a trap, driving a chocolate-colored mare on a trip through the south of France. It was as if I'd visualized one of my own memories, but it wasn't an image I'd ever seen before. As quickly as it arrived, the image was gone, and I was left asking myself how that sort of memory, which was not my own, could have come to me. Was it Autre's? No, because Autre was also me, or at least I'd invented him some hours earlier.

Disconcerted, I took another step. Then, almost immediately, I began to hear a wan foxtrot coming from the back of the room that ended up turning into a little Peruvian waltz. The person who had come in behind me stumbled against my hesitant body by mistake and almost sent me flying. Then, possibly frightened, she turned around and left the dark room at once, and I went after her, toward the light outside, as if in hot pursuit.

On leaving the room, I didn't see anyone ahead of me, just more light, just the craziness of light, that was all, though that was no small thing. I put out of my mind what had just happened and lingered in the doorway, listening to the end of the waltz, but then the music stopped dead. I did the same, brought up short, and remained there motionless for a few seconds, after which I raised my eyes to the ice-gray sky and saw a bird pass, and then another, and then many more, and it seemed to me they were all flying toward the Dschingis Khan.

Back on the street, I passed the hotel. First, I asked for an umbrella in reception. Then I decided to head for the outskirts, as if out in that area far from the city I might find something more associated with the avant-garde than anything I'd seen up to that point.

Soon afterward, I took the bus to the Dschingis Khan, which was not at odds with my desire to go in the direction of the outskirts. No sooner had I sat down in a good seat than I looked to the sky and saw the birds were following the same route, no doubt because (as everybody knows) birds always travel toward the outskirts.

35

On the bus, I started leaving my memories of the previous bad night behind, the remembrance of an extremely difficult session in the cabin. I suspect the most overwhelming thing about those sleepless hours wasn't just meditating on Europe's tragic fate, but also perceiving that I wasn't wrong to see myself transformed into a total Kassel native, one more citizen of that provincial German city. Once again, I told myself that my habit of informing everybody I was from whatever place I found myself in had made me the victim of my own words and ended up doing me real harm. The proof was that it was suddenly no trouble to see myself as a humble and eloquent, melancholy Kassel citizen, who spent the night hours meditating on the solitude stretching away beyond time in the feeble light of his fatherland ...

With visions this terrifying, it's understandable I barely slept a wink all night. I saw the world slipping through my fingers. I felt it was undesirable to have it with me any longer. I wanted to hurl it on any old galactic garbage dump, or perhaps into a Euro Sex Shop, or a butcher's in the Black Forest, or a carpet store in El Paso, or a laundromat in Melbourne. I did not know what to do with the world.

I spent the night turning over awkward questions in my mind and I was incredibly restless, sometimes twisting in a ridiculous, tragic way between the sheets, transformed into a sort of neurotic Sinbad, old and forgetful, devoted to summoning up, in a series of litanies, all the cities I'd ever laid eyes on. I remember myself that way, simultaneously tragic and comical. A homegrown Sinbad or a Kassel-made one, if you prefer, dedicated to evoking, from inside his precarious cabin, with a rosary-like rhythm, solitary refuges to which in times gone by great anguished minds had withdrawn to think.

But what really drove me to the most dogged insomnia and a near fatal nervousness—I went on remembering on the bus heading in the direction of the Chinese restaurant—were the visions that followed one another in front of my astonished eyes. However little credence I gave them to start with, I was unable for many hours to push them away. It all began when I suddenly felt enveloped in a deadly silence and noticed that not a breath of air stirred inside the cabin, not a sound could be heard, not a squeak, nothing. The utter conviction that Europe had long since been wrapped in a shroud hit me all at once. Or, more accurately, the feeling had slowly crept up on me over the last few hours. I was in the center of Germany, in the center of Europe, and there, in that center, it was more obvious than anywhere else that everything had been cold and dead and buried for decades, ever since the continent allowed itself to make its first serious unpardonable mistakes. Everything had been wiped out in the center of that actually inanimate territory, where by day (as I'd been able to observe during that now past and very regretful morning and afternoon), the sun had remained unchanging at its zenith and, nonetheless, had stayed hidden behind a haze that seemed to have been hanging in the air for centuries, traces of a sort of dust as fine as residual pollen, from an earth that was disintegrating with terrifying slowness.

You are in Europe and Europe is not here, said a singsong, obsessive inner voice, which seemed keen to do away with me at all costs, simultaneously reminding me that the weight of our most recent terrifying history was too much, a history in which horror was the dominant presence.

It was a difficult night. And my eyes were like lighthouses. Europe was infested with ghosts, like the ones in Sehgal's dance hall, and it was laden with symbols from the past. Europe, already a tragic composite, would never again manage to feel part of the world in a good or natural way, in fact would never again manage to feel *on earth* in any way at all.

At last, I could sleep, albeit only for an hour. At seven o'clock, I dropped off, and that drop drowned out my horror. I woke an hour later, and in a great frame of mind, which surprised me because nobody expects to find himself suddenly feeling so good after one hour's sleep.

"Life is serious, art is joyful," I said out loud, and then imagined cannon fire waking the whole of Kassel.

36

Time moved like lead and so did the whole city, but my buoyant mood didn't flag for a second.

Among other things, I wasted no time discovering that on the bus—unlike in my meditation space in the cabin—thinking turned out to be simply relaxing, and even helped most of the phantoms from my night of insomnia to evaporate. I should have had more sleep, but I wasn't tired. I sat at the front of the bus that morning, giving thanks to God and Duchamp for the existence of theories in art, conscious, too, that much as I'd had to put my shoulder to the wheel and knuckle down to the actual practice on so many occasions, the theoretical would always be my great passion. I was sitting there at the front when I decided to move down to the back, convinced the windows were bigger and I'd see the landscape better.

At that point it became Autre who was looking out at the rainy highway. And, quick as a flash, Autre thought up a character who resembled me and was supposedly part of the avant-garde, which was why he traveled at the front of the bus. I was feeling more and more lively thanks to my unexpected mental strength that seemed to increase the farther the bus ventured into the outskirts.

On reaching kilometer 19 of the Auedamm, we stopped for a few brief moments outside the Dschingis Khan. I looked at the place through my window and felt an immense weakness: an uncommon fatigue swept over me just at the thought that I was going to get off where nobody was waiting for me and where there might even be someone who would hate me, taking it as a given that I was a writer of no great interest.

Even so, I stood up with the intention of getting off the bus, but something compelled me to sit back down again at once. From my recaptured seat, I carried on looking in utter amazement at that place that appeared so innocuous, so insubstantial, so dreary in the rain. I still remember the horror, the tremendous horror, with which I regarded it.

Then the bus continued on its way. I was so utterly alone, knowing I was going to continue that way for so many hours, that I felt the need to see myself from the outside, precisely in order to be accompanied at least by the person who imagined he was seeing me. And that was how I ended up seeing myself: as the main character in a scene from an old Wim Wenders movie, one of those films in which the characters travel on every sort of public transport, looking out the windows of a multitude of different vehicles, with infinite longing, at cold German cities.

The bus continued on its way and I discovered that the route on that line was circular, so twenty minutes later we stopped again at kilometer 19. That time I was closer to getting off than before, but seeing again how dull and dreadful the place was in every way beneath the rain, I still didn't alight. That morning I was interested in everything, but I couldn't manage that sinister place. I went around another eight times on the bus, each turn lasting twenty minutes; some three hours in total sitting on public transport, resisting facing my Chinese destiny alone.

And the oddest thing was that I didn't even have time to regret not having the books from my suitcase with me, *Journey to the Alcarria* or *Romanticism*, that is, not having something I could read on such a long and obsessively circular trip. The thing was, I was very well entertained by the repetitive run through the outskirts of the city, due to a faint but strange euphoria, which, although it was slight, subjected me to a hitherto unknown mental activity. I imagined that I went into the Dschingis and felt not only Chinese and as though I were going home, but that once again my arms had become excessively long and my legs were too far away from me. Totally Chinese and totally monstrous, I saw myself going into the Dschingis and looking at the round table with its vase, discovering that none of it was nearly as bad as I'd thought. Was that the effect of my tendency to see things in a positive light in the morning? That's what I asked myself, imagining this scene on the bus, while outside the rain got heavier and heavier.

In that scene, totally invented from my seat on the bus going around the Auedamm, a young Chinese waiter looked annoyed and led me through the Dschingis Khan to my table for the damned invited writer. I noticed right away there was no respect for writers in that dive, but I didn't find his attitude worrying and simply thought the guy envied me and wanted to take my place in the restaurant, possibly because my soft red couch looked very appealing on that rainy day. Then I forgave the jealous man and took out my notebook, pencil, and eraser. I read the first thing I'd written. ("Change your life completely in two days, without caring in the slightest what has gone before. Leave without further ado. When all's said and done, the right thing to do is take off.") Then I wrote a few sentences about the worrisome problem of poor communication, though no doubt it would be better to say it worried Autre, since it didn't bother me one bit. Why should I concern myself about it, anyway, when I was a poor lonely soul from a sad Wim Wenders movie? Sad? Actually, quite the reverse. I'd better correct that, as in fact I was actually going along uninhibited and happy there on the bus and all I needed was to start singing like I was a radio. What's more, I wanted to, because the piped music on the bus kept repeating, as if wanting to overwhelm its passengers, the intensely nostalgic soundtrack from *Out of Africa*.

What a contrast, I thought, to a few hours earlier, what a contrast to the torment of last night when my radical isolation had started to impinge on my state of mind, causing me, out of pure desperation, to react against it and, by way of a natural defense mechanism, to try to create, all through that never-ending night, a potent mental antidote or an "emetic" against my demoralization.

I was thinking, or rather imagining, along these lines, and the longer I sat beside that window watching the rain falling, the more my imagination seemed to visit the Dschingis Khan. With my euphoria, my interest in everything heightened (except in personally going to that damned Chinese restaurant), the world seemed thought-provoking, worthy of study, utterly fascinating; there was nothing around that could not be praised. I judged everything, or almost everything, adorable; it was as if I were immersed in a complete celebration of the very fact of living, as if it were a year later and I'd decided to try a third of Dr. Collado's tablets, discovering over the last few months that he'd substantially developed his invention and ended up creating a happy pill that made the world seem less imperfect. Or perhaps it was the force of the same breeze from *The Invisible Pull* that was creating an extra impetus in me and making me see things with a certain enthusiasm. Or maybe the slight euphoria came from my intense and permanent contact recently with different works of art, different ideas and new concepts that I'd been seeing and discovering in Kassel and which had come to form part of my world. In the end, so many hours looking at such unconventional art had left me with very positive feelings. And it only remained to be asked—if it actually needed asking—whether there really was anything new in all that had been seen. The answer was no, but it hardly mattered. I had been fascinated by most of it, surely because I preferred to think it was the newest thing for thousands of miles around. Without my fascination for the new—or everything that at least tried to seem that way—I could not live, I'd never been able to, at least not since I found out that the new existed or could exist. And this was something that Kassel had the virtue of reminding me, because, through intermittent memories, it had brought back to me the bleak days of my extreme youth in Cadaqués, especially that day I saw a golden reflection of the sun in the mirror of a restaurant where at that exact moment the widows of Duchamp and Man Ray were having lunch. Back then, I didn't know what sort of work their husbands had left behind, but there were photos on the restaurant walls of one or another of them— enigmatic cultural traces—and I wanted to be a foreign creator like them too; I wanted the air of difference about me that I imagined these artists had always shown, and, if it wasn't too much to ask, when the summer was over, I wanted not to have to return to "backward" Barcelona. I wanted to be an avant-garde artist. I mean this is what I understood at the time by "someone breaking away from the dried-up artistic reality of my city." And, as I desired all this, I thought that the most direct way to become "avant-garde" would be to adopt an air like that adopted by Marcel Duchamp or Man Ray in those photographs at the restaurant: dressing, for example, as I'd seen Duchamp, in a different white shirt every evening, a sort of uniform of the avant-garde.

With every curve the bus took on the Auedamm, the strength of the invisible push carried me mentally further along. I felt at times an almost subconscious joy and now I imagined sitting at my table in the Dschingis Khan, making sure Autre wrote something about how radical solitude drives some people to an anguish of such proportions, it makes them wish the world produced something more than just anguish, perhaps something we don't yet know and have to seek at all costs.

The new, perhaps?

I remembered Chesterton said that there was one thing that gave radiance to everything. It was the idea of something around the corner. Perhaps it is this desire for something more that propels us to seek the new, to believe something exists that can still be distinct, unseen, special, something different, around the most unexpected corner; that's why some of us have spent our whole lives wanting to be avant-garde, because it is our way of believing that in the world, or maybe beyond it, *out beyond the poor world*, there might be something we've never seen before. And because of this, some of us reject the repetition of what has been done before; we hate them telling us the same as always, trying to make us know things all over again that we know so much about already; we loath the realist and the rustic, or the rustic and the realist, who think the task of the writer is to reproduce, copy, imitate reality, as if in its chaotic evolution, its monstrous complexity, reality could be captured and narrated. We are amazed by writers who believe that the more empirical and prosaic they are, the closer they get to the truth, when in fact the more details you pile up, the further that takes you away from reality; we curse those who prefer to ignore risk, just because they are afraid of loneliness and getting it wrong; we scorn those who don't understand that the greatness of a writer lies in his promise, guaranteed in advance, of failure; we love those who swear that art lies solely in this attempt.

It is the desire for there to be something more and this desire leads us without fail always to seek out the new. And this endeavor, this eagerness, this *toil*—I started to use this word I found and liked in some lines by Yeats—this toiling was something that was in me since those summers of my youth and is still there; I think it is my center, the very essence of my way of being in the world, my stamp, my watermark: I'm talking about that ongoing concern for seeking the new, or believing that the new can perhaps exist, or finding that newness which was always there.

There is eagerness in this voice that speaks for me when they ask me about the world.

"The world?" I say. "No, just art."

"Why?"

"Because art intensifies the feeling of being alive."

The new, I imagined making Autre write at his table in the Chinese restaurant, was what some sought to align themselves with, taking the most advanced positions on the "literary battlefield." These vanguard positions exercised a fascinating power over some writers. Innately optimistic, they thought that from those positions where they were making an unexpectedly intense search, they might perhaps find the only possible way out of their existential angst.

In fact, all known great novels are avant-garde in a way, in the sense that they bring something new to the history of literature. Dickens, for example, never presumed to be avant-garde, nor would he have wanted to be, but he was; he was because he changed the course of literature, while many presented themselves to literary society, putting on avant-garde airs and never innovating a thing.

I was wrapped up in all this when, next to my table in the Dschingis Khan, in my imagination, someone pointed a finger at me and said right beside me: "Look at him. He has an avant-garde world, a Duchamp's widow's world."

I felt not in the least ashamed of this, and anyway, it was only in my imagination. As far as real life was concerned, I was still on the bus. The rain continued to fall, relentlessly punishing that labyrinthine geography of the outskirts.

37

I imagined again that I decided to go into the Chinese restaurant and, over the course of the next hour, instead of getting bored doing nothing or sitting writing about noncommunication as the funloving Autre would have done, I devoted myself to spying on what an almost hundred-year-old couple sitting beside me was saying— the two of them really were very ancient—and also to interpreting a conversation between a Vietnamese cook and her boyfriend, a young man who was probably Austrian, plus the discussion between two Chinese waiters who were commenting in a very veiled way on the chat they'd had some weeks earlier with a writer who'd sat where I was sitting.

I also imagined suddenly returning from a quick visit to the restroom. I was shocked to see the guy with the crackpot air about him beside my table, that nuisance by the name of Serra from the day before. Under normal circumstances, I would have run straight out of there, but that morning I imagined being so disposed to finding life and the world interesting that, imitating the calmness of the Vietnamese woman's boyfriend, I sat down mildly beside the loon, who appeared to have something more interesting about him than the day before.

"What brings you here, good fellow?" I said.

"I went back to the *Sanatorium* and they haven't fixed what's out of order."

I offered him my sympathy with a few words that gave the impression I was agreeing to take on his clinical case. And, of course, I was immediately alarmed. I realized I had to tread very carefully, unless I wanted my participation in Documenta to consist of setting up a confessional at my table with its vase.

That scenic picture of "doctor and patient" had something of the *installation* about it but little that was avant-garde. It was also clear you couldn't expect much from Autre either, his being a conservative writer. Thinking about all this led me to finally take Autre's place and put in an appearance myself. With a swipe, I knocked the vase to the floor, pricked up my ears, and asked the crackpot to tell me his problem. The Chinese waiter came over and complained about the broken vase, but whatever he was spluttering was the only thing I didn't manage to translate all morning, nor can I say I was terribly interested in his reproaches.

To start off, the mustachioed Serra held back and asked what problem I was talking about. He said he didn't have any and asked whether I had perhaps forgotten he was a success. But it wasn't long before he crumbled. It was a trivial thing he had to tell me, he ended up confessing, but it had stopped him from doing anything his whole life.

"I collapse ..." he said.

"Excuse me?"

"I collapse what is the fact of Galileo, but it is obvious he escaped here the contribution of Kepler ..."

He was speaking like a Google translation into Catalan. And what he said was strange, too, assuming he was actually saying something. He was talking like a bad translation, but also like a Cheyenne Indian; the fact was, he spoke in a very disjointed manner, or at least in a way that seemed so. Looking at it from another perspective, his language was reminiscent of the jargon peculiar to psychoanalysts in the seventies, Lacanian jargon in particular.

I saw with a measure of dismay that noncommunication between two people was an even more catastrophic matter than I'd imagined and also that this type of problem interested Autre more than it did me. I was at the point of letting the conservative writer come back to the brazier table and staying on myself only in the capacity of rigorous observer, but in the end I preferred it to be me who attended the case, essentially an interesting one, because when all was said and done everything before me that morning was exciting. I found the good in it all and didn't stop appreciating what I saw the world was offering me. I felt it wasn't life I loved, but living; it seemed that those who did not experience delight in things showed little accomplishment, just as Democritus had once said: "Fools live without feeling joy in life."

"I not collapse," I said, "so not recovery."

The two of us sounded increasingly Cheyenne.

Serra cried and I stayed there a good long time, determined to prove my great capacity for self-sacrifice, which was perfectly tied to my unexpected labor of assisting the needy, attending to this patient, while also coming to understand, in its most tragic dimension, the terrible disgrace of not being able to communicate, being unable to do anything for that sick man.

We'll have to wait and see, I thought. I often had the impression—like right now—that the imagined was inseparable from what took place, and vice versa.

Outside, beyond the bus window, in the great ring of the outskirts, it was raining heavily.

38

I once heard it said that real life is not what we lead but what we invent in our minds. If this were true, it was somewhat agonizing that just a moment ago, I had locked up my imagination in the Dschingis Khan. Able to fly wherever I wanted, I'd stayed in a corner of that pitiful Chinese restaurant talking to the mustachioed Serra. Why such masochism? Was it that Serra's vulgarity was the very same coarseness Catalonia had sunk into in recent decades, and, not getting out of there in so many years, I'd become accustomed to the stench? Did I not remember that (as Autre would say) in any situation, come what may, even if it was marvelous, the right thing to do was always to take off, to travel to other spheres? Did I just want to invent an insipid life for myself, with no horizon other than a mustache painted over the navel of the Catalan fatherland?

39

I was reconstructing in my memory the bombardment reproduced by Janet Cardiff and George Bures Miller's loudspeakers when my cell phone rang very loudly. I hadn't noticed, but the volume was turned all the way up. The eyes of all the passengers on the bus—and there were quite a number of them at that hour—converged on me.

It was Boston, asking where I was right at that moment. She'd like to meet me in about four hours, since she couldn't get away from the office any sooner.

I preferred not to mention that I was on the bus and still less that I'd spent three hours watching the rain falling on the windows of the vehicle. So I lied and told her I was in the Dschingis Khan and already getting tired of hearing Chinese and German and constantly translating to myself what I overheard the customers talking about.

I kept quiet for a moment but I had the idea of explaining to her: "You know, when you expose yourself to languages you don't understand, you suddenly imagine you can decipher everything." I didn't say it, because it would have been too obvious I was out of sorts, she might even have guessed I was upset about being so alone.

Instead, I started to tell her I knew everything about the mighty power China and Germany wielded on their respective continents and how they planned to join forces to invade the world. It was anticipated that the future of humanity would be governed by those two immeasurable powers, exercising their centuries-old immutable imperialism ...

I stopped. I realized this chatter was obviously revealing that I was in a state, anxious, and had already spent too many hours alone. So I tried to dissemble. I pretended I was very busy with the people who were coming to see me, but it didn't do any good.

"And all this time nobody came along to interact with you?" Boston interrupted me maliciously.

I told her that in fact I'd only seen the same crazy guy as the day before, the crackpot Pim had possibly told her about. No, Boston said, I don't know anything about that gentleman. Then a silence fell. "Remember," she said finally, "you're having dinner with Chus this evening. I've sent you yet another email with the details of the restaurant." It was as if she were saying: In a few hours, I'll see what's going on with you. What's going on is that I'm running on empty, I mumbled, but I'm sure she didn't hear me because she'd already hung up.

Minutes later, the bus stopped for the tenth time outside the Chinese restaurant. For the hundredth time, the music played the theme song from *Out of Africa*.

Art is joyful, I thought.

And this time, I decided to get off.

The rain hit my face hard and forced me to shut my eyes tight. It was raining noisily on the restaurant roof, and, on the way to the entrance, the raindrops fell at such an angle and so strangely that I thought I could hear a wind unlike all others blowing at regular intervals. It was a wind that didn't seem to be from that place, almost frightening, especially if I remembered that now I wasn't imagining things but actually experiencing them.

The wind is cheerful, I told myself, and I carried on walking fearlessly. I didn't know I was on the brink of seeing that, as they say, there's always a lot going on if you look carefully. There was a slight obstacle for me in the doorway: a small man with a sullen air, around my age, who wore a checked cap. He protected himself from the rain with an umbrella that was also checked, and he was smoking a Montecristo. All of this made me think he might be Spanish, but nonetheless he turned out to be a Frenchman, who worked at a Renault office and was a lover of contemporary art. He'd just come from the nearby *Sanatorium* and, following the route marked by Documenta signs, had got himself to this Chinese restaurant, where he hadn't understood what sort of *installation* it was they were telling him to see.

"They've installed *me*," I said.

"What for?" he asked.

"I listen to problems."

He raised an eyebrow, as if he thought I might be a psychoanalyst, or perhaps just mentally unstable.

That frightened me because it reminded me of a popular claim that at the beginning of time, it was a single misunderstanding that led to our undoing. I remembered that everything that happened in the world was caused by those kinds of dangerous mistakes. The world itself was built on an initial misunderstanding, I thought. I decided to cut this error off at the root, whatever the error was.

"You're mistaken," I said.

"That is my problem," he replied unexpectedly. "That's my great problem, I'm always mistaken, and now I don't know where to turn for help to make fewer mistakes."

In my clumsy French, I told him not to worry, that I did nothing in life but make mistakes too and it was only human after all. I let him in on my sudden suspicion that my joy that morning—because that morning I was experiencing a constant and very controlled joy that caused me to take an interest in everything—my joy originated in a possibly erroneous reading of what had most captured my attention in Kassel: the invisible push of the breeze from the Fridericianum, upon which I was bestowing subversive, avant-garde powers.

Although he'd said he was passionate about contemporary art, I didn't expect him to understand me very well, so I was surprised when he assured me he knew just what I was talking about. More than you could imagine, he said emphatically. And he told me he was from Strasbourg and that my vision of the push from the unseen breeze reminded him of what he always imagined about the origin of the wind blowing around the cathedral in his city.

I had the impression, he said, that in former times the Devil was flying over the earth traveling on the wind, and one day he saw his likeness carved into the outside of the cathedral; he felt immensely gratified, and went in to see if there were any more images of himself, and once inside, he was trapped, which has resulted in the wind waiting for him on the porch ever since, impatiently and ceaselessly clamoring for him all around the place.

I was very direct and told him I was terribly sorry, but I didn't see any relationship between my breeze and his wind.

"No, no there isn't any," he acknowledged, keeping very calm.

I felt frustrated because I wanted to argue with him. And even more so when, to my surprise, immediately afterward, seeming happy in spite of all his mistakes, he hopped into a car that had come by to pick him up.

Suddenly, his problem of always making mistakes seemed to have evaporated.

"*Au revoir*," he said with a simplicity bordering on insolence.

For a moment, it was as if I'd lost an important client from my psychiatry practice. I was left only with the consolation that the place I had to sit in the restaurant was a soft, red couch, which, given its color and another detail or two, brought to mind Freud's divan in London. I felt bad about losing that good client, I felt very bad. And I felt even worse when, on entering the Dschingis, I experienced a sudden mistrust thinking of the breeze and wondering why, like the wind in Strasbourg with the Devil, it didn't ceaselessly clamor for me. What was it waiting for? Maybe so much joy stopped the breeze from visiting the forest in which I seemed to be trapped?

I would have liked it if, when Boston came in to the Dschingis, she'd found me terribly busy, attending a lady who was spending a good while telling me her innumerable problems. And that also sitting at my table was a young man who seemed despondent, a second patient gravely waiting his turn in my improvised, very active branch of the *Sanatorium*. He would be talking with his unsuitable muse, a very young girl with gray hair, who was against his visiting my practice for reasons that escaped me.

I would have liked Boston to find me in full-on medical activity, turned into an important psychiatrist, highly esteemed by the Chinese, overwhelmed by so many people anxious to tell me their problems; or I would have liked her to find me simply doing something worthy of a writer: and not the way she did, which was humiliating. I was fast asleep, snoring uncouthly, belly-up on Freud's divan.

40

When I opened my eyes and discovered her looking at me, somewhere between horrified and amused, I remembered—still befuddled by sleep, the sentence about nobody sleeping on their way to the scaffold. The striking thing was that I'd ended up being the exception to the rule and slept right there beside my own gallows. A few seconds had to pass for the situation not to seem quite so serious. After all, the bus journey had given me such an enormous jolt, and not having slept a wink all night weighed so heavily on me that in the end it wasn't so strange I'd ended up completely exhausted, slumped on my Chinese sofa, on my personal scaffold.

I quickly went back over the most positive aspect of that awakening: I'd managed to keep my excellent state of mind, as it had lost nothing of the high it had reached before I flopped onto the couch; in other words, I continued to feel extremely interested in everything and appreciated being alive like never before. Being so interested, I was even entranced by Boston's dumbfounded expression. You could tell my involuntary "Chinese number" had shocked her.

"The thing is, I couldn't sleep last night," I said.

"Were you engrossed in the cabin?"

Confused, ashamed, reining in my good mood, and at the same time trying to shake off the stupor of the Chinese nap, I resolved right there that, next day, when I had to sit down to write at that table, I would turn myself into another Documenta installation and set about pretending I was asleep.

It would be an installation that paid homage to the deep sleep I had just at that moment woken from, beneath Boston's almost protective gaze. To do it, to refine the Chinese number that paid tribute to my sleep of the day before, I would try to pretend the whole time that I was sleeping in the style of Benino (that figure from Neapolitan nativity scenes, the shepherd who slumbers eternally on and is aware of nothing). In reality, I would be devoting myself to meditation, in other words to covert cabin work, knowing (as I'd recently found out) that thinking during the day was much more relaxing and more productive than at night.

From the outside—that is, in the eyes of possible spectators—no one would know I wasn't actually sleeping but awake, isolated inside a perfect cabin, in this case a mental one, which perversely existed out in public.

A sign on the table would give some explanation of that installation and have everyone believe the writer was asleep and not thinking about anything. The sign, then, would assert the opposite of what was happening and say I was a guy who was completely convinced that—as an atheist schoolteacher had taught me—no religion was ever good for anything; sleep was more religious than all the religions put together, perhaps because when we sleep we are truly closer to God.

No doubt about it, that installation (which I was making up as I went along for the following morning) would contain a deceit, by making out that I professed that religion of sleep.

There's no meditating on anything here, not even on the figure of the sleeper, the sign on my table might also say.

Or perhaps (this would be Autre's version): *Here lies a genuine attempt to go toward nothing, literally toward nothing.*

Or rather this: *When we sleep, we're closer to Duchamp.*

I set about removing some irritating bits of sleep from my eyes, and just then noticed Boston had started looking at me with a great deal more compassion than she'd shown a minute earlier. She doubtless saw me as an old, bald, fat sleepwalker in that foreign city, and most likely at that very moment she was feeling very sorry for me. I could have made her feel even sorrier—or rather, more horrified—if she'd known that, while she was looking at me so compassionately from on high, I was seeing her from below as a representation of Documenta in the form of a housewife with curlers in her hair, with all the neuroses of a nosy, bourgeois woman …

The avant-garde in curlers.

In the end, what happened was that my scant faith in the existence of a visible avant-garde was weakened still further. If anything remained, you'd have to go look for it among the silent conspirators I'd seen, for example, in the woods adjacent to Karlsaue Park, who seemed to me to be moving through the outskirts of the outskirts: ultrasecret accomplices, as weightless as the invisible breeze at the Fridericianum; surely they were the last members of the avant-garde, although none of them were interested in being classified that way.

From my supine position, I kept my gaze fiercely on the housewife with curlers, who seemed to want to dislodge me from the red divan.

"But what is our man of the cabin thinking?" she asked.

In her sarcastic note of affection, I seemed to detect that she thought my recent solitude had unhinged me. Or maybe she didn't think anything of the sort and was simply a pleasant girl who'd always treated me very well and had actually shown me utter courtesy, elegance, and goodness. Had she simply given me the gift of the immense pleasure of hearing her voice, generously instructing me in what there was to see in that park of strange inventions and a thousand marvels (which ended up reminding me of the country estate in *Locus Solus*, the novel by Raymond Roussel)?

Even if it were so and she were just a charming woman with an unrivaled way of talking, even if there were scarcely anything to worry about, I couldn't bear the idea that there existed the slightest possibility of her seeing me at that moment as an Italian nativity-scene figure at the most central Chinese chapel of rest in Europe.

I turned over on the couch.

"And don't leave me all alone again!" I shouted at her.

That was a mistake. On a journey there is always one mistake that stands out above all others. Since I was a boy—a shy one like any other—I've always tried to hide from everyone the fact that I was very lonely. But I had ended up snapping at Boston and I couldn't turn back the clock.

She smiled.

"I think," she said, "that is entirely beside the point."

41

As soon as it had stopped raining, we shot out of the Dschingis Khan, leaving some unappetizing cakes half-eaten. We went straight around to the back of the restaurant and from there set out on a walk through the south of Karlsaue Park.

Half an hour later, we were looking up the pronounced slope of a steep and pretty path that seemed to hail from an earlier time. After a tough climb, we stopped at a precarious little stone construction, the front of which had a closed green door and two windows with drawn blinds behind rusty security grilles. The grilles boasted a number of hinges pretending not only to be gold but to be protected by a sophisticated-looking alarm system. If you went to the back of the house, you could get in via an open door and enter a large, sparsely furnished room. A wooden sign by the back door informed the visitor that what was inside the house could be associated with *The Last Season of the Avant-Garde*, the work of the Berlin artist Bastian Schneider. Inside, there was an easel with an unfinished canvas depicting one of the two battles of Smolensk in the Second World War. It was so well painted, you could almost hear the din of battle. As for the easel, there was a small machine attached to it that looked like an old wall-mounted telephone, but was in fact a tiny, peculiar printing press.

On the board at the top of the easel, you could read the inscription from the tomb of a great and almost forgotten genius, Martinus von Biberach:

> *Ich leb und ich waiß nit, wie lang,*
> *Ich stirb und waiß nit wann,*
> *Ich far und waiß nit, wahin,*
> *Mich wundert, daß ich fröhlich bin.*

> (I live and don't know how long,
> I'll die and don't know when,
> I am going and don't know where,
> I wonder that I am happy.)

If you pushed the button on the little machine beneath the word *fröhlich*, it would crank into motion and spit out a scrap of paper on which Schneider gave his opinion that the contemporary artist these days was in the same position as the traveling artist of the *pre-Aufklärung* (the period before the German Enlightenment), writing not for an established community, but rather in the hope of founding one.

Squatting down, I read the bit of paper the machine had spit violently onto the floor. I thought at length about the group in the forest: that improvised community I'd seen around Janet Cardiff and George Bures Miller's loudspeakers.

That message from Bastian Schneider was just right. When I finished reading it, I went outside the house and saw the park spread out below; the view was slowly narrowing on the horizon. A moment arrived, and I had the impression that with each blink of the eye the space grew narrower still. Even in the most immediate vicinity, soon there wasn't the slightest line or figure. And I thought: no doubt about it, we are at the center of the center of what was once a center. It's also beyond question that we're in the last season of the avant-garde, or perhaps the penultimate one. And the last does exist, but its whereabouts are unknown; being clandestine suits it.

I thought of the world of summer and the world of death and birth, of the world of collapse and recovery, of storms and calms: of the infinite cycle of ideas and action, of infinite invention, of supposedly endless experimentation. And because a dust cloud seemed about to swamp the place, I remembered the fearful handful of dust with which, according to T. S. Eliot, the Western tradition had come to an end. It was a fine dust that blew around out there, from left to right, from right to left, from everywhere to everywhere, reaching the heights and drifting down murmuring.

I would have given anything to know what it murmured.

42

An hour later, in a theater at the Orangerie, I was bewildered to see the Finnish singer M. A. Numminen adapting Ludwig Wittgenstein's *Tractatus Logico-Philosophicus* and blowing it to bits with jazz, pop, and punk rock.

I could hardly believe what I'd just seen. The swift and efficient destruction of the *Tractatus*. When I realized Numminen had wrecked the book, I tittered nervously, almost foolishly, and Boston had to calm me down. I haven't had much sleep, I reminded her, as if that might serve as some sort of excuse. Well, she said, don't forget you have a dinner date with Chus. I felt it was by no means certain I'd make it to that appointment alive, as my weariness was sapping my strength. On this occasion, unlike a year ago, I'd be going out at night without the assistance of Collado's tablets.

I went back to thinking about the Finn, Numminen, and recognized that none of us Anglo-Saxons or Latinos could understand his vein of humor; he was, for us, an incomprehensible comedian, albeit an extremely good one. I didn't quite know why, but he certainly was. Why, why was I sure? I didn't know how to shake off this doubt.

When Numminen left the stage, it was Boston who laughed, although not in such an unbalanced way as I had; *she* was laughing because she'd just read Numminen's bio in the program notes. The translation of his biography must have been taken straight from that anarchic Google tool: "M. A. Numminen was given birth to in 1940 in Somero, Finland, and studied philosophy, the sociology and the linguistics at the University of Helsinki ... He has composed philosophical intimacies, movies of pen, poems, and experiences in genius and tango."

Philosophical intimacies? Movies of pen? It was strange to see new genres of writing seeming to be invented daily. The encounter of genius and tango seemed an attractive combination to me, however unlikely it was that either Boston or I would ever end up fitting in anywhere. But surely it might be an enviable thing to experience genius and dance it in the form of a tango. Coming out of the Finnish show, we exchanged these jovial comments on the Orangerie terrace, noting that the storm had finally moved off.

Then Boston showed me she knew more than I thought by talking about a book by the Argentinean J. Rodolfo Wilcock, *The Temple of Iconoclasts*, in which (in one of the stories) a Catalan director named Llorenç Riber—a big fan of rabbits (he put them into all his work)—was summoned to Oxford to direct the stage version of the *Tractatus Logico-Philosophicus*, and many thought at first it was an almost desperate undertaking.

We had some coffee—rather a lot in my case—and set off in the direction of Rosemarie Trockel's pavilion to see her piece *Tenattemptsforonesculpture*, a work Boston didn't know how to explain to me; perhaps it had no explanation, though I decided to take it upon myself to interpret it as something that spoke about how choosing a daring path is often a good way out of adversity: an idea I made a mental note of, as I had the feeling it was something I'd already done at certain points in my life, and it would be a good thing for me to keep in mind.

Soon after, we saw the sculpture *Scaffold*, Sam Durant's gigantic gallows. That horrifying place was swarming with children: they were climbing all over the vast structure, confusing it, I think, with an amusement park. In the future, the world will belong to these children and resemble a lawless playground, I thought, all the while linking *Scaffold* to my red couch in the Dschingis Khan, that seat I tended to associate with a gallows.

We also saw the inverted, belowground reproduction (by the artist Horst Hoheisel) of the magnificent fountain financed by the Jewish businessman Sigmund Aschrott. The original had been erected in the middle of the city and was brutally demolished in 1939.

We took a long and agreeable turn around Karlsaue Park. The park was getting busier all the time—a lot of people were arriving at the last minute for Documenta's final weekend, and it was increasingly packed. We decided to head into downtown Kassel, and there we bumped into Lara Sánchez, blogger for the Spanish newspaper, *El País*. She had just seen *Fatigues*, the very show by Tacita Dean we ourselves were going to.

Despite beginning to feel worn out and fearing for my appointment with Chus, not to mention my mental stability, we paid a visit to the outdated, ugly branch office of a bank, the least poetic place in the world. It was in this old financial center that Tacita Dean had left her wonderful drawings on large chalkboards, which were a very intense green color and reminded me of the extraordinarily vivid green from my dream in Sarzana: that chalkboard-green that suddenly turned into the green of a doorway fitting into a pointed Arabic arch, on which my friend Pitol was inscribing, slowing down the rhythm of his hand, the poetry of an unknown algebra.

Tacita Dean was the only participant in Documenta whose work I knew something about, because two years earlier I'd seen *The Friar's Doodle* in Madrid, an exhibition centered on motifs she'd photographed that were engraved onto the colonnade at the cloister of the Abbey de Silos.

I'd been to see *The Friar's Doodle* on Dominique González-Foerster's recommendation and discovered an exhibition that interested me very much, focused on the strange traces of carvings a few unknown men had made in the stone of the pillars there over the centuries. Marks had been made by individual artisans in order to work out the price of their labor; there were rudimentary boards for playing games on, probably the work of stonemasons to amuse themselves while waiting for the newly carved columns to be set into the fabric of the building. There were also rough sketches of ornamental designs for the cloister.

While thinking about those carvings at Silos, I saw that a lot of people were forming a line to see Tacita Dean's Afghan chalkboards. Once again, María Boston resorted to those passes that got us in fast. As the line was in a narrow passageway, everyone was keeping a strict eye on everyone else, and it didn't seem okay to simply jump ahead of people who'd been waiting their turn for a couple of hours. I adopted a serious official demeanor, as if I were secretary to officer Boston on her routine inspection of the site.

I did everything I could to show secretarial nonchalance and convince them all that I belonged to Documenta's imaginary board of supervisors, but of course all that was only my conjecture and what everyone saw was a young woman with a seductive voice and an old man both brazenly flourishing bits of paper and getting straight in without any trouble. The protests were loud and even caused me a certain amount of reasonable panic, as the passage was narrow. In addition, I was becoming increasingly sensitive, no doubt as a result of having slept so little.

But once inside the old and antipoetic bank building, all was well. Tacita Dean's chalkboard murals had a blindingly green background and were an evocation of time suspended in the snowy Afghan mountains, although the truth is I was slow to realize that those perfect drawings—among the most elegant I've seen in my life—had been done in chalk in situ, in that very place with a long commercial history where, according to Boston, many artists had previously refused to show their work but which, on the contrary, Tacita Dean had liked from the outset.

The artist had spent several weeks in Kassel drawing that very lovely series of images for *Fatigues*, in which she depicted, with originality and great precision, the Hindu Kush mountains, and the glacial source of the Kabul River. The drawings showed the melting and annual descent of snow-water on the capital of Afghanistan, a phenomenon that seemed to be both welcomed and feared. But in that series, which Boston told me constituted Tacita Dean's return to drawing on boards (she hadn't touched chalks for ten years), the artist was also giving a nod toward Rudyard Kipling's poem "Ford o' Kabul River" (a moving piece about British soldiers who drowned in the second Anglo-Afghan War), as well as to the forces of nature and the Kabul River's terrible power.

María Boston said Tacita Dean's show was among the most visited at Documenta, which didn't surprise me, given the sober and impeccable, classical elegance of the drawings. It did seem strange that in an exhibition of the avant-garde, the closest thing to what could be considered orthodox should make such an impression.

While we were walking around what used to be the offices of the old savings bank, we ran into Carolyn Christov-Bakargiev, the head commissioner or curator of Documenta and one of those people you see right away, as soon as you meet them, who need no kind of push, not even of the invisible sort; she was someone whose gaze seemed to carry a certain brilliance, and you could tell she enjoyed stirring things up verbally. She was accompanied by Chus's assistant, Ada Ara, a woman from Zaragoza who lived in Berlin. Her name seemed made up or a pseudonym, all the more so if you knew that in Catalan *ara* means *now*.

"Ada Now," I said. "That sounds like a stage name."

No sooner had I let drop this remark—none too fortuitous, it goes without saying—than I blundered into what might be described as a brief and unfortunate loop of clumsiness. It all started when Carolyn asked me in English (which I understood perfectly) what I thought of Documenta. No doubt it was a routine question, but I wasn't ready for the artistic director, the one responsible for the whole show—it's always impressed me greatly to meet the person in charge—to ask me such a thing, and I became absurdly tongue-tied, as if the power of speech had been snatched from me.

"Carolyn's asking how the work you've seen in Documenta has made you feel," Ada Ara clarified for me.

"That ... well, um ... that there is no world."

Ada Ara translated my answer with a smile that sought to minimize the possible contradiction in what I'd just said. Carolyn, giving me what seemed a look of disappointment, wanted to know what there was if, as I maintained, there was no world. It was one of the most challenging questions of the day, but at that moment an invisible impulse—or perhaps it was just nervousness due to my extreme fatigue—pushed my energy level up another notch, as if it wanted to come to my aid.

"There's a corollary," I said.

But asserting this—possibly a bad move, influenced by the excessive energy I sometimes suspected flowed from that invisible inner current—was even worse. I bowed my head, conscious that what I'd said didn't make the grade as a McGuffin and also aware that I wasn't even altogether sure why I'd expressed it that way. I never liked taking exams and I had the feeling I was taking one there in front of Carolyn; maybe that's what had made me nervous and gotten me lost in the deranged muddle of my answers.

Ada Ara asked what a corollary was. It's an outcome, a conclusion, Boston said. They amused themselves arguing over what a corollary was, and in the end Carolyn, getting impatient, asked me again what on earth there was if there wasn't a world. There's a conclusion, Boston said, speaking for me. Carolyn pierced me with a terrifying look that made everything infinitely more difficult. She seemed to be saying: But, really, is this the writer they recommended to me, the one they told me we should select? Then she asked me, What conclusion? I was paralyzed, utterly mute. None, I ended up saying. I saw Carolyn was very upset and angry. Suddenly, she let fly: "So what do we do now? Accept it all calmly, implode with panic, or what?"

I remained impassive, thinking of those linguistic short circuits that are inevitably part of the most mundane conversations. "Nice day today, ma'am." "Don't even go there, sir." "Did you see that amazing light?" And the lady doesn't answer. Brusque interruptions, the breakdown of language in the most pointless exchanges. Of course, people contribute to the short circuit sometimes without even wanting to.

43

Toward evening we arrived at the Hauptbahnhof to see *Artaud's Cave*, a film installation made for Documenta by the Venezuelan artist Javier Téllez. It was showing in a strange space inside the old station.

On the way over, Ada Ara, Boston, and I talked about my ridiculous mix-up with Carolyn. The only thing that might have been worse, said Boston, is if you'd told her the world is kept spinning by two tsetse flies.

In that space in the Hauptbahnhof—designed as a cinema but looking like a grotto—Téllez looped his single-channel film. This was what Boston and Ada told me, thinking that since Artaud was involved the work would surely interest me. The installation showed a performance of *The Conquest of Mexico*, an Artaud text that I recalled sought to bludgeon the viewer, to create the harsh effect of an ax-blow on the frozen sea lying within us all. It was all very much in line with theories forming the foundation of the Theater of Cruelty, established by Artaud himself in his bid to make an aggressive impression on the spectator: "For that reason, actions, nearly always violent, come before words, thus freeing the subconscious to fight against reason and logic."

The video by Téllez was extraordinarily interesting and subconscious-freeing: it was acted out by mentally ill patients from the Bernardino Álvarez hospital in Mexico City. The video took place in two parallel time frames, alternating daily life in the psychiatric institution with the historical events of the conquest of Mexico as told by Artaud, which made the patients of the Bernardino Álvarez duplicate themselves ingeniously: playing themselves as patients and at the same time identifying with Moctezuma and other historical characters.

I didn't say anything, and it seemed as if I wasn't interested in the cave, or the video, or the conquest of Mexico. But that wasn't the case; it was that I'd just seen the young blonde German approaching, the woman in strict mourning I'd seen before at *Untilled*, enlightening people about the death of Europe. It was unmistakably her, still in the same dark clothing and once more shouting at people as she came toward us. Arriving where we were, she handed us a sort of pamphlet she had written and was distributing to inform us that Antonin Artaud was one of the first to condemn the Enlightenment for destroying the West. In fact, it was nothing very different from what she'd said previously from up on a pile of rubble.

I went so far as to think the vociferous young woman had reason on her side. Was she reasonably mad? Nothing was further from the spirit than rationality, and for that very reason, rationality was the peak of madness. The young blonde woman in unrelenting mourning was, moreover, quite right to remind us that Artaud was a pioneer when it came to identifying Europeans as the living dead.

Artaud screamed, too. Or was I thinking of Humboldt, that Saul Bellow character who used to reminisce about the day Artaud invited the most brilliant Parisian intellectuals to a conference and when he had them all gathered there, he read nothing, but went up on stage, simply yelping at them like a wild animal? It seemed Artaud went on letting out deafening shrieks, while the Parisian intellectuals remained sitting there, petrified. Yet, for them, it was an exquisite act. And why? Humboldt said that in some way Artaud had understood that the only art that interested intellectuals was one that celebrated the primacy of ideas. Artists had to interest intellectuals, the new class. That's why the position of culture and of the history of culture had become the main theme of art. And that's why a refined French audience respectfully listened to Artaud while he screamed. For them the sole objective of art was to suggest or inspire ideas …

If I thought hard about it, hadn't I acted that way too, since arriving in Kassel? From the word go, I'd been pleased by the prospect that theories running through Documenta might inspire me with ideas for my own work. In fact, I suspected that some of those ideas had already permeated my personality and, like a powerful drug, had left me in such a pleasant condition that my habitual despondency at that hour didn't even dare to put in an appearance. That was one of the things that was happening: despite it being close to dusk, anguish didn't arrive punctually for its usual appointment with me. It was without a doubt totally unusual; maybe anguish was just running a little late.

What was happening was that anguish appeared to have vanished and been secretly replaced by a great admiration for the complexity of what I'd seen in Kassel. That complexity had become part of my new personality. It was as if what was happening to me there had a direct link with those words of Mallarmé to Manet: "Paint, not the thing, but the effect it produces." The effect on me of some of the work at Documenta was altering my way of being.

That stunning complexity, that Alcarria of art, was truly a marvel, and I was seeing it with the eyes of Raymond Roussel.

So I was sorry to have to wreck the gloomy predictions so many friends were making about the end of art, which they unfortunately confused with the end of the world, an entirely different matter. It seemed to me that art was still holding up perfectly well, and it was only the world, with its two dizzying tsetse flies, that had crumbled.

44

It was there in Artaud's cave that I remembered my old conviction—still holding true from what I could tell—that anyone who dedicated himself to literature had not renounced the world; the world had simply evicted him, or never admitted him as a tenant. Nothing serious, then; in the end, a poet was someone for whom the world didn't even exist, because, for him, there was only the radiance of the eternal outside.

I was thinking all this, and it was as if the cries of the radical young German woman fundamentally appealed to me. I had to really force myself to move away from that unhinged ranter. I was helped by my tremendous accumulated fatigue as much as by the invisible breeze: for a moment they both seemed to have joined forces to try to hold my interest in everything except the shouting. And so I soon managed to dodge the young madwoman in mourning—with a slight twinge, because underneath it all I liked her madness—and I was able to concentrate on the video being shown in that artificial cave.

I noticed I continued to be interested in everything. Not long before, I'd even been interested in the soothing, ruddy sunset, which, going into the cave, we'd left behind and which plenty of people had been paying too much attention to, as though it were part of Documenta. My reaction to the anodyne sunset had been very emotional, as it reminded me of my father who, before going off to his daily labor year after year (which began at sunset), always sang "Pace non trovo," and his voice in the shower rang out with a succession of squeaks caused by excessive sorrow (perhaps at not having dedicated himself to opera). It resounded with excessive volume and excessive despair.

I was also emotional inside Artaud's cave, because on top of everything, each time I looked off into the distance, I thought I saw the sea. It was a receding sea, which revealed a more distant sea, and in the end only allowed me to surmise a series of seas without coastlines. This visual effect seemed to tell me I should dare to go farther, unafraid, far from any handful of dust or misunderstanding of this world, that I should dare to go toward other conjectures, also without coastlines.

Under the circumstances, I was barely able to follow the thread of the film by Javier Téllez: when I wasn't sunk in conjecture about a series of seas without coastlines, I was imagining what I could say to María Boston and Ada if they suddenly decided to ask me what I thought that invisible breeze (which possibly contributed to preventing the collapse of my mental state) was like. If the question arose, I thought I'd tell them it was like that well-known current vibrating between two poles of the tiny voltaic column that made the first electric telegraph possible; that fiendish spark was capable of leaping miles and miles over mountains and entire continents.

I don't know how it could have happened, but when we came out of that grotto, I thought I saw the star Sirius high in the sky, and then very soon afterward, as if there were a logical connection between the two, I again met the young madwoman in mourning proclaiming, in an increasingly imposing manner, her desperation over the destruction of Europe. Confronted by this juxtaposition, I was aware of being very conscious that I would long remember the majestic, somber beauty of the scene and that she was involuntarily forming a part of it; it would be one of the key images of my journey to Kassel. And that is because, among other things, on suddenly seeing the bereaved young woman's shadow in the night's first electric lights and taking into account the fact that Sirius was high up in *the radiance of the eternal*, the figure of the madwoman took on a strange sort of dignity for a moment, as if all of a sudden, there in the Kassel dusk, you could see that only she was telling the truth.

45

"The horror, the horror," whispered Kurtz, that Conrad character holed up in the Congo. For a moment, *Momentary Monument IV* struck me as the twisted prolongation of that madman's harsh mental landscape, but also an outrageous landscape that fit well with the figure dressed in mourning shouting about the destruction of Europe.

Momentary Monument IV was an immense mountain of industrial ruins, for which Lara Favaretto claimed responsibility. The monstrous agglomeration of four hundred tons of scrap was piled up on the other side of the Hauptbahnhof and protected by tense security guards who, at the possibility of a predictable accident (children were the most likely potential victims), made sure no one attempted to climb on that criminal heap of sharp, old bits of metal.

With some disdain, María Boston said that the work, according to the catalog, was about the instability caused by the fluctuation between the lasting and the fleeting. And saying it, she used a metallic voice that pitilessly distorted hers, which made me hate that momentary, monumental mound of trash by Favaretto even more.

But beyond feeling sad about the voluntary deformation of a marvelous voice, I wondered what the artist of scrap iron might have said about her own work. That mise en scène of a monumental destruction was, above all else, insufferably ugly. Without a doubt, we could have spared ourselves the visit and I would have been grateful. Although I felt enthusiastic about many of the things I was seeing in Kassel, I hadn't lost my critical eye, and looking at *Momentary Monument IV*, nothing better occurred to me than to think of *Las Meninas* by the painter Velázquez, and of the music of Mozart and Wagner, and I was on the verge of bursting into violent sobs.

We still had time to get back to the old station, where a project called *The Refusal of Time*, by the South African artist William Kentridge, awaited us in a large, old warehouse. As we were walking there—seeing that, in spite of the time of day, I was continuing to feel joy and an exaggerated interest and curiosity for everything—I again wondered if it wasn't strange for there not to be even the slightest sign of anguish in my head. Normally by this time, my body coincided with the loss of the day's energy, and along with my mental fatigue, anguish perfectly undermined my good mood.

Not that I hadn't seen a few signs of anguish, but I'd rejected them so emphatically and they'd disappeared so swiftly that even I was surprised. Normally, anguish erupts simply when I'm reminded of my age and how few years, long-lived or not, are left to me.

Maybe, since I'd modified my daily routine and slept so badly the previous night, the unimaginative, secret regulator of my moods had been misled, and I'd been brought to a new, long-forgotten sensation: a good mood at this difficult time of day.

I thought: Let's hope it lasts. It was perfect timing, since I didn't have any of Dr. Collado's pills and I had to have dinner with Chus Martínez and I'd better arrive with a good vibe.

Taking for granted that I'd like Kentridge's work, I started to look at *The Refusal of Time*, a spectacle on which the physicist Peter

L. Galison had worked, as well as several composers (Philip Miller and Catherine Meyburgh); it was an explosion of music, images, shadow play, with a Da Vinci-esque memory machine, easing the visitor into a fabulous, epic dimension, where time eventually began to be canceled.

The Kentridgean narration, Boston whispered to me, was a great dance of shadows, among which the artist—the artist in abstract—would appear and disappear, crossing an imaginary space of geographical maps. All this, according to her, should be read as a reflection on time that was refracted as it crossed places and people's lives and also in the different zones of the earth, the dawns and dusks, until all was united in a cosmic whole.

Though I was still keen to like Kentridge's work, Boston's words complicated everything for me. What did she mean? Had she memorized and recited this speech for me? Did she herself understand what she was saying? I arrived at the conclusion that she definitely did not, though I also thought it was much better that way. Because in the end, not having been able to easily follow its development, I found the work opening many doors for me; in fact, it had a beneficial effect, allowing me to sense that maybe art forms were changing and increasingly relating differently to one another and to everything else. Perhaps, among other tasks, it had fallen to me to guess where was the sign that stood out and made these new relations visible. Would I know how to find it? It seemed to me that this sign was an ellipsis. I sensed that, when Boston tackled the less well-known aspect of Kentridge as a draftsman, this was something she was undoubtedly better at explaining than *The Refusal of Time*. It was interesting, she said, this mania of his that in all his drawings you could see what was there, but you could also see a trace of the previous drawing … She didn't know anyone else who drew like this. He had, on the other hand, a brilliant and at the same time naïve side: he used dotted lines to make his characters' gazes visible, managing to show something as impossible to describe in painting or drawing as the visual behavior of people's eyes that we cannot see.

I understood that those dots that sometimes served to unite

glances were just a preamble to a sort of uncertainty that did not exactly invite Reason. Antonin Artaud would have so enjoyed feeling his way along those dots, shrieking intensely while touching them, maybe turning them into music for losers, heroes of our time, poets of our unique and ephemeral existence ...

Was there ever a better drawing of the human condition than ellipses, with their cheerful suspension of what, after all, only aspires to remain eternally suspended?

For me, the image most related to perpetual suspension will always be the patio of my school, when we pupils left for home in the afternoons and little by little the shadows grew and the patio was left abandoned like a quadrangular eternity—tidy and forever disturbing—offering us the condensed pearl of our school weariness.

46

A hundred meters from the Hauptbahnhof, on the ground floor of a building in a squalid alley—I was thinking of my younger days and an old terror that would have been upon me by now in the form of a dry, icy breath directly on the back of my neck—we went in to see *One Page of Babaouo*, the singular installation by the Portuguese artist António Jobim.

Ignoring the long line, we flashed our passes, going in to see that performance directly inspired by *Babaouo*, the film script Salvador Dalí wrote in the 1930s. As was to be expected, we saw a disconcerting show (considering that Kassel wasn't exactly known for dancing to a logical beat).

Boston had no information about that performance. She hadn't found the time to see it and, moreover, she hated Jobim because she remembered his first visit to Kassel in the middle of a February blizzard earlier that year. At eighty-five, he was the oldest artist invited to Documenta and he arrived in the city in February to set *One Page of Babaouo* in motion. He arrived with the strange reputation of having a tendency to disappear, to vanish into thin air, to get lost;

so Boston was ordered to make sure that didn't happen. But he's eighty-five years old! she'd said. It doesn't matter, they told her, this is an unpredictable man, who likes nothing better than to slip under the radar. That a man of his age, in the middle of a city where it was snowing copiously, was going to get lost still seemed impossible. But it happened. António Jobim was a genius of disappearances. He arrived on the coldest day of the year and went to that squalid building in the alley (that inhospitable ground floor by the Hauptbahnhof, where they'd begun to rehearse his version of a page from Dali's *Babaouo*). He had lunch with Carolyn Christov-Bakargiev and Chus Martínez in the Osteria restaurant, singing them an emotional rendition of the fado "Não Quero Amar." Afterward, they accompanied him to the hotel so he could have a siesta, and they put Boston in charge of setting up surveillance and looking after him as soon as she saw him reappear in the lobby.

They didn't see him again for two days. María Boston never found out how he'd outwitted her surveillance. She had to spend all her time looking for him all over the city, calling the police, hotels, brothels, anyone who might have seen him. Jobim was originally from Angola, and in the snow of that German city, if only by pure contrast, his blackness might have made him visible, but no one saw him anywhere. He didn't reappear until two days later, when they'd almost given him up for dead. All Jobim said was that the chocolate in Kassel—actually, all the chocolate of the Hessenland region— was very good. At that moment, if she'd been able to, Boston would have murdered him on the spot.

The work by that unexpected fanatic of Hessenlandian chocolate began with the first notes of the traditional Catalan tune "Per tu ploro" as a curtain representing a vast and desolate mineral landscape was raised. The convulsive and catastrophic shapes of the rocks offered a clear notion of an ancient geological delirium. A large, silver spoon came directly out of a rock of pure iron oxide and diagonally crossed the exposed, somewhat Angolan landscape. In the spoon could be seen two eggs on a plate.... Then the curtain went down and came back up again, now with the tango

"Renacimiento" playing in the background. The stage was full of cyclists, who, with loaves of bread on their heads and blindfolded, intertwined very slowly among tango-dancing couples. When the cyclists and dancers disappeared, a black woman could be seen center stage playing a harp and wearing a Chanel suit. Every once in a while she'd hit the harp brutally with loaves of bread she'd taken out of a basket set beside her. Then she'd calm down and just play. When her piece was finished, she threw the loaves and began to demand that the curtain fall, which it finally did so that everything would start all over again, that is, the Catalan *sardana* came back.

I do sometimes find *sardanas* moving; they remind me of unknown ancestors, making me cry out of a sentimental confusion. However, that spectacle essentially reminded me that I had to phone Barcelona, ask how everything was going back there. How was everything in my dull country? I noticed that it felt like an eternity since I'd left my city.

47

Ada Ara said goodbye, as she had to get back to the office. Boston said she was going to stay awhile longer, and we sat down in Die Büste Bar, near Kochstrasse.

There were children running around, chasing one another between the tables under the indulgent eyes of their parents and grandparents. The bar, full of adults crowded together almost fighting to get a drink, wasn't the best place for a conversation. But we talked. Boston told me she was looking forward to growing old, to being able to walk more slowly and dress like an elderly lady. She managed to surprise me.

"Walk more slowly?"

I looked at her feet. She was wearing the golden sandals that had so fascinated me before, and I imagined them destroyed by the passing years. At the same time, I couldn't help but be surprised at her sentimental, human notes infiltrating my cold investigation into the state of contemporary art (I might even say "too human"). What were those notes doing there? It occurred to me to ask her if her desire to walk more slowly might have something to do with the slow treatment of time she'd perceived in Kentridge's work. Not at all, she said. What an idea. What was true, she said, was that she was becoming an increasingly fanatical walker, so much so that she was confident that as an old lady she wouldn't have to give up her walks, they would just be at a slower pace, down the hallway of her house, better than ever. She would always be dressed in strange clothes; she dreamed of wearing very thin dresses with thick socks and, as night came on, falling asleep with her head back and her mouth hanging open…

I want to reach old age, she insisted, and have trouble sleeping. I want to wake up in the middle of the night and stay awake until dawn drooling and become senile and stupid. Her voice had curiously recovered all the charm of the first time I'd heard it. It was sounding immensely warm and so human. It even seemed *too* human. It was a voice that, despite what it said, managed to increase the power of its spell moment by moment. I would have stayed there in Die Büste Bar listening to her for the rest of the day, or the rest of my days, until she started to grow old. I don't know how I came to imagine that some of the grandfathers in the bar were practically on top of us and that they wanted to touch us, that their breath enlivened the red of the little dresses of the girls running around, the way oxygen enlivens fire. I believe it can be said that, in the company of old lady Boston, among the flames and little red dresses, I fully lived for a few moments in the tough hell of old age.

48

On my walk back to the Hessenland, I was tearing along at such a pace that I walked right past my hotel without seeing it; I kept on going, maybe because I was concentrating too hard on my old folks' experience in Die Büste Bar and going over and over my two quick farewell kisses to Boston.

Without noticing, I stumbled into unknown territory, in the unfamiliar area of Friedrich-Ebert-Strasse, and as I passed in front of the Trattoría Sackturm, I felt someone touch my shoulder. For a second or two, I thought I'd returned to Sehgal's salon. I looked around rather cautiously and saw it was Nené. (I call her that because I don't think the actual person would like me to give her real name.)

The moment has been engraved in my memory, not only because I was momentarily startled, but also because the person who'd grabbed me was Nené, an old girlfriend of my friend Vladimir (an ex-girlfriend from a very long time ago—to tell the truth, from the early seventies). I was quite shocked. I thought, if such things were happening to me—meeting a woman like her here—it meant when I got home I'd have to write about what had happened to me on this trip. Who could have expected things might still happen to me?

Nené was alone in the truest sense of the word. She was about to have dinner on her own when she saw me coming up the street. She was, she said, enormously thrilled. She was as high-strung as ever, though older, with a slightly crooked nose and shiny, bouncy auburn hair. She had just been left by her husband, a famous German artist. When? An hour ago. Horrible, she said. Her husband? No, that she'd been dumped again; my friend Vladimir had done the same thing, didn't I remember? I didn't remember that Vladimir had left her, was all I could say, and I thought this really took the cake; all I needed now was to have to justify decisions my friends had made in the seventies.

You've aged, she said maliciously. I'm not surprised, I thought. Was I not coming from experiencing a scene in Die Büste Bar with a decidedly elderly atmosphere? You're gaga yourself, I was about to answer, but I was bursting with such well-being that it was unthinkable I could hurt a recently separated old dame. She kept insisting I come have dinner with her. I don't know how many times I told her I had dinner plans with the co-curator of Documenta at the Osteria and couldn't have two dinners in one night, but the fact is, I didn't put up too much resistance going into the Sackturm, since I was really quite hungry and had been for hours.

I hadn't heard that you'd participated in Documenta, Nené said after ordering a salad to share, once we'd been seated at a table inside the Sackturm. I hid from her the fact that I was still participating; I didn't want to have to see her the next day in the Chinese restaurant or at my lecture. Nené was just as intellectual as she'd been in those distant days when I'd seen her often in Barcelona. I told her I had never seen anything like *This Variation*, but she made a gesture of absolute disdain. I would swear she hadn't heard of the installation, but there remained that gesture. While she was making it, I suddenly felt the beneficial stealthy company of toil, that concept so familiar to me since coming across it in a line by Yeats: "In luck or out the toil has left its mark."

I talked to Nené about this, and she half understood me.

"You can't live without art?" she said. "Well, I've had it up to here with my German husband, my artist husband. Germans are a pain and so are artists. Art is too, let me tell you, art is a complete bore, a big fat nothing."

Luckily, I was still in good spirits, which enabled me to survive all that.

Then I told her that in general a work of art—as in Sehgal's dark room—went by like life, and life went by like art.

It was very odd, she almost slapped me across the face.

Minutes later, when the irreproachable polipetti al pesto arrived, my enthusiasm for everything I'd seen in Kassel had reached such a height that even Nené seemed uncomfortable at my unstoppable praise, my long commentaries on all I'd seen. She told me I was "going way overboard with my enthusiasm."

It's not that I exactly believe in contemporary art, I told her, but every once in a while I'm able to see extraordinary details in it, and, besides, I don't think we're doing everything so badly in comparison with the ancient Greeks or the Renaissance. What do you want me to say?

She threw me a look of hatred. Maybe she'd guessed that I was thinking of leaving soon, without ordering dessert. I then started to tell her I wasn't praising what I'd seen in Documenta just for the sake of it, but that since I'd arrived in the city, I felt that an invisible force had taken hold of me, making me find everything exciting, as if Kassel had presented me with an unexpected shift of gears, an unforeseen impetus that would help me have more optimism in the future toward art and life, though not toward the world, which I'd already given up for lost.

I almost choked saying all this all at once, almost without a pause. And, to top it off, I felt her look of unbridled hatred on me again.

"I didn't get any sleep last night," I said. "And that's altered my behavior, my mood, both of which were always very regular until now, arriving in an orderly fashion and on time. In the mornings, I experience happiness and the idea that everything's possible. In the evenings, I experience fatigue and darkness. Suddenly—perhaps it's due to the Kassel climate—everything has changed. I've gone mad. I hope you'll be able to forgive me."

I said this and managed to get away from her much more easily than I'd expected. We agreed to meet at midnight in the foyer of the Gloria Cinema, but I had the impression neither of us would show up. I certainly wouldn't, because I didn't even know where that cinema was, even though a year earlier I'd downloaded a photo of it when I came across it on the Internet and it had reminded me of the neighborhood cinemas of my childhood.

49

I reached the street, finally heading in the right direction toward the Hessenland, and as I was walking, I started imagining that I had left the city and come back once Documenta had closed, and I went into the abandoned salon of *This Variation* to see what the place was like when it wasn't dark, with dancers lying in ambush. It didn't take long to discover that it was an uninteresting, rundown space. But there was someone there that I hadn't expected: an old Indian man, who asked me if I was aware that the soul survived in a "suprasensitive" world. I didn't know that, I said in fright. The soul survives, he told me, in coexistence with forces that those initiates of the ancient world understood very well, even their most mysterious aspects. I didn't know that either, sir, I explained, and almost felt the need to apologize for not knowing. A shame, he said, because you won't be able to connect with the superior beings of the celestial hierarchy. A long silence. Here in this room there was avant-garde art, I tried telling the Indian man. And to my surprise my words affected him the way a stake would have affected a vampire. So much so that I watched him leave completely horrified. It seemed clear to me that the term "avant-garde" caused serious problems for the densely populated, cosmopolitan colony of ghosts in Kassel.

50

Thinking about *art itself*, I thought that it was definitely right there, in the air, suspended in that moment, suspended in life that went by as I'd seen the breeze go by.

I was in my room now. Moments before, I'd waved to *This Variation* from the balcony, as had become my ritual. I sat down at my computer and googled the word *impulso* (which is how I thought of, or how I'd translated, the word *pull* in Ryan Gander's title). I discovered that it wasn't necessarily what I'd thought it was, because in physics, "impulse" is the "physical magnitude (usually denoted as *p*) defined as the variation in the lineal moment of an object within a closed system." The term is different from how we habitually think of it: it was coined by Isaac Newton in his second law of motion, in which he called it the *vis motrix*, referring to this force of movement.

In any case, I was enjoying a *vis motrix*, I'm almost sure of it. Then I looked up my next day's activity on Google: "The Lecture to Nobody," which I soon saw they'd programed for six in the evening. Would anyone attend? I expected to go along, propelled by my own *vis motrix*, but I hoped not a soul would show up. What was I planning to talk about, anyway? I kept looking for more information about Documenta 13 and found a feature article in which Carolyn

Christov-Bakargiev praised the confusion one might encounter walking around there. I remembered Boston telling me to bear in mind, when judging *The Brain*, that Carolyn Christov-Bakargiev was of the opinion that in art, confusion is a truly marvelous thing. "At the risk of unsettling people," Christov-Bakargiev said, "this Documenta does not have a single guiding concept. Due to the fact that there are many valid truths, one is constantly confronted with unsolvable questions; thus it has become a choice between *not* making a choice, not having a concept, acting from a position of withdrawal; or making a choice that one knows will also be partially or inevitably 'wrong.' What these participants do, what they 'exhibit,' may or may not be art."

I also found Carolyn's *Letter to a Friend*, in which she suggested that Documenta 13 was more than a big exhibition; it was actually a state of mind. I was on the verge of believing she had said that for me, since, after all, in a few hours I'd changed into someone enormously enthusiastic about everything he'd seen in Documenta, that great garden of contemporary marvels.

There were emails to answer in my inbox. In one of them, someone wrote to me from Neuchâtel to ask how I was getting on in Kassel and whether I was planning to write about it all when I got home. "If you do decide to, if I were you, I'd forget about genres and remember that every art, every science, operates by means of discourse; if it is practiced for its own sake as art, and if it achieves the highest summit, it is poetry."

As I read this, I thought that there are some friends who would like for you, not them, to take on great challenges. Still, I couldn't agree more with the idea of doing without genres. My favorite author was Nietzsche; I could never put his books down when I read him, so when I traveled I preferred to bring books in which he appeared only indirectly, such as *Romanticism*. To me, W. G. Sebald seemed to be just Nietzsche's distinguished disciple, though I had to admit he'd managed to give a poetic touch to his romantic pilgrimages. And, thinking of Sebald, I could never forget that lovely text of his on Robert Walser about how Walser seemed truly freed from the burden of himself the night he undertook a journey in a hot air balloon, from Bitterfeld—the artificial lights of whose factories were just beginning to glimmer—to the Baltic coast. A trip over a sleeping nocturnal Germany. "Three people, the captain, a gentleman and a young girl, climb into the basket, the anchoring chords are loosed, and the strange house flies, slowly, as if it had first to ponder something, upward," wrote Walser, the perfect rambler. For Sebald, that wanderer was born for this hushed journey through the air: "In all his prose works, he always seeks to rise above the heaviness of earthly existence, wanting to float away softly and silently into a higher, freer realm."

Another more prosaic email contained for the umpteenth time—I'd received no end of emails about this matter—directions to my dinner with Chus, including a detailed map of the neighborhood showing my hotel and the Osteria restaurant, separated by barely three hundred meters. It seemed like a simple trajectory, even though all the street names were in German. I felt insecure, perhaps because—for some reason that escaped me—the sensation of being just another citizen of Kassel had begun to fade. But I wouldn't say I'd gone back to feeling I was from Barcelona either; rather, I simply felt lost, lost in the center of Europe. In fact, it seemed increasingly obvious to me—as in the old song—that to get out of Europe I would have to get out of the forest, but to get out of the forest I'd have to get out of Europe.

Sometimes, when I noticed a change of light in my frustrated "thinking cabin," I felt lost, and that lost feeling led me to see myself as one more dead European.

51

I stopped to think about *One Page of Babaouo*, António Jobim's strange installation, and the more my imagination started to spin around it, the more interesting it seemed. An experience from the past helped: my visit to Salvador Dalí in May of 1978, an incursion into his house on the occasion of the publication of a Spanish translation of his book *Le mythe tragique de l'Angélus de Millet*. In light of what Dalí told me on that visit, *One Page of Babaouo* started to acquire greater intensity, which led me to recall that there are scenes from our past that with time—as we come across information we didn't have access to before—unexpectedly take on greater depth. One of those past scenes took place in 1963, at 87 Paseo de Gracia, in Barcelona's long-gone Libreria Francesa. Some classmates had taken me there, and to my absolute surprise, after an exchange of passwords, a sales clerk in blue overalls with a pencil behind his ear brought out from under the counter books by Sartre and Camus banned by Franco's censors.

I was so surprised by that sudden apparition of forbidden books that the scene was etched in my memory forever. Years later, when I read that Diderot's *Encyclopédie* had been banned in France in 1759 and Paris booksellers sold it from under their counters, there appeared to be a thread directly linking that eighteenth-century booksellers' gesture with the scene in repressed 1960s Barcelona.

An event, banal though it might be, is normally the consequence of others that precede it. That's why those drawings by William Kentridge that I'd heard Boston talk about attracted me, those works in which he deliberately left a trace of a previous drawing. It was as if Kentridge were saying: I don't want to hide the fact that many other drawings preceded this one, and it comes from them.

When back in May of '78 I was able to interview Salvador Dalí in his Cadaqués house, the painter kept going on about a Venetian painting: "A while ago, just before you arrived, I was looking again at Giorgione's *Tempest*. There is a soldier, and a naked woman holding a baby. It is a pivotal painting, though our fellow countrymen don't know it."

Pivotal? I didn't know who Giorgione was either, but I pretended otherwise. Years later, I saw *The Tempest* in Gallerie dell'Accademia in Venice and discovered it was a very enigmatic painting, with that strange scene of a man and a woman (with no connection to each other) and that storm brewing in the background.

Yesterday, that interview with Dalí unexpectedly took on greater depth when I read by chance Mallarmé's recommendation to Édouard Manet that is for some the founding statement of the art of our time: "Paint, not the thing, but the effect it produces."

I immediately thought of Manet's *The Railway*, that painting that dumbfounded the critics of the time. In it, a young mother looks at us, while her daughter stares at the plume of steam from a passing train. In the foreground, the little girl has her back to us. In the background, there's the great cloud of smoke that the train has left as it chugs through the center of Paris.

I noticed that the structure of *The Railway* reminded me of Giorgione's *The Tempest*. Looking it up, I saw I was not mistaken, many people had said the same. And then I thought if only Manet's picture had an actual trace of what someone had done before. A sketch or a hint of Giorgione would allow us to see the direct connection between the two, in the same way Duchamp's *Nude Descending a Staircase* would acquire greater depth if it contained an actual trace of Manet on the canvas. And might it not be that Dalí, lost in a very dark Spain, wanted to bequeath to me that day the effect that introduced modernity, the crucial Giorgione effect?

Se non è vero, è ben trovato, Dalí was known to say. That was, in fact, the expression he quoted to me in that interview when I told him that his book formed a sort of "obligatory perimeter," while leaving free in the center of language a great "shore of imagination," perhaps with no other object than for us to play on it. To this, Dalí replied that his wife Gala, when she read the book, had said: It would be great if what he wrote were true, but if in the end it turned out not to be, the book would be greater still.

52

Immersed in the subjects of Europe and death, I recalled a secondary character from Joseph Roth's tale "The Bust of the Emperor," the Jewish publican Solomon Piniowsky, that simple man with his natural intelligence, whom Count Morstin, gaining confidence in his ever reasonable replies, asked for his opinions on the most diverse subjects. "Listen to me, Solomon! That hateful Darwin fellow who says people are descended from apes, well, he seems to be right after all." And Solomon Piniowsky always had something interesting to say.

"You know your Bible, Solomon, you know it's written there that on the sixth day God created man, but where does it say anything about the nationalist? Isn't that right, Solomon?"

"Quite right, Count!" Piniowsky said.

One day, in the middle of the climate of general collapse—the Austro-Hungarian Empire having disappeared, causing a breakdown of secular institutions—the Count asked Piniowsky for his opinion of the world.

"Count, I no longer think anything at all. The world has perished," replied the tavernkeeper.

The world had gone to hell. In that apocalyptic climate, what could an individual like Piniowsky do, disappointed in the world, but still holding on to certain private convictions that endured within him?

For me, these convictions could be synthesized by writing the word *Art*. In some way, I resemble Piniowsky. Because on the subject of the sinking world, I no longer had anything to say, though I noticed that something endured within me: eagerness, toil, the old convictions, the same ones that led me at that moment to celebrate what I'd seen so far in Kassel and the fact that I seemed to incorporate some of the works I'd seen there into my own personality, injecting them into my own spirit.

I knew, as Piniowsky did, that the world had perished and was already disintegrating, and only if one dared to show it in its dissolution was it possible to offer some plausible image of it. I knew that the world had gone to hell, but also that art created life, and this path, contrary to what ominous voices said, was not exhausted. So I decided to change my name and call myself Piniowsky. Autre would drop his provisional surname and become Piniowsky. As him, I wouldn't have any opinion on the world (which had so disappointed us), but on art I would.

I soon felt an immense sense of well-being at having left behind the name that had accompanied me for sixty-odd years and of which I was so bored, among other things because it was the name I'd had during my youth (which I'd devoted myself to protracting far too long).

I logged in to Spotify and, thinking of Marguerite Duras, looked for the soundtrack to her film *India Song*. Listening to the music composed by Carlos D'Alessio, I returned to my past in Paris. It seemed odd: now being called Piniowsky, I resembled myself more. I'd been in Kassel all the while without being entirely me, and now that I was called Piniowsky, I was at last starting to be myself.

I amused myself reflecting on *Untilled*, the installation by Huyghe I'd already seen and that seemed to create an idea of a return to the prehistory of art—though it only seemed to, I wasn't at all sure. In any case, the installation seemed to be talking about the necessity of learning how to *stand apart*, to situate oneself on the metaphorical outskirts of the outskirts. Like me, Huyghe was attracted to fog and smoke, at least that's what Pim had told me. If there was a scene characteristic of my humble poetics, it would be a foggy atmosphere where a solitary man walked down a lonely road and smoke always got him thinking.

I evoked that characteristic fog sequence evident in so many of my stories. I perceived I was increasingly seized by the most extraordinary happiness, maybe just because of being Piniowsky: for calling myself by that name liberated me from the pressures of my own, and that allowed me, moreover, to cheerfully ponder a possible final dimension remaining to the avant-garde. Since becoming Piniowsky I resisted burying this dimension, seeing it as connected to some misty concepts that, as soon as the fog cleared, might have a future. Art could be a forest conspiracy in the outskirts of the outskirts, a flight from moral bewilderment, always discreet, not to mention invisible.

Now that some time has passed, I see that intuition has taken root in me, to the point where I would dare say that the more avant-garde an author is, the less he can allow himself to be labeled as such and the more he must be on guard not to be pigeonholed by that cliché.

This is what I wrote at the beginning of this novelized account of my participation in Documenta. Then, they were words that gave the impression of having little to do with what I planned to tell. They were just a sounding out, perhaps just a McGuffin. Now I see that what's happened over the course of this account—like Picasso's portrait of Gertrude Stein, which she eventually came to look like— is that my narration (in my books, the axis tends to be the journey about a writer who travels, writing of his displacement) has brought me back around to that phrase, now spoken with greater conviction. Now, I sense that a way to *not* be pointed out as avant-garde is to turn oneself, in broad daylight, into a sort of agile, very mobile forest conspiracy, as light as the most invisible breeze in the Fridericianum.

53

I thought, no one will ever know how obsessively I'm devoting myself to memorizing the route from my hotel to the Osteria restaurant; but it shall be known, because I'm going to confess. I won't tell it entirely, for fear it won't be believed. It was an exaggerated, meticulous, almost insane preparation.

I left the Hessenland and simply began to walk along the spacious sidewalk, up Friedrich-Ebert-Strasse, passing in front of the Trattoría Sackturm, and not turning left on Königstor but turning at the next corner, which was an alleyway I had to take briefly to get to Jordanstrasse.

It was a very easy route; in fact I already knew part of it. Nevertheless, I was afraid I'd get lost even though I'd spent a while memorizing it.

What kind of fear was making me act like that? Where did it come from? These questions reminded me of Tom Thumb, that tale of a tiny boy who left a trail of breadcrumbs along the path to be able to find his way back home again. It was the first story I ever heard in my life. In fact, my parents had made me learn it by heart and, at the age of four, when we had visitors, they'd make me recite the Catalan version out loud.

I was shocked to discover that Tom Thumb—or *Pulgarcito,* originally *Daumesdick*—the German fairy tale by the Brothers Grimm had been written in Kassel; they'd written it in a long-demolished house that once stood a few steps from where I was that very moment. It could be said that, instead of traveling to Kassel in search of the very center of contemporary art, I had actually traveled there to discover the exact place where the first story I'd ever heard in my life had been thought of and written down, the first of a series of tales I would go on to listen to over the course of many years.

You can't understand Tom Thumb's story without taking into account the terror or fear of getting lost. It was strange to see how that fear had just returned to me unexpectedly at dusk, sixty years after first discovering its existence.

My childhood fear had been summoned up as I left the hotel, as I walked along Friedrich-Ebert-Strasse toward my dinner with Chus. Although I already knew this fear of getting lost from the story of poor Tom Thumb, I remembered my discovery of the very essence of this fear one day in the summer of 1953, in a small coastal town north of Barcelona (a town with a long name, but known to everyone as Llavaneres). My grandfather's Swiss-style villa had been requisitioned as the Chilean Consulate during the Spanish Civil War. Later, the family recovered it, and in the fifties we spent all our summers there. In that town, on Sunday evenings, it was the custom for Barcelona families to go to the cinema. The first movie I went to see with my parents was a western. I don't remember the title or the plot. After all, I was only four years old. But I do remember, as if I were seeing it now, that we watched, up on the screen, the daily life of a happy family of farmers: an affectionate mother, an upright father, and a boy my age. Suddenly, normality was transformed by the appearance of a few strangers—later I would learn they were Cheyenne Indians—whose faces were painted and who wore feathers on their heads and communicated with one another using incomprehensible words; they were tremendously agitated, showing clear signs of hostility toward the poor, peaceful family of honorable white folks.

That unexpected incursion of the first alien people I ever saw in my life was etched in my memory, because up till then I'd never seen anyone who looked the slightest bit different from my own family. My terror undoubtedly arose from the discovery of true difference. In time, I would find out Nietzsche had said that fear is more beneficial for the general knowledge of human beings than love, for fear makes one want to find out who the other is, what it is that they want. And it's possible that's the way it is, I don't really know. But this distant memory of fear has always come along to warn me of the danger inherent in every first step one takes outside one's comfort zone, away from the familiar: that first step, which, if we don't pay attention, might just as easily leave us outside of a neighborhood association as outside a family circle of farmers in the American West, or just outside of everything. If one takes that first step into someone else's territory, one knows there will undoubtedly be, hidden, sometimes invisible, that sudden, first childhood fear. That fear we all discover in childhood, that terror of the inhospitable that I discovered one day in the summer of '53, when I saw, at first amazed, and then with the greatest panic, the alien world of the Cheyenne. The panic was accentuated by the fact that the Indians were speaking a strange language. It took me years to find out that their language wasn't so strange (it was Algonquin, after all). The name Cheyenne comes from the Sioux *sha hi'yena*; it wasn't so strange either, because it actually means "the people of alien speech."

Almost without noticing—caught up in the evocation of my first terrors—I passed the Königstor intersection and came to the second intersection, with the alleyway that provided a shortcut to Jordan-strasse (the street the Osteria restaurant was on). There wasn't a soul in the alleyway and, since I was remembering so many early fears, I proceeded with caution. I couldn't help but think that in badly lit side streets like this, surprises were always waiting; sometimes it was even pleasant in a solitary spot to feel a dry, icy breath on the back of your neck when it turned out nobody was there.

After so much indecision, in the end I passed through that little alleyway over to Jordanstrasse without the slightest problem or fear, perhaps because I went along absorbed in other thoughts, for I had begun to wonder what I would tell Chus about my time at the Dschingis Khan; I didn't know how to explain that, apart from a Catalan success story called Serra who'd first been cured in Hollywood and then been harmed in the *Sanatorium*, no other onlooker had come to see my "Chinese number," that is, to see how I wrote in public.

I was worried about what I was going to tell Chus. Ever since I was at school, I'd felt guilty about not doing my homework. I was also worried about the possibility of arriving at the Osteria and finding Boston there telling me that Chus couldn't make it but that, anyway, *she* was there, and *she* was actually Chus. Then I'd enter into a loop, into a new "Groundhog Day cycle," where everything repeats ceaselessly and pitilessly.

I was already seeing myself smiling like a poor fool, saying to Boston: "You're Chus, of course. You always were. What an idiot I am. I should have guessed, but I never learn."

54

I walked along the extremely dark Jordanstrasse toward the pale lights of the Osteria, the only illuminated place on the short street. And, making sure—almost like a blind man would—that I was now in front of the restaurant, I climbed the two big steps up to the porch leading to the entrance and decided to have a look from outside to see what the place was like inside. It was packed. Leaning my face against the big window, I saw Chus sitting there on the other side of the glass. It was her. The same person whose photo I'd seen on the Internet. There would not be a Groundhog Day or anything like that. It was Chus Martínez herself staring at me from inside the Osteria. She seemed to be saying: What are you looking at? Get off the damn porch and come in!

Whether it was from not having slept or from the constant impulse of my breeze, or from the delirium of having already had dinner before going out for dinner, which had generated an energy greater than I'd had two hours earlier, I felt increasingly outside myself, with a mental strength that gave me an unexpectedly enhanced audacity.

As a private joke, I went inside the Osteria as if I were Chinese, not like one who was finally finding a home along the way, but like a Chinese man simply going inside the Osteria for the first time with the word *Shanghai* written across his forehead. The way I walked in with my head bowed, I frightened myself, but at the same time I felt I was bringing the fiesta with me and that calmed me down. I greeted Chus, a kiss on each cheek, while I mumbled something about how nice, we meet at last, or something along those lines. I immediately saw that Chus didn't see me as Chinese, and I laughed, relaxed even more, and sat down across from her at the table. My private game was over. She was, as one might expect, a woman full of ideas, actually an unstoppable ideas machine, but also not lacking grace, a sense of humor, or beauty. And of course she was very self-confident. I found this charming and I also loved seeing that my state of mind almost couldn't be better, especially after I was seated.

"I hear you were a dramatic tenor," said Chus.

"Where did you get that from?"

Chus had managed to make me feel very confused. I wasn't even sure what a dramatic tenor was. Maybe it was a calculated phrase on her part to reduce my possible pretensions, perhaps it was a phrase intended to warn me that any protest on my part for having to spend useless hours in the Dschingis Khan would be given short shrift. Finally, it all became clear when she revealed that she knew I was fond of McGuffins, so that phrase about a dramatic tenor was just a McGuffin, a way of welcoming me. Had I lied, she said, and confirmed that in fact I had once been a dramatic tenor, the first minutes of our conversation could have constituted an exemplary McGuffin scenario.

A big laugh from Chus.

The menu was Italian—almost the spitting image of the one at the Trattoría Sackturm—not at all appetizing to me for the obvious reason: I had already eaten too much. Perhaps I gave too many explanations for my complete lack of appetite, when a simple excuse would have been enough. Probably so she wouldn't have to hear all my justifications, Chus interrupted me to point out a nearby table where some friends of hers were eating. They all waved in unison with icy British and Germanic affability. I got the feeling that she'd be joining them as soon as our dinner had finished. That struck me as perfect, since it would facilitate my early withdrawal to my "thinking cabin" (in which I'd barely managed to concentrate enough to think, because I seemed to truly ponder things only when I was outside of it).

In those first minutes, waiting for the tortellini alla panna, the single dish we finally decided to order—my first nonmelancholy night in a long time was well on its way to being a great night of Italian pasta—I reminded Chus of our brief phone conversation the previous day, and we went back to talking about Barcelona, of the horror the city inspired in us, every day more stifled for a thousand reasons, especially by the mediocrity of a truly inept political class.

I don't remember how we got onto the subject of art, which for Chus was not a question of aesthetics or taste, but of knowledge. There were some things, she said, that produced knowledge and others that did not. In Kassel, I had seen things that hadn't struck me as so aesthetically pleasing but that had brought me knowledge, hadn't they? Indeed, I said, and I noticed, by the way, that there were very few people who were, say, architects, urban planners, or commercial film directors here. Exactly, said Chus, no neuroscientists, but there were biologists, philosophers, quantum physicists, that is, people who went in search of knowledge, creative people operating on the least practical side of life, people trying to invent a new world. I wanted to believe I was one of them, which gave me a certain sense of security. From that moment on, everything I said to her was with the conviction—reinforced by my increasingly supernatural enthusiasm, I can't find a better adjective—of one looking to invent a new world.

We talked about the difficulty Spaniards had accepting art without a message, accepting literature without the necessarily humanist touch or a communist dimension. Spanish realist literature, Chus said, was pre-Manet, that's why she'd left the country, really, she couldn't take it anymore; the economic crisis had served as an excuse to revive the same old, early twentieth-century naturalism. What obstinacy, insisting on reproducing what already exists!

I noticed it was hard to say which of the two of us was the more fervent enthusiast. I'd arrived there in a great mood, but Chus's vitality, her desire to have an influence on every point, every angle of the art world, did nothing but get me even more revved up. And, in the middle of so much animation—conversing with Chus was very strange, because it was as if we'd spent our whole lives talking like this—I don't know how it was that she asked me something about the world, I think she wanted to know how I saw it.

That question caught me completely off guard. At that moment, I was thinking of the incredible amount of sleep I had to catch up on and how my fear had begun to inspire the joy that was now my traveling companion. It was logical that this should alarm me because on one occasion of great fulfillment and unbridled happiness, on one warm afternoon in the past, after a great seaside feast by the Mediterranean, I'd felt this unique moment so strongly, I'd thought of committing a theatrical suicide along the lines of Heinrich von Kleist's, which he'd staged like a play. It was as if I already knew—I do know now, but didn't so much back then—that early Romanticism was the only beautiful Romanticism: mad, imaginative, rapturous, and profound. The fact is, I thought a death by my own hand would allow me to never get away from the ecstatic beauty of that powerful afternoon: a ridiculous beauty, because after lunching copiously that day, at the very moment I thought of killing myself I was tasting a melon.

"How do I see what?"

"The world," said Chus.

It seemed as if she had realized perfectly well that I was Piniowsky. She was almost handing me my answer on a silver platter.

"I no longer think anything of the world, Chus. Nothing at all. It's perished."

"Really, nothing?"

"I think I've become like Marcus Aurelius. He announced one day that he had stopped having any sort of opinion about anything whatsoever."

"Then you don't have an opinion about me, either?"

I noticed again that with her excessive enthusiasm, she might be playing another dirty trick on me. I sensed that with my Marcus Aurelius quote I'd made a fool of myself. An avant-garde author like I claimed to be would never quote someone like that. Or was it the reverse? Wasn't it very avant-garde not to be intimidated by a classic? Besides, Marcus Aurelius had written *Meditations*, and that went beyond the classification between classic and modern …

I calmed down when she wittily summoned up the figure of Petronius, who, she said, reminded her—admitting an unmissable disparity—of *my* Marcus Aurelius.

Petronius, said Chus, one day told Nero that he was ever so sorry but he was totally fed up hearing him recite his "doggerel verses, wretched poems of the suburbs" and also seeing his "Domitian belly." Of course, after such interesting words, Petronius committed suicide.

Well, yes, I said to Chus, when I think of the world, I no longer think anything about it. I'm tired, even tired of having to see the world's deplorable belly of a Domitilo. Domitius, Chus corrected me. Of a Domitius, I said. And then she wanted to know what I'd seen of interest so far in Documenta. I immediately started talking to her about Sehgal's *This Variation* and how much it had impressed me. I was so emphatic that Chus was on the verge of not believing me. But I finally managed to get her to see that the sparkle of the authentic was in my words, I was not deceiving her. And then Chus, more relaxed, said that, regarding Sehgal, she was more than convinced we needed other voices in art, because what we'd been hearing for a long time, she said, were monotonous repetitions of things we already knew. What was urgent was inspiration from ideas, an energy that was different …

"An impulse," I hastened to say.

Never in my life had I said anything with such assurance, such self-confidence, with such happiness. And it seemed to me that the word sounded smooth, like a whipcrack. It began to expand with potential in the night, inviting us to flee down paths without logic. And for a moment—it felt like forever—I thought the word "impulse" was more than a single thing racing down those logic-less paths. Expanding, its physical magnitude was greater than the plain old, succinctly dry impulse—that is, the single run-of-the-mill impulse inhabiting our dictionaries. Newton had given it its second sense and opened a new door, and now whoever desired could bask in the glory of this new type of impulse, so different from the one known up till then.

55

"There is a logic to be changed," said Chus in her unique way of talking. "If you are feeling that you're being pushed and have been for hours by an invisible impulse, which you consider neither normal nor Newtonian, what you have to think is that you're in the grip of the *third* sense of impulse."

And somewhat later:

"I don't think people have any problem with art; in general they don't have any problem with culture. It's politics that creates the problem, it doesn't really know what culture is. When there's no money, people simply treat it as if it were an added extra, no? And that is the logic that needs to be changed. If artists are intellectuals, then obviously they're not a luxury, they're a necessity, they can change our lives. And today more than ever we need other voices, because the ones we're hearing just tediously repeat what we've been hearing all our lives. What we need are new ideas, a different energy. We need to listen to those who are formulating something new and trust them and say: 'Okay, maybe I don't fully understand you, but I believe in what you're proposing, at least it sounds different.' We have to give opportunities to those who've been silenced and to the insane, to tell them to carry on, to not look at them with mistrust and cynicism or with an air of having seen it all before. That's precisely what we've lost; we believe that it's all been done before, refusing to see that there is still ingenious, complex, wise art that pushes our limits. We need to *listen* to artists. Never before has it been so necessary as in our time. Artists are the opposite of politicians. Do you remember Flaubert's letter about going to the palace to see Prince Napoleon, but he'd gone out? I've heard how they talk about politics, writes Flaubert, I've listened to them and it's something immense. Human stupidity is so vast and infinite!"

56

For a while, as I was eating my tortellini, we got marvelously caught up in Chus's idea that art was essentially thought more than experience, which led her to conclude that artists should play a fundamental role in our society, as should poets, if art and poetry weren't the same thing. As for politicians, they all came off looking really bad.

It was perhaps the key moment, the most fascinating of my trip, because I noticed how her words were gradually restoring a lost atmosphere from my past, a former climate of rupture with conventional art, a way of considering things that I'd almost forgotten. It was as if I were reencountering what I would enjoy encountering most, my inner truth. It was a truth, however, that I'd been constructing on the basis of four initial misunderstandings. Maybe that's why many of my past mistakes began to file through my mind and I remembered the supposed avant-gardist I was for years and dreamed of being, as well as my yearning to go beyond provincial rupturism.

I remembered when I was barely twenty, I randomly wanted to be like the cineaste Philippe Garrel, who visited Barcelona for a showing of some of his underground movies at the Filmoteca. Garrel's "sad young man" appearance and his very radical attitude toward art attracted me. Back then, unknowingly, what so fascinated me about my contemporary's pained figure was the romanticism emanating from everything that he did and said; in fact, he was—though I didn't know it at the time—Romanticism itself in its purest and most original form: that of its beginnings, when that movement, that "odyssey of the German spirit," was the first of all vanguards (though its followers didn't gather under that emblem since the word had only a military meaning back then). These followers invented Literature as we now know it, also inventing the cult of genius (in which life sprang forth in freedom and developed with creative force), an outrageous cult to the so-called geniuses of vigor, who took the stage to announce what ended up being called *vanguardismo* many years later: Jakob Michael Reinhold Lenz playing the fool, Friedrich Maximilian Von Klinger showing off by devouring a piece of raw horsemeat, Cristoph Kaufmann sitting down at the duke's table bare-chested to his belly button, his hair a mess, with a colossal knotty walking stick … I was, unknowingly, an heir to Garrel, who in turn, also unknowingly, was an heir to Kaufmann and company. But if someone had spoken to me of Klinger or Kaufmann in those days I wouldn't have understood, apart from the description "geniuses of vigor."

When I was most absorbed in German avant-garde inventions of a now -distant century, Chus suddenly asked me if I'd seen anything else in Documenta apart from the dark and brilliant work of Sehgal. Luckily, I reacted in time. Of course I'd seen other things, I said. Essentially I was there to be a wanderer; I considered myself Documenta's rambler. That's what I said, and I told her that the invitation to Kassel had reminded me of another that had made me happy years ago, a proposal that came from Yvette Sánchez that I should be— and I was—the official rambler of the Basel Book Fair. In Kassel, as I walked around what seemed to me more and more like a huge estate full of oddities, I felt like the rambler in *Locus Solus*, that profoundly leisurely, erratic, perplexed wanderer, the inexhaustible visitor to the estate where Martial Canterel would show anyone around who wanted to see the strange inventions collected there.

Of course I'd seen other works, I said, I'd seen lots and in all of them I'd found ideas that connected me to an exceptional creative energy. In Huyghe's impressive *Untilled*, I thought I saw that only art in the margins and distanced from galleries and museums could really be innovative and present something different. I said I was planning to spend the night there in that installation, in the middle of the landscape of humus with an Ibizan hound with one pink leg.

Naturally, hearing my plan, Chus looked up from her plate and stared at me, as if trying to guess whether I was truly insane. I wasn't at all crazy. In fact, I was thinking of something Chus had said in an interview I'd read on the Internet: Documenta was not a traditional exhibition; it was not just for looking at, it could also *be lived*, something that could be visibly inferred from quite a few of the installations, such as that created by Pierre Huyghe with his surprising intervention.

I've observed, she said, that you speak seriously and jokingly at the same time. That's true, I said, but you'd do well to take it all seriously.

I'd announced I'd be spending the night out in the open, beside the statue with the built-in beehive for a head. I couldn't back down now. Actually, I'd announced it to her so I'd have no choice but to carry it out. As soon as dinner was over and Chus went to sit with her friends at another table (which she surely must have been eager to do by then), I would try to transfer my "thinking cabin" to the freedom of the open air in a corner of *Untilled*; it would be my way of paying homage to a hypothetical art of the outskirts of the outskirts.

It might be a strange experience to spend the night in an installation I considered very odd and which must be even more so in deep darkness. I saw myself out there at the mercy of the elements, following the pink-legged Spanish dog's progress. At the same time, I imagined traveling by balloon in those nocturnal hours as Robert Walser once did toward an abyss of frost and stars. Would I be scared? What would I see? Would I be alone or would I discover that at night the place filled with secret conspirators from the world of the outskirts of the outskirts of art? Would I manage to travel a very long way while essentially staying right where I was?

Chus didn't want to say that spending the night with the pink-legged dog was a bad idea. She simply asked me if I'd seen Scorsese's film *George Harrison: Living in the Material World*. In it, she said, you could see lots of thinking cabins, though in the form of "transcendental meditations." I hadn't seen it, I said, but I'd stumbled upon many things in Kassel that had dazzled me. I thought she'd want to know which ones, but she didn't ask. Like someone downing a shot of vodka without thinking about it, Chus suddenly dropped a question, maybe the question I would have most liked not to be asked, since I didn't have a suitable answer for her.

"I almost forgot. How's it going at the Chinese restaurant?"

The color and expression of my face changed. And I was more Piniowsky than ever.

Luckily, when I started to tell her something, I saw that she was not overly interested in my reply. In fact, she'd turned her face away and started exchanging signals with her friends at the nearby table. When she finally turned to look at me, she encountered my absolute Piniowsky face. She must have grasped my immense distress and taken pity on me because she suddenly started talking about hammocks strung between palm trees and the sounds of coconuts falling. She was talking about Gino Paoli songs and bathing suits and deserted beaches, salty breezes and love stories, and what was always, she said, hidden in the middle of the invincible summer.

57

When dinner was over, I said goodbye and went out onto the dark Jordanstrasse. Chus stayed with her friends, but I had the impression that her eyes possessed a strange power and were somehow binoculars, allowing her to see beyond the restaurant. If so, she was surely following me with her long-distance gaze and not planning to stop until she saw that, retracing my earlier steps, I'd turned into the dark alley leading to Friedrich-Ebert-Strasse.

I remembered for a moment that a friend had wondered in his latest novel whether *acting out* life was the only way to live it and if life were less true when it was performed. Those questions came to mind at the very moment I left the Osteria. I think it was because there wasn't a soul on the street. I observed that I wasn't going to be seen by a single human eye for a while, so I began to speculate that Chus might be following my steps with her binocular gaze. Then I began to act—literally to act—for Chus, as if I were sure she was observing what I was doing. It was possibly my only way of not feeling so alone. I reaffirmed once more the great truth that we need to feel we are seen by someone, since the opposite is insufferable.

Acting for Chus in the deserted streets, I felt that life was more intense when one put on a performance, for everything seemed to take on more importance, even if I just perceived someone following my steps on the big stage. Just as I approached art to turn my back on the world, it seemed to me that dramatizing my own life, my footsteps in the dark, was a way to intensify the sensation of being alive, that is, one more way of making art.

Initially, my performance leaving the Osteria consisted of simulating being undecided about whether or not to retrace my exact steps, turning again into the shortcut of the dark and lonely alley, or taking the well-lit street in front of the restaurant that also led to Friedrich-Ebert-Strasse.

These doubts I pretended to have didn't last long, because I quickly chose to take the well-lit street. The other option—retracing my steps—was shameful, because it would be acting like any old Tom Thumb who'd left a trail of crumbs so as not to get lost on his way home.

I went up the slope of the well-lit street and, arriving at Friedrich-Ebert-Strasse, turned right expecting to find myself, after a few steps, passing the same places I'd seen before. But instead of finding them, I ran straight into the illuminated foyer of the Gloria Cinema, which disconcerted and unnerved me, making me think I was lost. Hadn't I been wondering a few hours earlier where that cinema was and why I hadn't seen it when I'd tramped around practically the whole downtown? Well, there it was. There was the added danger of running into Nené again, for this was where I was meant to meet her at midnight, though most likely she wouldn't show up.

Probably, somewhere just past the Gloria Cinema, were the shops and businesses of Friedrich-Ebert-Strasse that I'd seen on my way out, so I kept walking, leaving behind the cinema that held within it a certain danger. I kept walking, but I didn't come to any of those stores and eventually I had the sensation of beginning to travel back to my childhood terrors, as if the story of Tom Thumb (*Daumesdick*) had projected its long shadow over my adult footsteps.

In other words, I was lost. I ended up making the difficult and humiliating decision—humiliating in my eyes at least and probably also to anyone who might be watching me through binoculars—to turn back, to return literally to the front porch of the Osteria and, once back there, this time singing Tom Thumb's song, begin the walk over again using the shortcut of the alley.

In about four minutes I got back to the porch of the Osteria and, though it was not at all necessary, I peered in the window to see what Chus was doing at that moment. She had sat down, as was to be expected, with her friends, and it looked like she was having another dinner. This is the night of the double dinners, I thought. Chus didn't see me, but I believe one of her friends did, at least he reacted in a way that made me think I'd been spotted. I was so embarrassed at having been discovered there with my nose pressed up against the window that I shot off the porch, straight to the alley, happy for a moment knowing I was going the right way this time.

It was admirable to observe how, through all that, the *third* sense of impulse hadn't abandoned me. I overacted as I went down the alley, as if I thought Chus would be interested in watching my second attempt to get back to the hotel through her binoculars. But when I saw two young people suddenly burst out of one of the alley's doorways in animated conversation, I felt less inclined to care about my own drama and more inclined to protect my own life. Those strangers, with their laughter and exaggerated liveliness, deserved to be looked on with total distrust. But they walked quickly off into the night, both with their hands behind their backs. They were inoffensive, just laughing at their own business. Even so, I was aware of the risk of walking around unprotected and I modified my will to exist as a performer. I stopped playing my solitary role and started concentrating on what I was doing, trying not to get lost anymore.

I reached the end of the alleyway and stepped out again onto Friedrich-Ebert-Strasse, walking down it, finally past familiar scenery, toward the hotel. It was somewhat frustrating that no one else could be seen on the streets; I would have preferred to cross paths with someone who would at least look at me. I was very happy in any case. My childhood fears had vanished, and with them the Brothers Grimm's great Tom Thumb. Though I felt physically exhausted, mentally I kept going, to the point where, when I passed the door of my hotel, I didn't stop but kept walking in the direction of Friedrichsplatz. I crossed it fifteen minutes later at a serene pace, especially as I passed by Horst Hoheisel's reproduction of the old fountain funded by the Jewish businessman Sigmund Aschrott. I ambled along, entering Karlsaue Park without the slightest fear. At that hour, the park wasn't exactly teeming with people, but there were still quite a few strolling around.

I tried to encourage myself as much as possible by thinking I was about to encounter a brand-new experience in my life, but I couldn't stop wondering if it wasn't absurd that, despite how much mental energy I felt, I wouldn't have rather retired to my hotel room.

It was odd to have chosen this pilgrimage to the most sordid spot in the park. Sordid? Perhaps it was, but I sensed that Huyghe's contribution was one of the high points of that Documenta, since among other things it had the virtue of not wearing thin in a single visit; it was an installation that was open to all sorts of interpretations. After seeing it for the first time, a person was left with the memory of a strange harmony between the animate and the inanimate. Maybe that's what I had wanted to see there. I was sure that the mystery of that place was endless. It had been accompanying me since María Boston had shown it to me.

I don't know when I started passing fewer people and walking more and more slowly through the park, as if reluctant to arrive at *Untilled*, reluctant just when I'd decided that all that dug-over land (where an Ibizan hound with one leg painted pink prowled around) was practically my promised land.

After walking for a good stretch and passing near Anri Sala's oblique *Clocked Perspective*, I approached the big greenhouse where Jimmie Durham had sited *The History of Europe*: a work that, seen from outside, seemed to consist only of two lumps of stone, each deposited in a glass display case in the very center of the immense space of that giant heated greenhouse.

In the middle of the night, unable to enter the warm enclosure, I found it difficult to understand what kind of history those two stones were telling. A metal plaque, found by chance as I was leaving, allowed me to discover that the rocks were in reality Neanderthal remains, indicating that Europeans had identity issues: for ever since they were invaded by the Romans, they'd thought they were Occidentals and Orientals were people in Asia. However, the plaque said, the most ancient finds of Neanderthal remains—like those two sleeping there in the gigantic greenhouse—had been discovered in Georgia, which forced us to rethink everything.

When I got tired of looking at the Neanderthal remains and pondering the history of Europe, which was happening more and more in my Kassel itinerary, I continued my walk through the park and sat down under the oblique clock with the idea of having a rest. In the meantime, I asked myself if I really considered it necessary to get as far as *Untilled*, or if I could turn around and go back to the hotel, where, though sleep might collapse my great mood, it might also do me a lot of good.

I had doubts about whether or not I should go as far as *Untilled* because to get to the area of disturbed earth I had to go into an even denser, leafier zone of Karlsaue Park, an area that, no matter how lively I might be feeling, instilled a certain respect at night. For the last five minutes or so I'd detected no signs of human life, and that whole pilgrimage seemed to have something of an "end-of-the-trail" feel to it, *finis terrae* …

There was a strange peace, seemingly resulting from the absence of the loudspeakers that during the day disseminated the uproar of the bombings of *FOREST (for a thousand years…)*. It was very peaceful and I didn't know if it would be worth going to the enigmatic calm of *Untilled*, which I was increasingly seeing as my personal Manderley. Everything in it reminded me of the atmosphere of the famous opening scene of Hitchcock's film *Rebecca*: "Last night I dreamt I went to Manderley again.... The drive wound away in front of me, twisting and turning as it had always done, but as I advanced I was aware that a change had come upon it. Nature had come into her own again and, little by little, in her stealthy, insidious way had encroached upon the drive with long, tenacious fingers. On and on wound the poor thread that once had been our drive. And finally, there was Manderley, our Manderley, secretive and silent as it had always been ..."

Untilled was also arrived at by a winding path, which hadn't worried me in daylight, but I guessed it might cause me some problems visiting at that hour, for there was a slight mist and the moon wasn't casting much light. Finally I decided to risk it. After all, I said to myself, I hadn't gone that far to turn back at the last moment. I remembered reading that Huyghe was constantly anxious about forces we so often know are lurking in the fog, the smoke, the clouds. Had I not always had this anxiety too? I'd had less anxiety about clouds than about fog or smoke, but that didn't prevent me from thinking of the words of the aviator Daniele Del Giudice in *Takeoff: The Pilot's Lore*: "Remember that beneath the sea of clouds there is nothing but eternity."

Some of my fictions start, or end up, in cloudy or misty lands, in Manderleys of the spirit, in extraordinarily secretive and silent places. In these fictions, there are misty nights in port cities like Detroit, thick fog through which a solitary hero glides until finally entering a bar.

I was going toward *Untilled* in the hazy night, walking with cautious steps toward that strange territory. Deep down, I felt that traveling toward Huyghe's uncultivated place was turning out to be like moving toward a certain atmosphere of my own fictions. More than that, perhaps I was moving toward pages I hadn't yet written; it was like traveling toward the future without seeing anything.

I tried to turn my way of walking into a performance as well, as if Chus's binoculars could see me where I was and I thought she might be pleased by her image of me as a one-eyed metaphysical excursionist in an interminable, sinuous ascent.

When I arrived at the threshold of *Untilled* territory, the first thing I tried to find out was whether there was anyone else in that sordid place. There wasn't. I was as alone there as Robinson on his island. That shifting earth would probably have to wait some hours before another man's foot would leave a print in it. Neither of the dogs was there. Really, it was to be expected, Documenta couldn't expose itself to the risk that someone might steal those animals. I'd reached the place and didn't actually have anything to do there; I could have left. But I immediately thought that would be turning my back on uncertainty and I stayed. I absolutely didn't have to worry about being bored, I thought, I could be well occupied all night just wondering, for example, what kinds of things God had got up to before He created the world.

58

I sat down on one of the piled-up logs, in a corner of *Untilled*, beside the chunks of reinforced concrete. I was aware that what I was doing was a bit crazy or, to put it a better way, illogical. But my state of euphoria was *in crescendo*, and I felt in marvelous harmony with almost everything in Kassel. Almost everything bewitched me, exactly at the time when I should have been laid completely low by my anguish. My contact with contemporary art, or whatever it was that had achieved that miracle, had left me in an extraordinary state, though I had no doubt that, sooner or later, I'd return to my habitual nighttime melancholy; that was the way it had to be. Otherwise, without that sadness that hit me every evening, I'd be nothing.

Hidden in the moonlit woods, the last conspirator of a dream on dug-over land, I slowly and treacherously whispered the song that said that to get out of the forest, we had to get out of Europe, but to get out of Europe, we had to get out of the forest. I thought I discovered that without the two dogs at that hour, the environment of decomposition—possibly a metaphor for our cultural decomposition—lost some of its force. The night was infinitely more powerful than that environment.

I looked for the little mound of rubble on which I'd seen the young blonde German woman announcing the news of the death of Europe. When I thought I'd found it, I looked up toward the starry canopy that I felt was the only thing that could really accompany me in my solitude. And though at that moment I didn't remember his name (Brian Schmidt), the Australian astronomer came to mind who had discovered, along with other colleagues, that, fourteen billion years after the Big Bang, the universe was accelerating, not slowing down, all owing, perhaps, to a dark energy, just as was happening with my mood, which I felt to be accelerating all the time, pleasantly unstoppable, as if my interest in everything kept expanding, and, because of this—possibly because of this dark energy—I couldn't close my eyes, thus perhaps confirming what that friend had said: it is night's own essence that keeps us from sleeping.

I wasn't at all uncomfortable in spite of being in a place that normally would have struck me as terrifying. I had a thought for that astronomer, who said he was exploring the very frontier of knowledge, penetrating the new and, therefore, daring to commit errors. As if I were the actual astronomer, playing at what I imagined that Australian did when he was alone with the stars, I began to pose to myself a problem, which I was obviously not the first person in the world ever to pose.

A question I wouldn't know how to classify, whether philosophical, logical, Cartesian, mathematical ... it consisted of wondering if one could prove what one stated. For example, one might look toward the nearby statue of a reclining woman on a pedestal beside a puddle and state the following in a moderately loud voice: "On the face of the statue on the pedestal there are bees."

So far all was going well, but the trouble began when I asked myself what form my verification might take. Would a quick look from various different angles suffice, or did I have to touch the beehive that took the place of the statue's face with my hands, then touch the pedestal, and so on? Here were two ways of considering the matter. One said that, even if I put my mind to it, I'd never be able to completely verify my proposition, because deep down, a back door was always kept open, an uncontrollable flight, and the possibility remained that one might be mistaken. Another view said: "If I could never completely verify what I'd stated, then I didn't mean anything by the proposition either. Therefore, it meant absolutely nothing."

I didn't know what to go with. Even though I knew I was obsessing too much over the matter, I posed the question to myself again, this time changing the proposition:

"I am sitting on a log at night."

Then I asked myself how I could *verify* that. Was a glance at the log enough, or did I have to touch it with my hands, checking that it could serve as firewood in the winter, and so on? Here, two ways of considering the matter opened up again, the same two that had become apparent with the statue beside the puddle.

I spent a long, very active time pretending to be an astronomer who, instead of looking at the stars, posed this problem to himself. It was perfect to play at something so illogical in a city like Kassel, which did not invite logic. It was not very connected to logic, for it demanded that the invited creators operate within the avant-garde parameters of a high-grade madness.

I remembered my last visit to the wonderful city of Turin in northern Italy. I'd been struck by how contained and elegant that place was—actually a French city, due to the long shadow of the House of Savoy. Etched in my memory was the serenity of its daily life, which one sensed as a dangerous creator of unexpected absurdities or impressive outbreaks of madness, like Friedrich Nietzsche's, when in January 1889 he left his hotel and on the corner of Via Cesare Battisti and Via Carlo Alberto, sobbing, hugged the neck of a horse being whipped by its owner. That day an unstable border broke open for Nietzsche, which had seemed to separate rationality from delirium for several centuries. That day, the writer distanced himself definitively from humanity, however you want to look at it. To put it more simply, he went crazy; although according to Milan Kundera, maybe he was just apologizing to the horse for Descartes.

The great Italo Calvino, Turinese by adoption, saw in this perfect, geometric city an invitation to logic. "Turin is a city that entices a writer toward vigor, linearity, style," he wrote. "It invites logic, and through logic opens the way toward madness."

In Kassel, I thought, something different was happening. The city invited illogicality, opening the way toward an unknown logic.

I spent many hours reflecting on how to verify various propositions. I no longer know how many hours I spent completely entertained by this game. The subject of verifications came to an end after I put forward a proposition that demonstrated that mathematics was either inconsistent or not entirely complete.

"I am an indemonstrable truth," I said to myself.

Just by saying this, I had the impression I had ruined the prestige of mathematics, the formal science that, starting with axioms and following logical reasoning, studied the properties and connections of abstract entities.

If I was an indemonstrable truth, mathematics wasn't what it was purported to be—it wasn't the superior language, the language of God, as some call it.

A few hours went by before I finished off mathematics and began to feel my mind distorted by unwanted interference; I became intimidated—I find this word very fitting—by a rare chinoiserie: the torturous story featuring two tsetse flies of Pekinese origin, a nightmarish tale undoubtedly proceeding from the impact—I wasn't so aware of it at the time—the vision, hours earlier, of those two minuscule, sleep-inducing insects I'd seen trapped in the Fridericianum in a gigantic display case.

That Chinese tale—a sort of dream that was putting me to sleep—was probably caused by my own weariness (generator sometimes of the most incredible nightmares). In the end, I gave in to the tsetse pressure and nodded off. The time flew by, and when I came to my senses, the first thing I saw—I thought I was still in my dream—was the docile, pink-legged dog at my side. Totally confused, I attributed the vision, the whole dream, to the proximity of the Dschingis Khan, which after all was very close, right behind Huyghe's territory, on the edge of the park, beside the Fulda River.

I realized it was getting light and I had somehow managed to live and dream on the outskirts of the outskirts of art, like a secret conspirator in the Kassel night. In spite of the two tsetse flies seriously tormenting me, I felt a certain pride in what I'd achieved: staying so long in such a difficult place hardly designed for nocturnal use. As for the dog, I ended up seeing it was the real one, she was really there, alive and well, wagging her tail.

I touched her.

"The dog is an indemonstrable truth," I said.

I observed that she was still there, indifferent to what I was saying, converted into an immovable, indemonstrable, immutable truth: a truth that, being a dog, moved.

59

And the other dog, the less media-friendly one? Just as I was wondering that, the caretaker of the two animals appeared. He wasn't just in charge of the dogs; he kept the forces of nature in harmony, in that complex but balanced territory, all in a tense equilibrium.

He spoke French and had a shaved head with an impressive diagonal scar; his ferocious appearance contrasted with his affable character. He'd been sleeping, he told me, in a hut nearby, with the two dogs. He'd been staying there since Documenta started, prudently taking the dogs in each evening when it got dark.

Was I there to steal the dog with the pink leg? I didn't know if he was serious or joking. The question offended me, I said. Imperturbable, he asked the same question again. It's my duty to know these things, he said, the hound has many admirers. I asked: If I had come to steal her, what would happen? I asked him. You're pretty old to be doing things like that, he replied. I'd put your head in the beehive and the bees would do away with your urge to take the hound home. I don't have a home, I said, just a cabin, but I don't sleep there because I can't think inside it. I'm not sure he completely understood these last words, spoken in my broken French. He looked at me first with profound astonishment and then with contempt.

The hound seemed to get bored with our conversation and went for a walk around the territory. I was observing her closely, and at first she actually managed to surprise me with her apparently infinite eagerness for all smells. When she found something that caught her attention—always an enigma for me, because I couldn't understand what was so alluring in what she was smelling—her snout stuck to it with absolutely amazing obstinacy, with such anxious, frenzied enthusiasm, the rest of the world seemed to have stopped existing for her.

The dog was like a little Piniowsky. Obstinately interested in everything and prisoner of a great enthusiasm for whatever crossed her path, she seemed ready at any moment to ignore the whole damned world. I reached the conclusion that she was enjoying herself and that was all there was to it. She seemed to be living on a permanent high, lost in a nasal nirvana that she couldn't detach from.

60

The caretaker seemed obsessed with keeping other people's affections away from his hound.

Suddenly, he came over and started to tell me a story.

"Once," said the caretaker, "I took a night train from Paris to Milan. I traveled in one of those classic compartments they used to have, those little four-man pigsties. In Paris there were only three of us. One of the passengers was a curly-haired young man with a parrot in a cage that said 'Je t'aime, je t'aime' to him every once in a while. The little creature seemed to know only this one phrase. When it came time to turn off the light in the compartment, the young man put a pink cover over the cage and told me that he'd had a similar parrot before but had to get rid of it because it refused to say loving words to him, which had led him to discover that he wasn't loved. What a drama, I commented. I had to do away with him, he said. And while he gave me horrible details of how he'd suffocated the bird, the murdered parrot's successor—now hidden under the cover—punctuated the story every once in a while by saying 'Je t'aime, je t'aime.'

"In the middle of the night, the train stopped and a fourth passenger boarded who was very careful not to wake the rest of us and politely got undressed quietly in the darkness. All of a sudden, when the fourth traveler had just lain down in his berth, the voice of the enamored parrot rang out again through the whole compartment, from the depths of his hiding place: '*Je t'aime, je t'aime*.'

"The next morning, when we arrived in Milan and the young man took the cover off his pet, I asked if I could take a photo of the two of them: the enamored parrot and his owner. I took a Polaroid and later showed it to my girlfriend in Milan, so she'd see I hadn't invented anything in my story. In spite of having such conclusive photographic proof, my girlfriend refused to believe me. That's crazy. You're always making stuff up, she said, sounding very disappointed."

Once he'd told this story, the ferocious-looking, funny caretaker began to walk away. Had he divulged that story to tell me that he was enamored of his hound and recommend I mustn't try to come between them?

I let my gaze wander among the hallucinogenic plants and the frog pond and then turned away fearlessly, flippantly, toward the lunacy of the morning light.

All the signs of a great morning were in front of me, by which I mean, it would be ideal not to overlook any of them. However, I ended up confining my grand panoramic view to go to observe some minuscule spyglasses I could see on top of a tower that seemed to be situated even beyond the remotest distance.

61

Was Chus keeping an eye on me from high windows? Was she really spending her time spying on my attempt—my secret, perhaps my only, contribution of real interest to Documenta—at turning time into space? Did I really believe that she had picked up on my desire to spend the night in the territory of putrefaction called *Untilled* because, once immersed in this disconsolate chronicle of universal history (that process of incessant decomposition), I would escape from history and try to restore the timelessness of paradise? Had Chus discovered that I saw *Untilled* as a paradise, which could be something difficult for any sensible person to accept? Had she guessed from the high windows that I was trying to merge my life with the environment? Did she know I believed that in time you could only be yourself, while in space you could become someone else? Did she know that it seemed to me time didn't give us much of a chance, that it only knew how to send dry, icy breaths on the backs of our necks in fascinating alleyways? Space seemed wide and full of possibilities, where logic, out of pure logic, always lost its footing.

Thinking about all this, I smiled. How could I imagine that from high windows Chus was spying with binoculars on my tranquil frame of mind in that far-flung corner of Karlsaue?

The smile stayed on my face for a long time, until I saw that for the umpteenth time, the hound was going toward the puddle near the statue with a beehive for a head, and I noticed a soft sound that was difficult to locate, a noise that seemed to be trying to give me a clue to help me decipher the intangible, the incomprehensible aspects of that territory.

The intangible? I kept my eye on the dog, who had gone toward the statue as if she'd guessed that I was buzzing with ideas and I desired to disorganize the insufferable order of the bees. I discovered that the slight but insistent sound was coming from the big puddle: from a tiny red toy boat that had been abandoned by some child the previous day. As it rolled on the water, it emitted a sad moan, perhaps mistakenly trying to provide a complete coded key to that mysterious place.

Perhaps that noise formed part of the secret history of *Untilled*'s territory. But I didn't want to investigate it, preferring to concentrate on Tino Sehgal's idea that art goes by like life. Did we not yet know how to see that life and art were walking together forming a unity, just as we experienced, for example, in *This Variation*? I was thinking about that when I started wondering where the caretaker of the dogs was at that moment. He was nowhere to be found, he'd disappeared; maybe he'd thrown himself into his work now that he knew I wasn't planning to run off with his hound.

That pink-legged dog seemed increasingly persistent about the puddle. Helped greatly by the first light of the day, I focused my concentration on the territory (mine again, momentarily) and observed the perfect harmony between the different elements that composed the, let's say, "very difficult" space called *Untitled*. In a short time I came to the conclusion that Huyghe's whole intervention was a sort of brilliant synthesis of what was in this Documenta. I remembered something Boston had told me. Huyghe had been a member of Documenta's "honorary advisory committee," which took part in preparations for the grand exhibition, and this probably brought him close to the works that would be shown, and possibly everything influenced him, making his participation very special, for in fact, according to Huyghe himself, without realizing it he had absorbed the projects of all the other artists. "Encountering many works being created gives a certain energy to your own; it's stimulating," Huyghe had said.

As soon as I knew that Huyghe had said this, I thought with an obvious sense of humor—admitting the unmissable disparity—that something very similar had occurred to me at Documenta. It was beyond doubt that, since I'd arrived in Kassel—surely thanks to the *third* sense of the impulse, the indirect effects of "the push" from Ryan Gander's invisible breeze—absorbing everything had given me an absolutely unheard-of creative energy and enthusiasm, and had even left me feeling happy at my habitually melancholy time of day.

Kassel had infected me with creativity, enthusiasm, a short-circuiting of rational language. Moments and discontinuities had me searching for meaning where there was no logic in order to create new worlds.

Maybe so much optimism was due to the fact that there in Kassel I'd recovered the best memories from my beginnings as an artist, as well as my admiration for those who had made writing their destiny: Kafka, Mallarmé, Joyce, Michaux, those for whom life was barely conceivable outside of literature, who made literature with their lives.

María Boston had also told me that being on the advisory committee had allowed Huyghe, in his own words, "to understand Documenta as the coexistence of thoughts, not all necessarily subjugated to theory and not all anthropocentric."

A unique, memorable spot—that Manderley of my spirit would be difficult to forget. While I was saying this to myself and thinking how life and art went by at the same time, the dog, tired of the puddle, came over to where I was, and for a few minutes the poor animal and I became inseparable. We even came to compose, in those first rays of the day's light, a single lonely, tragic figure, the way a bull and torero sometimes fit together in the most celebrated bullfights. And the curious thing was that the dog seemed to tune in with what I was feeling; her mood also seemed to be in a state of constant expansion. Dogs may not always understand the nuances of thought of the humans they make friends with, but they feel what they feel, and in this case there was no doubt that the pink-legged dog was with me, participating in my discreet but profoundly euphoric mood.

The caretaker reappeared all of a sudden and with him the other dog, and in a few tenths of a second the hound betrayed me and went off with them to where the cement slabs were piled up, as if she was deliberately moving away from where the secret history of *Untilled* emerged.

I decided to leave the territory, but first I had some doubts. I'm going, but I'm staying, I began to say. Then I began to play in my mind: I'm going but I think I'll stay, because in reality, after my hours spent here, I *am* the place, the place itself, I am *Untilled*, and a place never moves. I'm staying because I have only calm where I've been, only calm where nobody tells me who I am or knows who I've been. I'll stay because this dawn is slow and splinters, because all these things are familiar to me: this mist without fog, the warm cloths applied to my injuries in childhood, that winding drive I have to descend if I decide to leave.

After saying this to myself, I left.

And leaving behind those good moments, I thought it would be possible to remember that farewell to *Untilled* territory with the same exactness I remembered a work of art when I desired to: a work like my favorite Édouard Manet painting, *Le serveuse de bocks* (*The Waitress*).

Art, I thought then, is something that is happening to us.

I left aware that just leaving there was art, and knowing that when I had completely gone away, I would occasionally dream I'd returned to that territory, that I was returning to *Untilled*, and the drive leading to the place was winding away before me, twisting and turning to reveal, as I advanced, the silhouette of some kind of imposing space, secretive and silent, where everything—absolutely everything, even what I didn't notice—had great importance, because actually nothing there had been tilled, nothing there had ever been truly cultivated; deep down—notice I say *deep down*—everything was all still to be done.

62

I returned to one of the places that most intrigued me in Documenta. I went back to *The Last Season of the Avant-Garde* and took another look at the easel with its unfinished battle-scene canvas. There was the tiny press and the wooden board with Martinus von Biberach's great epitaph. And once again I activated the button Bastian Schneider had installed beneath the word *fröhlich* (happy), which once again spat out a little piece of paper, this time with a different message than the one it threw on the floor the day before: the text warned that at night, when there was no one there, the place was taken over by beings wearing Polynesian masks, singing songs from the future, songs that will be sung six centuries hence in a very different Germany, but one where Lichtenberg will still be read, even if only out of respect for that passage in which he expressed his conviction that, without his writing, such different things would be discussed "between six and seven on a certain German evening in the year 2773."

Unlike my previous incursion to that spot, there was no one around me this time. I was alone, because it was very early, so early that I understood I'd probably have a longer time to try to see things than I'd been able to on the previous occasion. But I soon had the impression that everything was just the same as the day before, so it was going to be pretty difficult for me to see anything very different from what I'd already seen. Even so, I began to inspect that interior again in case there were other secret springs, like the tiny printing press that produced leaflets. I looked in the drawers of the single piece of furniture in the room and found photographs of the gold hinges that were protected by the fake electric alarm system. But I didn't find much else. In *The Last Season of the Avant-Garde*, it would be deluded to hope to find surprises or novelties.

I was about to leave, when it occurred to me to go to the green door of the main façade and look through the keyhole. I don't know what I expected to find. Perhaps that Bastian Schneider might have set up something like *Étant Donnés*, Duchamp's famous last work (twenty years it took him to make it), where the spectator, looking through a crack in an old Cadaqués door, saw a cryptic scene with a woman stretched out on a bed of twigs, her legs spread, her sex very open and off center, with a gas lamp in her left hand.

I looked through the keyhole of the green door of *The Last Season of the Avant-Garde* but I saw nothing but darkness and more darkness. I tried again. Nothing. I looked again. Darkness. When I turned around, I saw a woman my own age, still beautiful and not too tall, smiling at me. She was a strange blend of the writer Lydia Davis and my Aunt Antonia. The woman was American, though she wasn't actually Lydia Davis. And I knew the whole time that, in fact, she wasn't Davis, because I'd once had dinner with her in Brussels. Obviously she wasn't my Aunt Antonia either, because this woman was American, from somewhere in the States, although she'd spent time in Zaragoza, and also in Girona and in Begur, so she spoke a mix of broken Catalan and Spanish. This woman found my voyeurism immensely funny. We began a conversation, and she immediately declared herself curious about everything, though she didn't go, she said, to such extremes as I did. Her favorite hobby, she informed me, had been collecting medieval weaponry, but that wasn't all: she'd studied Hebrew philosophy, written about China and religious leaders in India, and been a friend of numerous paint-ers and writers (she named several but I didn't know any of them).

When I took my leave to begin descending toward Karlsaue Park to continue my early morning walk, and somehow search for, I told her, other happy moments, she asked how I imagined one of those might be. Absurdly, I didn't know how to answer her. My euphoria didn't stop growing, but I didn't know what to tell her about hap-piness. And so she told me that she'd once read about an English teacher in Shanghai, who'd asked a Chinese student what had been the happiest moment of his life. The student had hesitated for a long time and finally smiled, blushing. He told him that his wife had once gone to Peking, where she'd eaten duck, and she'd often told him about that trip, so he could say that the happiest moment of his life was his wife's trip when she'd eaten duck.

After this, I was even quieter and felt blocked. Why did I encoun-ter China so often on the paths I took to avoid it?

63

I went for a walk along the Fulda River, past the terraces that would soon be filled with indefatigable German retirees.

Pretending to have a retired air, I went into a bar overlooking the Fulda. There was a jukebox playing "Parisien du Nord," by Cheb Mami, an Arabic protest song from the French *banlieues*. I soon dis-covered that the jukebox was part of *Die Gedanken sind frei* (*Thoughts Are Free*), Susan Hiller's project for Documenta. The work was com-posed of a hundred popular protest songs for the hundred days the exhibition lasted.

There were five jukeboxes in five bars in Kassel, one of which was this one. As I left, I was cheered by the young voices I could suddenly hear amid the mist rising off the river. They were Arabic women who'd just gotten off the bus and who, by their way of speaking Spanish, I guessed might belong to the big Saharan tent set up on the Karlsaue grass, beside the Orangerie.

I approached the group and I hadn't been mistaken. They were going to *The Art of Sahrawi Cooking*. Pim had told me about this tent. It was a project, if I was not mistaken, realized by Robin Kahn from New York, and also a Cooperative, which (I'd later verify at the hotel) was called The National Union of Sahrawi Women, an association from a refugee camp in the Western Sahara.

From what Pim told me, visitors received tiny glasses of tea there and sat on cushions, maintaining a climate of permanent conversation in low voices; the tent functioned as a research station, providing information about the Western Sahara: about the history of the occupied territories, the refugee camps, and the so-called Wall of Shame, which is a dividing wall in the south of Morocco, and scandalously unfamiliar to most Europeans.

I walked a long way along the Fulda. I hadn't had a call on my cell phone for an infinity of hours. No one in Kassel seemed to remember I was there or that I would be giving a lecture that afternoon. Maybe I'd now been forgotten by Boston, by Ada Ara, by Pim and company. The fog of the place reminded me of those scenes in my books, which began or ended up in misty lands, in Manderleys of the spirit. All this stemmed from adolescence, from the days when, if a movie began with a melancholy scene and an enigmatic guy walking along a road in the middle of nowhere through fog on his way to a seedy bar, from the start (and to the finish too) the scenario made my eyes as wide as saucers; it was something that interested me enormously.

The mist rising off the Fulda seemed to arrange things in a way in which a mystery story could burst out at any moment. However, the biggest mystery was within me and it was the unbreakable perfection of my mood. I was tired, sometimes sleepy, but excited at the same time, the enchanted accomplice of everything that crossed my path.

After a long rambling wander without getting lost thanks to the river, I felt that my physical fatigue had become an absolute reality, and then, almost providentially, I remembered I'd decided that, when I had to sit down again to write at the table in the Chinese restaurant, I'd turn myself into one more installation at Documenta and pretend to be sleeping. I would pretend to sleep in the style of one of my idols, the marvelous Benino, that shepherd who slept the whole time, not noticing anything, in Neapolitan nativity scenes.

The idea was for possible spectators to leave me in peace during my working hours, that is, during the hours of writing in public. If they saw I was sleeping like a log, that would happily frighten them off. But who was I expecting to come and see me? Nobody had been interested in spying on me, and in reality, I had never been left in such peace and so abandoned as during those hours they made me spend in the Chinese restaurant. Still, a short phrase on a sign on the table would give some clue about that installation, making anyone believe that the writer was sleeping and not thinking about anything.

Somehow, I needed to pretend to profess the religion of sleep, which went on about how sleepers were closer to God. Not thinking about anything was like connecting to that divine sleep that sustains the world.

ASLEEP, ONE IS CLOSER TO DUCHAMP

That's what I would write on the sign to leave there on my table. I decided this as I left the Fulda behind, crossing the road to go to the Dschingis Khan. At that moment, I was struck by the intuition that it wasn't going to be difficult for me to pretend to be asleep. I could tell I'd surrender to sleep as soon as I stretched out on the comfortable red couch. I was happy, but somewhat unsteady, a bit zombie-like at times. I didn't even know if I'd have the strength to write the sign where Duchamp would take the place of God.

On the threshold of the Chinese restaurant, I hesitated. The more one vacillates before a door, the stranger one feels, I told myself. And in I went. This time they didn't even recognize me, nobody seemed to register that a writer who was working there had entered. Perhaps my appearance was to blame for that misunderstanding. Or perhaps I hadn't been exerting myself enough as a writer, maybe since I was Piniowsky, I had a slightly different air; or perhaps being so tired and unshaven and wearing smelly clothes—nobody passed through *Untilled* with impunity—all that disoriented them. But the fact is I noticed that they'd gone from indifference to not even remembering I was the invited writer.

"I am Piniowsky," I said.

That, of course, did not help matters.

I saw an isolated, glacial Chinese smile from behind the circular bar in the middle of the restaurant. When the staff finally remembered that I had a table reserved there, they resigned themselves to suffering as many mishaps as they imagined must be coming. I wrote the sign, but at the last moment I put down a different text from what I'd planned:

APOLOGIES FOR DESCARTES

Writing at top speed, that's what I begged on the sign and left it on my table. Obviously, it was a phrase taken from Kundera, his interpretation of what he supposed Nietzsche had said to the horse in Turin.

Half an hour later, I was lying down but still awake. Crisscrossing through my mind were Chinese and German words, which seemed increasingly attracted to each other and seemed even to be creating a new language (the language of Galway Bay). I remembered some beloved Robert Walser pages that, admitting the unmissable disparity, I could practically have written myself. In his delightful diary of 1926, Walser spoke of walks with cheerful young women that sounded rather akin to my experiences in Kassel.

Today, said Walser, I went for an agreeable little walk, brief, minimal, without going too far away. I went into a grocery shop and saw a nice girl inside ... He began like that and a little while later, in a burst of sincerity, said that what he wanted to explain was that in this city he'd had occasion to meet some really adorable and very nice women. He ended by asking who could be bothered by the affection he'd grown used to feeling for people who radiated confidence, overflowing with joie de vivre!

I was also cheerful that morning, although at the same time I lacked sleep and felt disconcerted. After a short while, I fell asleep for real; I curled up in the fetal position on the red couch and didn't even apologize for Descartes, nor did I feel close to the god Duchamp, nor did I stroll with young girls. I slept and I dreamed that having traveled to Kassel in an intensely red and Chinese room, I was submitting the trite idea of *feeling at home* to incessant though skeptical scrutiny, until I finally understood that I had found my home, that place I'd always expected to find along the way, on the road of life. In this friendly home I'd searched for so long, a stranger was writing signs I'd never seen; he was writing them on a chalkboard in a very intense green, a chalkboard that ended up transforming itself into a door in a pointed Arabic arch. On this door the stranger was inscribing—while slowing down the rhythm of his hand—the poetry of an unknown algebra. Through what seemed a secret code, it ended up revealing to me with startlingly bright clarity something very private, something I'd not detected until then: the Chinese logic of the place.

64

The bright clarity evaporated as soon as I opened my eyes, but the Chinese logic remained in place.

That was my home along the way.

I remembered the Hungarian professor with the unruly hair in a Russian short story I had read a few months ago. He affirmed that if we isolated the stray, passing thought of indiscernible origin, then we were beginning to understand that we were systematically unhinged, that is, that our madness was an everyday matter. The students of this professor loved the idea of daily madness. As for the professor, wouldn't he also be an expert in the Chinese logic of place?

In the depths of our minds was the enormous bestial, territorial back room, full of irrational fears and murderous instincts. That's why we invented Reason, to oppose the great muddle, the general emptiness that is so lethal. At least that's what the Hungarian professor in the short story said, and every time I remembered that story, I liked to think that the professor was entirely right, which would mean that deep down he wasn't; but it was better to believe him, for if what he said weren't true, one might end up outside oneself or out of one's room, no more and no less than how I'd ended up the night before at *Untilled*, the night spent out in the open.

I looked at my watch. It was past noon. They still hadn't called me on my cell phone; luckily they hadn't phoned while I was sleeping and dreaming, so I was able to get some rest. I felt excessively enthusiastic, which didn't take long to create a conflict for me when I began to smile at the waitresses. It was deplorable (it goes without saying). The worst of it was that I was attracting attention. I was acting stupidly and my euphoria might end up arousing suspicion. So I tried as hard as I could to control myself. Everything seemed to indicate that when I wasn't at my desk in Barcelona, I felt empty, like a skinned, boneless hide, lurching through life. Even so, I tried to improve the situation. With elbows propped up on that Chinese corner table with its vase, I pretended to search for something I could write on. From so much pretending, I ended up searching for real. I finally thought I should say something on that oh so overused idea that nobody can step twice in the same river. I'd heard it so many times and I'd never been convinced. I remembered that in my role as a writer in public I could write whatever I wanted to in my notebook and, as if debating that commonplace about the river you step in twice, I finally wrote:

"Hummm …"

Thirty times I wrote that out as a drill. In another thirty lines, in a somewhat cynical homage to Germany, I strove to reproduce a Goethe phrase:

"Everything is there, and I am nothing."

Then I carefully described in my notebook the carpet of larch needles I'd walked across before I got to *Untilled* territory. It was an even more masochistic exercise than the previous two; I hated writing lingering descriptions that belonged more in other eras of

197

narrative history. But I thought that the one there, writing in the Chinese restaurant in public, much as he was called Piniowsky like me, couldn't be anything more than a conventional writer and, therefore, he should believe in the "power of descriptions." This so unbalanced me (nobody likes to turn into a poor, old crock) that I had to say to myself several times:

"Calm down, Piniowsky."

On the other hand, though what I was writing wasn't all that serious, not a single person approached to see, which, occasionally, slightly undermined my self-esteem (even if it was the other Piniowsky's morale). I called Barcelona and calmed down, but not enough. A friend wanted to know why he had to tell me everything that was going on in the city and why I wouldn't tell him anything about Kassel. Because, I told him, absolutely nothing has happened to me since I got here, nothing at all, I've barely spoken to anybody. I walk around, sleep. My life lacks action, I told him, but I was thinking that surely, in a very Borgesian way, everything that was happening to me—which was nevertheless very little—was happening to the other Piniowsky.

I let the conversation with my friend dwindle down of its own accord, just die out. And so I didn't tell him anything about my red couch like a scaffold or the lecture I needed to prepare and might not prepare for. I was undoubtedly right not to tell him, for that friend surely wouldn't have understood what I was talking about. When I finally said goodbye and hung up, I stared at the figure of a dragon over by the door and remembered that some oriental dragons were said to carry the palaces of the gods on their backs, while others were known to determine the courses of the streams and rivers and protect subterranean treasures. I remembered the dragon at the entrance to Parque Güell in Barcelona, which I saw so often when I lived in the upper part of my city, and which sometimes, for no reason, I imagined secretly alive and ceaselessly devouring pearls and opals: something impossible, for it was simply a sculpture to which more and more tourists, especially Chinese tourists, were becoming addicted every day.

I ended up devoting myself to writing the first words of my afternoon lecture in the Ständehaus. I decided it would begin like this:

> I left for Kassel, via Frankfurt, searching for the mystery
> of the universe and to initiate myself in the poetry of an
> unknown algebra. I also left for Kassel to try to find an
> oblique clock and a Chinese restaurant, and, of course,
> though I sensed it was an impossible task, I also left to
> try to find my home somewhere within my displacement.
> And now all I can tell you is that it is from this "home" that
> I am speaking to you.

As soon as I finished these lines, I realized that Piniowsky had never written anything so authentic in his whole life. He was saying that he was at home, that the table in the Chinese restaurant was his destiny, and that he was giving the whole lecture as if he were sitting at his private gallows in the Dschingis Khan. As long as no one was asking about the logic of it all, he had the impression of knowing it all by heart; but if anyone asked him, he wouldn't know how to explain it.

Not know how to explain it?

The Chinese logic of the place was him!

Or to put it a better way, the Chinese logic was me.

I was a bit nervous, too.

"Calm down, Piniowsky."

65

Hours later, I crossed Karlsaue Park at a slow pace, and then walked through downtown Kassel until I ended up taking refuge in the hotel. I'd lost count of the hours spent on my own. Except for minor incidents, I was staying in a constant good mood, perhaps I would never again feel as marvelously good for the rest of my life. I increasingly attributed it to the creative atmosphere of the city, and to the works of art I'd seen over the course of those last days, and the recovery of the juvenile impulse that had once led me to break with the obsolete forms of so many dull, non-avant-garde artists.

Who had said that contemporary art was on the decline? Only the intellectuals of uncultured, depressed countries like mine could reach such backward conclusions. Europe had died—maybe the young madwoman in mourning had been right to wear black from head to toe—but art was very much alive in the world, it was the only open window left for those still searching for spiritual salvation.

As soon as I entered my hotel room, I went out onto the balcony and sent a new greeting toward *This Variation*. Since Kassel was inviting madness, seeming to open up many complex paths to my own Chinese logic, I decided to greet the dark room this time with the most horrible grimace I knew how to make. I greeted it the way I imagined one of the many Chinese mandarins of the ancient legends I'd read in childhood would have. I said as if speaking from a public platform:

"The twentieth century, a film from Germany."

In the street my slanted words were perfectly audible, and some young people on their way to see Sehgal's work in the annex of the hotel looked up.

Those were the words pronounced by an engrossed, very intense character in *Hitler: A Film from Germany*, an avant-garde film from the seventies made by Hans-Jürgen Syberberg, one of the cineastes who had most impressed me in my youth and whom I remember asking for his autograph one night in the course of a long party in the port district of Barcelona.

After the Chinese grimace, I went back inside. I decided to lie down on the bed with my arms behind my head and my knees raised. I looked at the ceiling and stared at the cracks: at the German cracks, I said to myself. And then I started fixating on the peeling paint, the stains, and the chips. Suddenly, I didn't feel like seeing anybody, much less speaking in public, or going outside, or even moving. However, there wasn't much time left before I had to move, to go out, and give a lecture.

I remembered that not so long ago—on a day and at a time like this—I'd been overcome for the first time by this sudden apathy. I had thought I'd discovered I didn't know how to live, that I'd never known how to live. That day, the sun beat down on the roof tiles of my house. I hadn't yet met the people who would be decisive in my life and would help me to know a tiny bit how to be in this world, the same world I'd turn my back on many years later, on behalf of Piniowsky.... That day, sunk in the deepest depths of my tragedy, I spent an infinity of hours with my eyes glued to a white wooden shelf on which I thought there was a washbowl; I concentrated on that bowl, which later turned out to be imaginary, though by the time I found out I'd already spent hours thinking about that basin and death. It was the first time in my whole life that I had a serious anxiety attack, though with an undoubtedly slightly comic or ridiculous touch.

I got over this brief moment in which I'd remembered the day of my initiation in anguish. Then, I managed to recover my desire to see people, to speak in public, to go out, to move. But it served as a warning that any triviality might end up breaking my general state of great enthusiasm.

For a few moments, I imagined what my two Chinese neighbors might be doing in room 26. I thought I could hear a string quartet. Maybe they had found two lovers who were musicians. These things sometimes happen. Accompanied by the good music coming from that room, I stayed for quite a while reading page 193 of *Romanticism*, about "Aimless Journey," a poem by Eichendorff, whose verses expanded on the traditional motif of a great voyage and the losses that sent Odysseus on his way, the motif from which the romantics extracted the voyage without arrival or goal, the endless journey, and that Rimbaud would continue with his "Drunken Boat" and Roberto Bolaño, among others, would prolong saying that journeys are roads leading nowhere; nevertheless they are paths down which we have to turn and lose ourselves in order to find something again: to find a book, a gesture, a lost object, maybe a method, with luck, something new, which has always been there.

"So the avant-garde doesn't exist?" I asked Dalí when I interviewed him in his house beside the sea.

"No, but there's Giorgione's *Tempest*, which revolutionized everything."

I looked at the clock. I didn't have much time to keep reading or to do anything else, because it was almost time to leave for the Ständehaus and give my lecture. I thought it strange no one had phoned to arrange to take me there, but since that's how things were, I'd better get used to the idea that I should get there under my own steam.

I looked at my emails again to see if there was a message telling me someone was coming to pick me up, but there wasn't. I double-checked my Google map and the notes I'd made so I wouldn't get lost downtown. I looked to see if there were any messages accidentally lost among the spam, but there were none there either. Then, precisely at that moment, my cell phone rang and it was Ada Ara saying she'd come by and get me at five. I relaxed, but not entirely, because it was very close to that time. In any case, I took the call as a good and almost providential sign, even thanking Ada for remembering me, for I had the impression, I told her, that going on my own, without anyone to accompany me, I would never arrive at the Ständehaus.

Then, remembering that the lecture should have a certain amount of content and seeing with some terror that all I'd prepared was the beginning ("I left for Kassel, via Frankfurt, in search of the mystery of the universe ..."), I decided that in the first minutes of my talk, since I was going to be forced to improvise something, I would talk about how over the last few years I had learned to escape from my sole and exclusive obsession with literature and that I had opened the game up to other artistic disciplines.

This big opening up to other arts, I'd tell the audience, might never have happened if not for a telephone call I'd received seven years ago from Sophie Calle. I would tell them, at length, about meeting her at the Café de Flore, in Paris, and the strange proposal she'd made to me: to write her a story that she would try to live.

Then I would talk about Dominique Gonzalez-Foerster and my modest collaborations in some of her brilliant installations. In my memory, above all her other works, was her setting for after a universal flood in the Turbine Hall of the Tate Modern.

In telling these two stories about my recent relationship with artistic disciplines other than literature, I hoped to fill as much time as possible. But in case I didn't manage to fill it all, I could always start listing how many things happened to me in my life, even though I didn't notice most of them when they were actually taking place, but rather as I went back over them and examined them under a magnifying glass; writing them up was the most interesting way to extend them—taking a long time over them and studying them in depth—to see how very true it was that we tend to think that things we ignored have no relevance but in fact they always do, they have a great deal.

While I was organizing this final part of the lecture, I inopportunely felt an impulse to go outside again and directly visit *This Variation*. I was somewhat disoriented. It might be said that the permanent good mood I was enjoying was very interesting, undoubtedly a great positive force, but it sometimes dragged me into an undesirable true bewilderment and chaos; it was as if on occasion the invisible wanted to take me pitilessly to the center of whirlpools that were getting more and more excessively wild.

The fact is, I suddenly felt this impulse to go outside and, for a moment—as if I'd sensed that I needed to hold myself back and reflect—I tried as hard as I could to cut it off at the root. I stopped to think of what is termed "physical magnitude," which, according to what I'd read, characterized the movement called "impulse" in physics . . .

But this attempt at distraction was futile. Trying to immobilize myself was a wasted effort. Because in a few seconds, propelled by unexpected *physical magnitude*, I was out on the landing, going down in the elevator and waving to the girl at reception as I went outside (not the one who spoke Spanish, but a Japanese one; they'd swapped, and I made a note of it in my red notebook, as if it were a sign of something I should study in depth).

I was so convinced of having imbued myself with models of Chinese conduct that I entered Sehgal's room as if I were just another component of the Ming dynasty. I tried to confuse the dancers who crouched in the shadows of the place. Someone from the Ming dynasty, I thought, would have had flat feet and walked slowly. I convinced myself of this, even aware that I knew nothing about the people who'd lived under the Ming dynasty and the only thing I could be sure of was that someone from then and there had to have other characteristics than the ones I was attributing to him.

In any case, I entered the total darkness of the room pretending to believe myself transfigured into a man from the Ming dynasty and hoping to confuse the hidden dancers, who, more invisible than ever, allowed me to advance without giving any indication of being there.

Confident and now breathing freely with relief, I decided to turn around, forgetting for a fraction of a second to keep moving the way I thought a flat-footed man in the long-ago Ming dynasty would have. Then, at that very moment, everything changed and someone whispered in my ear:

"*Last bear.*"

I had seen a film with that title. If that was what the dancers were talking about, it seemed to lack logic. The last bear? Or was it the *last beer*? I took two more steps in the darkness and headed toward the exit light. When I was about to reach outside, I saw something phosphorescent in the shape of a crescent moon and at first I tried to catch it, but I failed utterly. It completely dazzled me, and I ended up going outside with my sight cloudy while hearing again: "*Last bear.*"

Back at the hotel, I couldn't get that whisper out of my head, and I even strayed down grammatical paths looking for hidden intentions in the two words. Finally, I calmed down very unexpectedly: a memory buried in time was resurrected, the memory of when I was little and my sister dared me to stay in a corner until I stopped thinking about a white bear. The more I tried not to think of the white bear, the more I thought of him. For years, I thought of that animal often. I forgot him the day I tried to mock that image, forcing myself to really see the way the language of logic laid traps for me. I forgot the bear then, but defusing deceptions immersed me in an even more disturbing obsession.

66

At the last minute, Ada Ara couldn't make it, and María Boston showed up at the hotel to take me to the Ständehaus. She arrived accompanied by Alka, who I suddenly remembered had been introduced to me by Pim as "the person in charge of your visit to Kassel." Since she hadn't taken charge of me at all, everything led me to think that up in the offices of the organization—so invisible to me—they'd decided to relieve her of that job. Now she reappeared with Boston, more smilingly than ever. Each time I saw her, I wanted to ask her what she was laughing at, but I was aware that could lead to a tremendous, endless spiral of misunderstandings and linguistic short circuits. Of course, since arriving in Kassel I'd discovered a special pleasure in studying those short circuits that seemed to rebel against the logic of our common language. But I preferred not to study Alka too much because I sensed that could end up driving me crazy.

As we entered the Fridericianum, the invisible breeze welcomed us forcefully, as if it were an old friend (in fact it was), as if it had recognized us and was so pleased to see us again that it wanted to squeeze us in the most exaggerated way possible. Right then, I discovered that the exact title of Ryan Gander's work was *I Need Some Meaning I Can Memorise (The Invisible Pull)*, which made me realize that this *need for some meaning I can memorize* could in time take on an immense significance. When I needed to better "memorize" what those glorious days in Kassel were like, I'd always have within reach the memory of that breeze that stretched through my mental fabric, leaving with me "a meaning" of renovation and optimism that would be difficult to forget.

Swayed by that old friend and the cheerful force of its invisible pull, I told Boston that in Sehgal's room, that same afternoon, someone had whispered *Last bear* twice in my ear. It didn't seem to surprise her too much. More than that, it gave her an idea to take me to a white room in the Fridericianum where Ceal Floyer's sound installation *'Til I Get It Right* was.

I asked her for the best possible translation of *Last bear*—I was sure it was very simple—but there was no way to get her to tell me, because she insisted on talking to me about an old work by Ceal Floyer that she'd liked very much; she'd seen it three years ago in Berlin and it was called, if she remembered correctly, *Overgrowth*. It was a bonsai photographed from below and projected on a slide that increased the image to the size of a normal tree, as if situating the spectator beneath, or rather the bonsai above, or both. It seemed, said Boston, a marvelous way to take apart the stupid act of manipulating a tree to dwarf it. Ceal Floyer's work restored its proper size at the same time as alerting us to the number of sinister people we come across in life who try to pulverize our aspirations, whatever they might be …

My only aspiration at that moment was still for her to translate *Last bear* into Spanish for me, but she didn't seem to be up for that task and preferred we talk about *'Til I Get It Right*, another phrase, she said, that seemed like a slogan. In *'Til I Get It Right*, you could hear the American country singer Tammy Wynette repeating continuously: *I'll just keep on / 'til I get it right*.

I asked Boston why we hadn't gone to see and hear this on the first day. And I saw that Alka was laughing, as if she knew what I was talking about. You can't do everything at once, said an ironic Boston.

In Ceal Floyer's white room, the artist's need to always search out the difficult was exposed, which reminded me of the afternoon at a talk when a woman in the back row asked me when I planned to stop sinking my poor, lonely characters in the fog. When I get it right, I'll stop doing it, I told her. And then I informed her that fog and solitude were not my principal obsessions, I'd simply started a series of books that always prowled around that image of the solitary man in the mist and I felt I had to conclude the series. The woman then reproached me for the darkness of my texts. Señora, please, I said angrily, don't you see how dark and complex the world is? But a little while later I noticed the daylight, which was soft and beautiful. And I thought: If one could only see everything with such clarity.

67

After a long search through the Fridericianum we came upon Salvador Dalí's *Le grand paranoïaque*. I seemed to observe that the voice singing *I'll just keep on / 'til I get it right* was continuing at my side and seemed to form part of the painting, the same way that in Kentridge's drawings, there was always a trace of the previous drawing.

The voice only disappeared when we arrived at a room with paintings of apples that Korbinian Aigner had grown and painted when he was a prisoner in Dachau. Within that huge insanity he managed to create four new varieties of apples, designating them KZ 1 to 4 (KZ is the German abbreviation for concentration camp).

Once more, the horrors of the Nazi delirium showed up in a Documenta piece, on this occasion in a very special way. Those admirable, simple little paintings of apples left one impressed by the human capacity for resistance in the midst of difficulties; even in extremely adverse circumstances, to create art is the one thing that actually intensifies the feeling of being alive.

I looked at those apples, noticing that fragments of *Le grand paranoïaque* seemed to have lodged in them as if the apples too needed the trace of a previous work of art to feel more complete. I reflected on human courage, thinking of the case of a young woman from Moscow, a specialist in English romantic literature, who I'd been told had been sent to a prison in the Brezhnev era to a cell with no light, no paper or pen, because of a stupid and completely false denunciation; that young woman knew Byron's *Don Juan* by heart (seventeen thousand lines or more) and in the darkness she translated it mentally into Russian verse. When she got out of prison having lost her sight, she dictated the translation to a friend, and it is now the canonical Russian version of Byron.

I thought about the totally indestructible human mind and that we should meditate on everything better and be happier. And while I was thinking this, I felt the air of the breeze, which seemed to turn the corners of the galleries of the Fridericianum, catch up to me fully. It was exactly at that instant when I saw the young blonde woman who'd announced the death of Europe walking past, serene and silent, in her elegant mourning. I was shocked to see her this time so calm, so appeased, without her lost look. I observed her closely in case I was mistaken. But yes, it was her. She realized she was being observed and flashed me a slightly complicit smile, as if saying, It's me, you're right, I'm the one who believes that Europe has been dead for centuries.

I was about to carry on walking when I stopped and asked Boston whether she'd noticed that we'd just crossed paths with the mad-woman in mourning whom we'd first seen at *Untilled*, and then later, on another occasion, at the door of *Artaud's Cave*. It's true, said Boston, without attaching any importance to it, she seems calmer now, we could invite her to your lecture, I think she goes to all of them.

She said it with a smile, possibly as a joke. Just ask what her name is, I said, I'd just like to know what she's called. Boston assigned Alka that mission, which she carried out immediately without any prob-lem: she went over to where the madwoman in mourning was, asked her name, received a reply, and came back. The blonde had told her she was called Kassel. Are you sure, Alka? She nodded, she was sure, she said, the blonde's name was Kassel, she'd repeated it three times.

A little while later, when Alka—maybe this was also part of her job—told us it was ten to six, we left the Fridericianum almost at a run. It felt like the last straw that I should have the feeling—there in Kassel, where I'd always had more than enough time for every-thing—that I was going to be late for something.

We were rushing, but as we passed the Documenta-Halle, we lost a few seconds stopping to see Kristina Buch's *The Lover*, an enclosure full of plants that Boston wanted to show me. If not for her, I would never have noticed that apparently anodyne enclosure, which turned out to be a whole Documenta installation. I confirmed that often what moves us tends to arise in the most insignificant-seeming cir-cumstances: in what looked like merely a big container full of weeds, Kristina Buch had grafted plants that attracted butterflies who lost their characteristic liberty and went on to spend the sad lives of hostages, trapped by the plants that so loved and nourished them and, therefore, also tyrannized them with their overwhelming love.

68

Kassel was lucid, mad, obtuse, clairvoyant, calm, desperate. Who knows anything about Kassel with any certainty? Blonde, mourning, shrieking, young German, spreading the news of the death of Europe in all directions.

Kassel. There were so many ways to define her. Kassel was also a city. According to the old encyclopedia I sometimes used to escape from Wikipedia to feel that I was still living in another era, Kassel—surface area 106.77 km², with 196,345 inhabitants—is a small city on the banks of the Fulda River (one of the headstreams of the Weser) in the region of Hesse. Industries include lignite mines, car manufacture, precision engineering, optical and photographic instrument making, leather tanning, and textile production (cotton and artificial fibers). In the 1930s, there was the manufacture of military hardware, especially tanks.

Kassel's Ständehaus was for the most part destroyed during the last war. Originally the old Parliament Chamber of Hesse, it is once again today a solid and imposing three-story building, architecturally influenced by the Italian Renaissance. Every five years, when Documenta comes to town, its main hall is fitted out as a venue for many lectures related to contemporary art. Mine was announced for six o'clock in the evening on Friday, September 14. On a discreet sign at the entrance, you could still read "Lecture to Nobody," a title now totally out of context, for I had previously believed that the talk would be given in a place beyond the farthest forest, bordering the edge of Karlsaue Park.

When I arrived with Boston and Alka at the Ständehaus, they took me to an office near the entrance hall, and there I signed a few documents I assumed were to do with the lecture fee. I chatted in French about the Brothers Grimm with some people I didn't know from Adam. Then I escaped from the office for a few moments and went to spy on the hall where I would have to speak, wanting to know whether the lecture had attracted a little bit of expectation, or none at all. There was none, as was to be expected. But ten innocent people were sitting there, waiting for my lecture to begin. Since the hall was huge, it looked very empty. Perhaps worst of all was that the ten audience members showed not the slightest sign of knowing what they'd gotten themselves into.

"Here before you, Piniowsky," I imagined telling them.

Given the circumstances, I would have been content with a single spectator knowing something about me, about my books. And, while I was telling myself this, I ran into Chus Martínez, who told me that Carolyn Christov-Bakargiev was thinking of coming to my talk and was apparently very interested in what I might say there.

"Why?"

"You intrigue her," she said.

Accompanied by Chus, I returned to the office by the entrance hall, where I was surprised to see Alka sitting there with her legs crossed, leafing through *Journey to the Alcarria*. That was my copy of Cela's book, which I'd brought with me in case I was caught empty of ideas mid-lecture and had to resort to reading someone else's text. I was sure I wouldn't require it, but I needed it as a nearby object that I could touch; I needed to know that something as concrete as a book by another writer could save me if I got into a tight spot. I was really very surprised to find Alka leafing through the book, but even more so by the casual conjunction of Alka and Cela. I remembered at that moment that Carolyn Christov-Bakargiev had said that everything the Documenta participants set out to do "did not necessarily have to be art." This wasn't a bad idea, it took away the absurd pressure of having to do something artistic. That said, the image composed by Alka with Cela's book was pure art, actually a good stab at what I'd once imagined a great aesthetic instant to be like.

In that same office, Boston handed me a second document, which I also signed, without knowing this time what it was. And a few minutes later, escorted by Boston and Alka, I headed for the hall, which

I found slightly fuller than I'd left it. My uncertainty with respect to the kind of audience I'd have for that atypical lecture made me experience a moment of fear. I wanted to convince myself that my talk was just a formality I had to go through, but when I saw Carolyn Christov-Bakargiev arrive, accompanied by a large retinue, I confirmed what I always knew: there is no such thing as a talk in public that is just a formality, and if anyone takes it that way—I'm going to exaggerate somewhat, but not much—he runs the risk of losing in a single hour all the prestige he may have accumulated over decades.

By way of introduction, I improvised lightly on the little bit I'd written (I'm reconstructing here quite faithfully because I still have what I wrote for the beginning of that lecture, nor have I forgotten, the changes I made to it as I went along):

> I came to this city, via Frankfurt, in search of the mystery of the universe and to be initiated into the poetry of an unknown algebra. I also came to Kassel to try to find an oblique clock and Chinese restaurant, and, of course, though I believed it might be an impossible task, I also came to try to find my home somewhere within displacement. I did find it. It's not far from here. In fact, I'd say that I am in it, because I believe this evening I'm speaking to you from my homey scaffold in the Dschingis Khan.

Then, thinking of the place from which I was theoretically speaking (it's well-known that to situate yourself in the world, you have to do as much as possible to seem already situated), I quoted Wallace Stevens's "Notes Toward a Supreme Fiction":

> From this the poem springs: that we live in a place
> That is not our own and, much more, not ourselves
> And hard it is in spite of blazoned days.

From my scaffold, in this case, sprang the lecture. Surging from that charming Chinese gallows, the talk reflected the roughness of living in a world that was not mine and was sometimes tough, though Kassel had given me blazoned days, infecting me with enthusiasm and creativity and categorically refuting that contemporary art was finished. Finished? I had seen only splendor, and certain great changes that were finally bringing this art toward life. Had I not learned from Tino Sehgal, Ryan Gander, and Janet Cardiff and George Bures Miller that art *is what happens to us*, that art goes by like life and life goes by like art?

I tried to transmit this in some way to the audience, but they were so glib and restless, there was nothing to be done. I'd barely been speaking for three minutes and already more than half the people— seeing that I was addressing them in neither English nor German— had gone to look for their simultaneous translation devices, or had simply left. With so much movement on the part of the public (I had never had so many people coming and going at the beginning of a lecture), it was difficult to concentrate. It wasn't until ten minutes had passed that I had the feeling of being able to count on a stable audience of about thirty people, Carolyn and Chus among them, in the front row.

Just when I started to feel that sensation of stability, I saw—first with surprise and then with fear—that young Kassel, the frightening blonde in mourning, had entered the hall. She settled down—in a manner of speaking, because I've never seen anyone sit in a less settled, more dislocated way—in a seat in the back row. She didn't seem to need simultaneous translation, she seemed to be following my words attentively, and every time I pronounced the word "Kassel" she stirred in her seat as if she felt alluded to.

I tackled the story of Sophie Calle and told how thanks to her phone call, my ever-delayed yearning to escape from literature and open up to other artistic disciplines finally became reality. Perhaps thanks to that, I said, I was here, in Kassel, such a legendary place for me ever since I'd first heard people talking about it back in 1972, when the best minds of my generation spread the rumor that the essential and most audacious avant-garde in history gathered here: it was a subversive breeze that would change everything.

I told them that at the meeting in the Café de Flore, Sophie Calle showed me a book by Marcel Schwob, which featured a text on the imaginary life of Petronius, the Roman poet, who according to Schwob, when he'd finished writing sixteen books of adventure stories, read them to his slave Syrus, and Syrus laughed and hooted and clapped, and when Schwob finished, the two of them agreed to live those written stories out in real life.

I opened a parenthesis here to tell them that Jules Renard—observing that at the end of his life, Schwob traveled to Samoa with his Chinese servant Ting to contemplate the tomb of one of his favorite writers, Robert Louis Stevenson (and in the end he didn't see it)—wrote this: "Before he died, Schwob lived out his stories."

Closing the parentheses, I returned to the afternoon in the Flore with Sophie Calle, when she invited me to imitate Syrus and Petronius, and I immediately accepted her proposal to write a story that she would try to live.

Then I talked about Dominique Gonzalez-Foerster, of my friendship with her and my small collaborations with some of her installations, such as the one she did in the Turbine Hall of the Tate Modern, where she depicted an apocalyptic London in the year 2054.

Although in fits and starts, I was delivering a lecture, and figured I'd filled about half my time, when I suddenly started to feel an indescribable emotion: given the excitation of my mood, I was communicating to everyone my great enthusiasm for this glorious moment of contemporary art.

As I spoke, I felt noticeably more and more authentic. And I seemed to see in a very obvious way that calling myself Piniowsky had made me reencounter my own self and that my previous name, my name of so many years, had come to be a huge burden to me, because in reality it was nothing more than the name from a youth that had gone on too long.

The entire audience was either confused or calm, except for young Kassel, who was fidgeting in her seat in the back row and seemed increasingly restless; she looked disappointed and I didn't know why, though I feared it was because she grasped too well the lack of rigor in my extremely improvised talk. But I was not prepared to modify the method I was employing to communicate with my audience, who, by the way, seemed only to be listening to me to try to figure out what the hell I was talking about. Maybe they thought I was on drugs: I might have looked it, because my enthusiasm bordered on the supernatural.

Trying to keep my distance from what the madwoman or the rest of the audience might be thinking, I devoted myself to narrating the infinitely profound impression that William Gaddis's novel *The Recognitions* had made on me; most especially, the treatment of the characters had left a strange trace on me, particularly one of them, a certain Wyatt who suddenly stopped being Wyatt to hide beneath the name of Reverend Gilbert Sullivan, and later behind the name of a certain Yak, who soon went on to be called Stephan (though only somewhat later do we recognize him by that name).

Could we say that Wyatt was Wyatt at every moment? Was it the same Wyatt in each part of *The Recognitions*?

I asked this question, and as I did so, I looked up for a moment and saw that the audience was looking more and more astounded, as if wanting to warn me not to carry on down that path.

"Wyatt!" shouted Kassel from the back row, and I'd never heard a shout inviting less logic.

Even so, I carried on. I began to talk about contemporary writers, about those I claimed could all be called Wyatt and had supposedly inherited the sacred flame of literature, but only on rare occasions could we see that they were indeed Wyatt. To explain such a huge debacle, I said, we had to talk about the abandonment of moral responsibilities on the part of all living writers, but that argument, not necessarily wrong, was insufficient to explain so much desertion and disaster. It was quite true that at present all contemporary writers, instead of taking up positions against capitalism, were working in tune with it; they were all well aware they were nothing if they didn't sell books or if dozens of admirers didn't show up when they signed copies of their novels. It was no less true that liberal democracies, by tolerating everything, absorbing everything, made any text futile, no matter how dangerous it might appear to be ...

Here I stopped because I felt on the verge of asphyxiation; I'd suddenly been talking in a sort of compulsive outburst. I'd felt extremely uncomfortable at every moment as well, especially since I detected the absolutely false tone of my melancholy: I had wanted to deploy a sullen discourse, as I tended to do lately when I made literature, and I simply felt like a faker speaking so sadly.

When I regained my composure, I made a humorous allusion to "Collapse and Recovery," explaining that more than once during the days I'd spent in Kassel, I had physically played out Documenta's motto.

Then I talked about Paul Thomas Anderson's film *The Master*, which I'd seen the first day of that month at the Venice Film Festival, and which had impressed me with its moving description of people who were lost, unable to recover after the Second World War.

The Master brilliantly described the mental climate of recovery. I would undoubtedly think of this film if one day I had to write about finding in Kassel these optimal circumstances that allowed me to leave behind a creative collapse and enter into a process of Recovery, leading me to mental spaces where euphoria sometimes seemed limitless. Then I spoke briefly—dispensing with any taciturn tone that might sound false—about some of the works at Documenta that had helped me rethink my writing, concentrating especially on Janet Cardiff and George Bures Miller's installation in the woods, *FOREST (for a thousand years)*.

I spoke about this work and the random subversive groups it created, how I'd been overcome by the impression of being on a battlefield hearing, as if it were all happening right there, the yells of men in hand-to-hand combat, the overflying airplanes, the breathing, real footsteps through dry leaves, the nervous laughter, the wind, twigs snapping in the densest part of the forest, thunder of an approaching storm, the noise of ancient battles, bayonets tearing through the air, consternation ...

And in the background of it all, I said, an obsessive song warns us that to get out of the forest, we have to get out of Europe, but to get out of Europe, we have to get out of the forest.

If these last words of my lecture had suddenly blended with the glacial, heartrending cry of young Kassel, everything would have been perfect.

But it didn't go like that; I looked toward young Kassel and she was simply scratching her head.

The floor was opened for a discussion, which was soon closed. There were no questions and only Carolyn Christov-Bakargiev took the floor to tell me in French that the whole lecture had struck her as "Martian."

She didn't specify whether she meant "admirably Martian" or just Martian, but since my joy and frenzy for life were ongoing, I chose to take it as a compliment.

69

Hours later in the hotel, I would read on the Internet in English, without understanding any of it, a summary of that lecture written by someone on the Documenta payroll. The Spanish version supplied by Google Translate was strange, as was to be expected, but it helped me to believe that I really had delivered a lecture in Kassel, even if, according to what it said, it wasn't exactly the lecture I'd planned to deliver, but a slightly different one:

> A literary analysis of the event of the lecture by the Catalan writer could only fairly be said to have demonstrated the potential of a resourceful event like the Ständehaus, where an insomniac has spoken to demanding listeners calling for shortwave radio headphones. In the medium term, you can expect the Catalan writer to publish from behind prison bars his account of his flâneuresque steps through Kassel and his Chinese home, and infamous adhesion to a subversive breeze.

70

In *Untilled*, one had the experience of not knowing whether one was stepping on a work of art, or whether it was all real or imaginary. I felt the same way leaving the Ständehaus and saying farewell to the whole curatorial team that had gathered there. I found out from Chus that they'd arranged for a taxi to take me to the Frankfurt airport the next morning so I could avoid the train.

I said goodbye to the whole curatorial team, with a special hug for Boston, who was moving to London in a week. She said she hoped to see me again one day somewhere. Maybe we'll end up having dinner with the McGuffins on a foggy night, she said, smiling. I've always hoped to find that fog one day in London …

The taxi was coming to pick me up at seven in the morning, an early hour, and the sole representative of Documenta there would be Alka, coordinator of my stay. I looked at the Croatian woman, who immediately smiled at me, and who, moreover, seemed content that we were talking about her, though she didn't give the impression of knowing what we were saying.

Minutes later, after all the farewells, I began to walk aimlessly around downtown Kassel, feeling lonelier than ever in that city. It was all over, and I had too many hours to kill before the taxi would arrive the next morning. It would have been ideal to leave immediately. After an hour of wandering, I came out onto Königsstrasse by surprise and decided to set out for a fixed destination. I headed for the Gloria Cinema and once again was fascinated by its anachronistic foyer and box office that sent me back into the past. I stood there almost hypnotized. No matter how much time passes, I thought, I'll never figure out the exact reason for the great magnetism exerted over me by the façade of the Gloria Cinema, so similar to the neighborhood cinemas of my childhood.

I was standing there half hypnotized when, to my astonishment, I saw the lights go out in the windows with the posters in them. I saw a man up on a ladder starting to change the letters to the next day's film. I waited until I could read it: *Shanghai*. Directed by Mikael Håfström. A Chinese title and, if I wasn't mistaken, a Nordic director, probably Swedish.

I stayed there a while longer, and a childhood memory came to me: halfway through a movie, I heard a bell ringing and started wondering if it had rung in the movie or if it came from outside, from the steeple of the neighborhood church.

Then I left. I left the Gloria's foyer as if it didn't matter to me, when actually I felt very moved because I had the impression I'd left behind something very important to me. I left and began walking back the way I came. Finally, now somewhat tired, after contemplating Horst Hoheisel's reproduction of the fountain for a long time, I sat down on the terrace of a café on Friedrichsplatz. I called Barcelona and said I had a taxi for the next day. All I had left, I said, was the most tedious part, the return, now that it was all over.

What hadn't ended at all, I suddenly noticed almost incredulously, was my creative mood and absolute enthusiasm for almost everything. Sitting on the terrace of that café, from my position of vigilance over that big public space, I suddenly realized everything that evening was splendid, magnificent, marvelous. I lacked adjectives. The sun, though now setting, still shone a little. The streets transmitted a contagious joy of bustling people. An agreeable breeze moved the leaves of the trees in the square. I loved most of the things I noticed, and I did so almost instantaneously. I did have disdainful glances for people I saw rushing past, as if wanting to make them comprehend it was incomprehensible that they weren't stopping to contemplate such beauty.

I sat on that terrace for about an hour, contemplating things I'd been going over for years now, although perhaps tackling everything with an excitement and complexity far greater than I had at other times. I wondered how long that great vital impulse would last and also what could have happened to humanity that made it so difficult to give literary interest to joy, to the excitement of being alive, to the exaltation coming from what we were seeing.

Leaving that terrace, I went to the hotel. I had a thought for *art itself*, which seemed to me to definitely be there, in the air, suspended in that moment, suspended in life, in the life that went by as I'd seen the breeze go by when art went by.

I was walking up Königsstrasse, wondering why glorious moments always announced storms or misfortunes.

It was late now, and I suddenly noticed that everything had gone dark.

I had a sudden, complete sensation of being orphaned. As if a tiny break had caused a switch in the cheerful rules of the day and my mood had changed in the most radical way.

Walking toward the Hessenland, I stopped to contemplate the earth, air, and sky from within the darkness. And I remembered the dead, all the many people I'd known and loved who had died. And I also remembered that for the living there was only a gloomy path, to the grave, to the earth; there was no other route to any other world than what went by way of the grave. All the marvels of life—the nice colors, the charm and joy of certain days, family homes, unforgettable days, the sweet and gentle paths, the marvels of small and great art—everything was on its way to expire and disappear, everything was oblivion. The sun on high would pass away, and all the best emotions, and with them the eyes of men who cry.... It had really grown dark. I took refuge in the hotel, went into my room, went out on the balcony, waved for the last time to Sehgal's invisible room, came back into mine, that enclosure that hadn't even provided me with a thinking cabin.

One hour later, I was sitting on a plain chair in my room, my bag packed, totally ready to embark on that return journey despite having so many hours left to wait. My computer was in its case. And I was there in the chair as if petrified, as if in hell. The invisible impulse, the effect of the breeze, seemed to have reached its end. I looked toward the black hole that had originated inside myself, and it showed me my own face. As if with my brain I was going through this zone without a bit of good humor; it was a region with no jokes at all. I wanted to go back to the world, although it had perished some time ago and was no longer within my reach. I had been trapped inside

Piniowsky since the moment he was born in me. I was a victim of my own mask. It was no longer possible to have any opinion on the world. Every axiom of my life had turned out to be false, it felt, and I didn't see anything, there was nothing, I was nothing; everything was, from top to bottom, a false illusion. The invisible impulse had vanished entirely.

I barely moved from the chair the whole night, thinking of all the dead I'd once known and who had gone with an inadmissible ease. I spent the night in this misty humorless zone thinking that what was happening to me was going to stay with me forever. But at dawn, everything changed: at first just slightly; then, in a more dynamic way.

At seven on the dot the taxi arrived. I went downstairs with my suitcase and my laptop. At reception, as I'd imagined, Alka was not there; she probably hadn't set her alarm. It was obviously too early for her. The day looked splendid, magnificent, marvelous. Stealthily and slowly, the black taxi slipped through the deserted streets, and for a moment, I feared I might encounter the image of young Kassel leaning against a rough wall, weeping in silence for the end of Europe.

But no. Kassel too, like all the dead I'd once loved, had disappeared, as if it were the most natural thing in the world.

The taxi driver was Chinese. I was grateful for this last detail from the curatorial team. Even his Chinese cap had meaning, and noticing it led me to understand that I was back in a zone of luminosity and joy.

Art was, in effect, something that was happening to me, happening at that very moment. And the world seemed new again, moved by an invisible impulse. Everything was so relaxing and admirable, it was impossible not to look. Blessed is the morning, I thought.

penguin.co.uk/vintage